Saavri

The Mind's Last Mirror

Ashfaq Ahmad

GRADIAS
PUBLISHING HOUSE

Gradias Publishing House
448/843, Ghasmandi
Thakurganj, Lucknow— 226003
Ph. 9616066930, 9473926431
E-mail: *gradiaspublishinghouse@gmail.com*

Book: Saavri— The Mind's Last Mirror
Genre: Fiction/Horror
Author: Ashfaq Ahmad

First Published by **Gradias Publishing House** 2025

Edition: 1
ISBN: 978-81-995620-0-4

For those who have ever tried to bury a memory—
and found it waiting for them in their dreams

"When reality is born inside the mind, who decides what's real?"

—Unknown Monastic Fragment, 14th Century

Introduction
The Mind's Last Mirror

This story is written as an autobiographical document of Soumitra Banerjee. When it reaches its conclusion with a striking and suspenseful turn, the central character realizes that, in physical reality, he had remained asleep on his bed in his room the entire time. Yet within a virtual world, he had come to know everything about the life of another mysterious man named Soumitra Banerjee— one who, after living a cursed existence, attains liberation from his life through him.

Everything that unfolds in the story may take place within an illusory world, but several key characters carry real pasts, filled at every step with mystery and intense suspense. All the characters are real in essence, yet instead of existing in physical reality, they inhabit a virtual world created inside the mind, where their powers become, in a sense, limitless.

This is the story of a matrix that does not operate in the external, physical world, but within a realm constructed inside the mind— where the story's most powerful characters can draw others into their world against their will. Within this domain, they can engage in romance, inflict physical harm, and even take lives.

Soumitra Banerjee, raised by an English couple, encounters a mysterious girl named Saavri while returning home after his twentieth birthday celebration. She reveals the truth of his birth, tells him about his father, and helps him reach a diary that had been preserved specifically for that day by his father, Soumik Banerjee.

Through the diary, Soumitra learns the truth about his father— that Soumik belonged to an influential family in Calcutta but separated from them due to his eccentric pursuits. He risked his life attempting to master a mysterious goddess known as Agashi, found deep within the forests of Assam, and as a result of this pursuit, reached a state where he was neither truly alive nor dead.

In the past, Soumik had travelled with others who shared a similar obsession with mastering dark forces. In search of a crucial power needed to control Agashi, they journeyed into the deep, shadowed forests of Africa. In their attempt to obtain this power from cannibalistic tribes, all the travellers except Soumik Banerjee were killed after a terrifying experience. Soumik alone succeeded in acquiring the power and returned alive.

After this, he travelled to the forests of Assam, where Agashi's dominion prevailed— an entity that did not exist in physical reality at all. She was a princess who had died hundreds of years ago and now resided in a different dimension. She commanded a dangerous army of nocturnal beings who constantly brought her prey. These beings fed on human blood and flesh, drawing strength from it and sustaining their own immortality.

Soumik confronted them and attempted to subdue Agashi in order to gain her immense powers and immortality. Despite relentless effort, his battle ended inconclusively. He neither obtained Agashi's powers, nor was she able to consume him like her other victims— but he did gain immortality, which had been one of his goals. When Soumik began to endure the curse of that immortality, a desire for liberation took root within him. Driven by this longing, he secured his accidentally born son in Calcutta, along with a diary filled with the experiences of his life.

The time had now come for his son, Soumitra, to complete his father's unfinished task and defeat Agashi—and for that reason, he was being summoned to the forests of Assam. Saavri arrived as his father's messenger to call him there— but this was not the complete truth. He could not prepare himself for such a journey, yet by the time of departure, it was as though some unseen force had readied him. He could not perceive that his decision to leave had little to do with his own will, and that he had been prepared from elsewhere.

As the journey begins, a new character enters in the form of Maling, who, along with his disciples, draws Soumitra into his dreams and attempts to kill him. Amid the challenges that confront him at every step, Saavri continues to help him, and through the consequences of these trials, he receives rare opportunities to discipline and refine himself, preparing him for a confrontation with Agashi.

Who, then, truly prepared Soumitra to stake his life on this journey to Assam? If Saavri was not who she claimed to be, then who was she— and what was her purpose in taking Soumitra along? Who was Maling, and why was he determined to end Soumitra's life? How could Agashi, who did not exist in physical reality, be defeated at all? In the realm where she resided, her will alone governed— a virtual world of her own making, where she drew people from the real world and consumed them. How could a human overcome such power? What was the outcome of Soumitra's journey? And was he able to face a force as formidable as Agashi?

Contents

CHAPTER 1

Stepping down from the rickshaw, Debu adjusted the bag slung over his shoulder, pushed his slipping glasses back up his nose, and began walking in the direction he had roughly guessed. This was one of those old corners of Kolkata where colonial-era buildings still stood— their fading grace now sheltering the few remaining descendants of those Englishmen who, after Independence, had chosen India over home.

Debu himself was a writer— not particularly famous, but his books earned him enough to keep things afloat. The rest was managed easily enough by his wife, who worked with the Kolkata Municipal Corporation.

He had come here on someone's invitation. The address he had received was far from precise— not the kind one could follow without asking around. So, once he had gone as far as he could on his own, he stopped at a small roadside paan stall for directions. The stall-owner was alone at the time. When Debu asked for a cigarette, the man gave him a sharp, assessing look before handing one over.

"You look like a writer, dada," he said, sliding his lighter across the counter.

Debu smiled faintly. "Yes— I am."

"Oh really? What do you write, dada? Novels, TV shows, web series, films?" The man's curiosity had clearly grown.

"Ever heard of Debashish Dutta?" Debu asked, lighting his cigarette.

The man frowned, thinking, then shook his head. Debu sighed— a small sound of disappointment. Curse this digital age, he thought. People had stopped reading altogether. There was a time when authors' names were as well-known as film stars— even if not their faces, their names carried weight and wonder.

"Well, no use knowing what I write then," he said after a moment. "Just tell me— which way to Soumitra Babu's house?"

"Who, Soumitra?" the man squinted, uncertain.

Debu pulled out his phone and read the entire address he had saved on WhatsApp.

"Oh, Hedges Babu!" the man exclaimed. "That road you see there— go straight to the very end. His house is the last one. You'll recognize it easily— of all the mansions around, his is the most rundown. Looks less like a home for people and more like one for ghosts."

"You know him?"

"Everyone around here does, dada, though most call him Hedges Babu. A few years back, he could still walk around. Every morning and evening, he'd go out for a stroll— that's how we saw him. Haven't spotted him in years now. Must be well past ninety."

Debu nodded. "Hmm."

"No one visits him anymore," the man added. "What business do you have with him?"

"Not me— he's the one who has business with me. He knows my editor— called me through him. What he needs, I've no idea," Debu said, finishing his cigarette and paying before walking off in the direction of the mysterious Soumitra Hedges.

He indeed had no acquaintance with the oddly named old man, nor any knowledge about him. His editor, Binod Das, had been the one to send him here, saying that Hedges needed a writer. Naturally, the word "writer" had sparked a hopeful thought— perhaps a filmmaker or a web-series producer was looking for a scriptwriter. It was the trend these days. Debu had agreed on that hope alone. He had tried to confirm, but his editor had refused to disclose more.

Now, after what the paan seller had described— a frail nonagenarian living in a crumbling mansion— that hope seemed rather misplaced. Still, "I'm here now— might as well see it through," he thought, walking on.

It was only ten in the morning. The rush of office-goers had passed, and those with shorter commutes were just stepping out. At the far end of the lane stood a few ancient bungalows— and the one he was headed for truly looked ready to surrender to gravity any day now. The gate was half-broken, its iron letters rusted and incomplete.

Finding no doorbell outside, he pushed the creaking iron gate open. Inside lay a short courtyard— littered with broken concrete and iron rods. Ahead stood the door, its frame chipped and ancient, but there, on the wall beside it, a small old-fashioned switch for a doorbell was still visible.

Despite his waning enthusiasm, Debu pressed it.

Two minutes later, the door opened. An elderly man stood there— perhaps in his seventies, wearing a white dhoti-kurta and thick glasses. He squinted at Debu, trying to place him.

"Nomoshkar— Debashish Dutta. Soumitra Babu asked me to come," Debu said, joining his hands politely.

"Yes, yes— please come in. Soumitra Babu has been waiting for you," the man said, stepping aside.

Debu entered, and the door was shut behind him.

"Your good name?" Debu asked.

"Bhagatram, babu. I look after Soumitra Babu— been serving him for forty years now. He's like family."

Bhagatram led him down a narrow passage into a room that was surprisingly well-kept compared to the rest of the mansion. The walls were painted in a pale, velvet-finish color; a large oil painting hung above the bed; several framed photographs adorned the opposite wall. A soft carpet covered the floor, and silk curtains framed the windows.

On the bed sat a frail old man whose eyes lit up faintly when he saw Debu.

"Ah, you've come, Debashish babu— master," Bhagatram announced softly.

Debu greeted him with folded hands. The old man nodded in return, then, gathering his strength, leaned back against the headrest. Bhagatram gently helped him sit upright.

"Please, sit," the old man said, gesturing toward a chair near the bed.

"Thank you," Debu replied, sitting down.

"I'll get some tea," Bhagatram murmured and left.

"At this age," Soumitra said, glancing at the doorway, "he's all I have left. My wife's gone, my children are settled abroad, but he still stays— tending to me like always."

"And your wife and children?" Debu asked politely, though without real curiosity.

"My wife passed away long ago. Two sons— both in England now. They want me to live with them, but I can't leave my soil. I'd rather breathe my last in this air."

Debu nodded thoughtfully. "So, why did you call me?"

"My old friend Binod— your editor, has known me for years. I told him I need someone to write my story. He sent you," the old man said, studying Debu's face, as if weighing whether he was worthy of the task.

"Your story?" Debu asked, a bit startled.

"Yes. You write stories, don't you? So far you've written about imaginary people— now write one about someone real. About me. Believe me, my life has every element a fine book or film could ask for."

"But why do you want it written?" Debu asked, still uncertain.

"Because there are questions— many questions— that my family and others have never been able to answer. They don't know what happened to my wife, or why I kept my sons away. Even your father's generation knew my name, but no one ever knew the truth. Before I die, I want the world to know it. I want to unburden my life— to free it from its secrets."

Debu leaned forward, intrigued now— "Secrets? What kind of secrets? What could still interest the world today?"

Soumitra's eyes gleamed. "Tell me, do you believe in spirits— in ghosts, witches, or dark forces?"

Debu hesitated. "Well… in this modern age, such beliefs are often dismissed as superstition. I wouldn't say I truly believe, but I can't deny them either. I suppose I'm somewhere in the middle— open, but skeptical."

A faint smile touched the old man's lips. "After hearing my story, you may change your mind— if you can believe me."

"That," Debu said quietly, "I'll decide once I've heard it."

The old man's gaze drifted to the framed photographs on the wall. Debu took out his phone and switched on the voice recorder. Slowly, Soumitra's expression changed— as though he were slipping into another time.

"The two English faces in that top photograph," he began softly, "they were my parents— the couple who adopted me before I could even speak. They gave me the name Hedges. I never knew who I was or where I came from. They said only that they had no children of their own and that I was their only hope. My life was simple— studies, friends, laughter— until the day Saavri entered it.

It was 1950. I had just turned twenty that evening. After celebrating my birthday with friends, I was driving home when she appeared— as a messenger from another world."

He paused, his eyes distant.

"It was around eleven. I had dropped my friend Bimal off at Bagbazar and was driving down the empty road toward home. The streetlights— old yellow bulbs— glowed faintly against the night.

And then I saw her. A figure standing by the roadside, signaling for me to stop. The spot was between two lamp posts— cloaked in darkness— so I couldn't see clearly at first. As I neared, the shape grew distinct.

She was wrapped from head to toe in a dark cloak. The fabric hid her form, made it impossible to tell if she was young or old, man or woman. But since she was waving for me to stop, I slowed the car and pulled over.

"What is it?" I asked through the window.

"You are Soumitra, aren't you— Soumitra Banerjee?" The voice was unmistakably female— soft, young— though her face was hidden beneath the hood.

"Soumitra Hedges," I corrected her firmly.

"Son of William and Irene Hedges?" she asked again.

"Yes— but my name is Soumitra Hedges, not Banerjee."

"Hedges is only a gift— a borrowed name," she whispered, leaning closer. "You are not their child. You were adopted. Your real father's name is Saumik Banerjee."

A chill ran down my spine. How could she know this? Yes, I had always known I was adopted— but from whom, where, under what circumstances— that was something my parents had promised to reveal only when I turned twenty.

Twenty. The word flashed like lightning in my head. I had turned twenty today.

"Who are you?" I asked, my voice unsteady.

"A messenger— from your father. He left something for you, something meant to reach you only when you came of age. The time has come. Tomorrow morning at ten, I'll be waiting for you here. You must come with me to claim what's yours."

"And if I'm not interested?" I asked, gathering my nerve.

"Then your father's life— his sacrifice— will all be in vain," she said softly, "We have waited sixteen years for this day. Don't waste it. Go home now. You'll understand tomorrow."

With that, she straightened and stepped back.

I stared at her, uncertain what to say or do. She didn't move— still as a statue. The message was delivered; her part was done. I finally drove off, but after a few yards, I turned to look back— and my breath caught.

She was gone.

There was nowhere to hide— no alley, no wall, no open gate. She had simply vanished. My hands trembled on the steering wheel, and the car swerved slightly.

I didn't know it then, but that night marked the beginning of everything that would change my life— and perhaps, the end of what I thought was real.

●●

Chapter 2

That night passed in restless confusion.

For a long time, my mind kept circling the same questions — what was my past? If my father knew of my existence, why had he left me to grow up in someone else's home? What kind of mother could bear to part with her own child so easily? And who was that messenger girl who had appeared so fearlessly at that hour of the night— and vanished so completely afterward?

My present parents had often told me that when I turned twenty, I would receive the answers to all such questions about my origin. But they had never said who would give me those answers— whether they themselves would, or whether I would have to find them on my own.

When I'd returned home that night, Father was awake but Mother had already gone to bed. I didn't think it right to disturb him with my thoughts, so I simply went to my room, deciding I'd speak to them in the morning. But the night stretched endlessly in unease, sleep evading me until the distant call of fajr azaan reached my ears. Only then, as dawn began to melt the darkness, did I drift into sleep.

And since I had fallen asleep late, I awoke late as well. By the time I came down, Mother and Father had already had breakfast. I sat down at the table, and while eating, brought up the very subject that had kept me awake.

"If I was supposed to know about my past when I turned twenty," I said, "then now that I'm twenty, shouldn't I be told?"

At once, both of them grew silent and exchanged a long look. They must have seen something firm in my face, for they came and sat down at the dining table with me.

"What exactly do you wish to know, son?" Father asked, his gaze fixed deep into mine.

"First of all," I said, "how did you even know my date of birth when you adopted me? Usually, children who are found abandoned— on the streets, temple steps, or at orphanages — have no records of such things."

"Because you were not a stranger to us," Father said gravely— "And we did not find you in any of those places you mentioned."

"Then?" I asked, puzzled.

He sighed, then began, "I once had a friend— Saumik Banerjee. Came from a respectable Bengali family. We studied together. Most of my friends were British, but he was among the few Indians I counted as close. An intelligent man — but withdrawn. He spent his life obsessed with the dark and the unknown— ghosts, spirits, pishachas, witches, demonic forces— things we dismissed as superstition.

But he believed. He wanted to prove their existence, to communicate with them. After completing his studies, he joined a group and set out for Africa in pursuit of his strange research. He was gone for seven months. When he returned, I met him— weak, pale, nearly broken— yet his obsession burned fiercer than ever. He said he'd succeeded in something, though he never explained what. He only said he was going to Assam to finish what he'd started. His family tried to stop him, but nothing could. He came to meet me one last time, then disappeared. He never told me where exactly he was going. And after that day, I never saw him again."

He paused, his expression hardening under memory.

"Five years later," he continued, "A tribal man— ragged, half-starved— appeared at my door carrying a small child, a few belongings, and a letter. That child was you. You must have been about three and a half, maybe four years old.

In the letter, Saumik wrote that he would likely never return. He was entrusting his son to me, asking me to raise him as my own. The child had no name yet— I was free to give one— but he insisted that I replace the family surname completely, that no one should ever learn you were his son. I was never to speak of it, not even to you, until you turned twenty.

He wrote that by then, you would receive a message— one that would lead you to complete a mission he could not.

At that time, your mother and I had been married six or seven years, but we had no children of our own. So, when you came into our lives, we saw you as a gift from God."

He fell silent then, his eyes glistening faintly in the morning light.

"Didn't people ask where you got me from?" There was still so much left for me to understand.

"They did," Mother replied softly, speaking for the first time— "But it was easy to explain. We had just returned from Banaras that night, and we told everyone that we found you during that journey."

Father's tone grew thoughtful again— "But tell me, son— what made you bring all this up today, so suddenly? You only turned twenty yesterday."

I hesitated. Should I tell them about the girl from last night? Would they even believe it? Or would it only worry them unnecessarily?

"Nothing, really," I said, forcing a smile— "It's just been on my mind— you always said I'd get my answers when I turned twenty. So… I thought I'd ask."

Even as I spoke, my eyes drifted toward the wall clock in the hall. It was a few minutes before ten. The girl's words flashed in my mind— "Tomorrow at ten, I'll be waiting for you."

I quickly finished my breakfast and stood up— "Sorry if I ruined your morning," I said lightly, "But I've to meet a friend at ten— he's waiting."

They looked at me with quiet, worried eyes as I left the table.

Back in my room, I changed quickly and left home around a quarter past ten. It took me five minutes to reach the place where I'd met her the previous night.

The day was bright and open, the streets alive with rickshaws, bicycles, cars, and people engaged in their morning chatter. Yet, even in that crowd, I spotted her instantly— for the moment she saw my car, she lifted her hand to signal me to stop.

I pulled up beside her. Without waiting for a word, she opened the door and slipped in.

Last night I hadn't really seen her face, but now, in daylight — she was breathtaking. She wore a light fawn-colored gown, the kind British women often wore. Her hair fell freely over her shoulders, catching the sun. And her eyes— deep, dark, and magnetic— seemed to hold a power that could enslave anyone who met them once.

"You— it was you last night!" I breathed, stunned.

She smiled faintly, and the curve of her lips made my heart stutter.

"So, where are we going?" I asked, steadying my voice.

"Towards Girish Park," she said. Her voice matched the one from last night— only now it sounded richer, because I could see the face it belonged to.

I nodded and started the car.

"Last night," I said after a pause, "I thought you were just an ordinary woman— but walking alone at that hour, unafraid… now I wonder how you dared. After Partition, the city is full of refugees— not all of them harmless."

"I know," she said calmly, without looking at me— "I can take care of myself."

"Good to know. By the way, how did you vanish so suddenly last night?"

"I didn't. I was right there," she said with quiet indifference.

I could tell it wasn't true, but I didn't press.

"May I at least know your name?" I asked.

"Saavri," she said simply.

"Nice name," I smiled— "But it sounds incomplete. Surely there's more to it?"

"No— that's all there is." She looked at me in a way that made it clear I should not ask again.

"So… how do you know my father?" I shifted the subject.

"Why such hurry, Soumitra babu? You've just begun a new journey," she said, smiling faintly— "You'll know everything— slowly. It's better for your mind that way."

In other words, she was telling me to keep quiet.

"Can I ask something else?" I teased.

"What?" she glanced at me, half-curious.

"Just whether anyone's ever told you that you're beautiful."

A pause… then that same careless smile— "Yes. And I already know it."

No trace of embarrassment. No hint of amusement. Just calm, composed indifference.

I tried a few more light remarks, but she remained reserved. My college friends used to joke that I could charm any girl, but this one— this woman… seemed immune.

Soon we reached Girish Park. She began guiding me through narrower lanes until we stopped before an old mansion— one of those that must have been built in the time of Job Charnock, when Calcutta was just beginning to rise as a trading post. It now stood decayed and weary, more a haunted ruin than a residence.

"So," I said, turning to her before stepping out, "is your part just to bring me here for my father's so-called bequest, or does it continue beyond this?"

"That depends on you," she said, getting out— "First, see what your father left for you."

We walked to the heavy wooden door. It was shut. Saavri knocked hard several times. Footsteps shuffled within— slow, dragging— until finally the door opened.

A frail old man stood there, stooped, leaning on a cane. His dhoti and kurta were stained and worn; a round cap covered his head; his thick spectacles magnified eyes filled with irritation. His beard was wild and unkempt, his manner gruff.

"What is it?" he barked, glaring at us.

"This is Soumitra— Soumitra Banerjee," Saavri said quietly.

The old man stilled. His eyes narrowed, then widened, studying me closely.

"Hmm... yes," he muttered at last, nodding— "He's Saumik's son, no doubt."

He stepped aside to let us in.

Following his gesture, we entered. He shut the door and motioned for us to follow. Through narrow, peeling corridors we reached a room lined with bookshelves— a library of sorts. In the center stood a dark ebony table, flanked by wooden chairs. The old man sat on one side and gestured for us to sit opposite.

"I remember Saumik saying his son would come one day," he said— "You do resemble him. But that's not enough for me to hand over what he left. I need the seal— the one I gave Saumik for identification."

He extended his hand.

I stared, puzzled. What seal? I'd learned of my real father only yesterday. How could I possibly have it?

Saavri's eyes flicked toward the pendant around my neck. My breath caught.

"This?" I whispered, "But this locket— I've worn it since childhood. My parents told me never to take it off."

"The time has come to remove it," Saavri said evenly.

Both of them were watching me. After a pause, I took it off and placed it in the old man's hand. He turned it over several times, then pressed a hidden point— and the locket sprang open with a soft click. Tiny mechanical parts slid out — like a secret device.

I stared in shock. All these years, I had thought it solid— just a trinket.

The old man rose silently and left the room.

"I didn't know it could even open," I muttered, glancing at Saavri.

"You don't know many things yet," she replied, her tone flat, distant— "You'd do well to stop being surprised— and start being ready."

I wanted to answer but didn't. A few uneasy minutes passed before the old man returned, carrying a thick, hardbound volume— like a Bible— and placed it before me.

"What's this?" I asked, confused.

"Your father's own handwriting," he said— "A book he left seventeen years ago— filled with his life, his secrets, his experiences. Through this, you'll know everything no one else ever did."

"Why is it important for me?"

"Because he left something unfinished," Saavri said softly — "Something only you can complete. Your life's purpose is to finish what he could not. Only then can you reach your parents."

"What do you mean— reach my parents? Are they alive?" I asked, startled.

"Yes," she said, stepping closer, her eyes holding mine, "And they will remain so— but their return to life depends on what you decide."

"Where are they?" I asked, breathless.

"The answer," she said, tapping the book gently, "lies in here."

And I found myself staring at it— that strange, heavy book — feeling a shiver crawl down my spine.

●●

Chapter 3

They handed me the book and sent me away. Saavri did not feel the need to accompany me; in that same impassive manner she only said that I should read the book as soon as possible— and if I ever felt I needed her afterward, she would find me somehow.

Two questions nagged me. How would I even know that I needed her after reading the book, and how would she know that I had felt that need? She answered both with a mysterious smile and silence that implied the answers would come to me in time, just as she had said on the road.

The leather-bound volume was actually a diary— two hundred pages, each one either written on or bearing a photograph. I had glanced through it in the car and thought that if it hadn't been tied to the man who called himself my father, I might never have dared to open it. But since it belonged to him, and since his presence had become increasingly mysterious, the book aroused a hunger in me I could not resist.

Even so, another thought stuck in my chest like a thorn. Had I not met Saavri that morning, I would have focused on this first. Until yesterday I had no idea who my biological father was— now I knew he was from this city and of some standing. That meant his other relatives should be here too. How, then, could they have handed their kin over to some dark place and never inquired after him or his child— a child left to be raised as an orphan in another household? I wanted to meet them, to ask why they had abandoned a son to such a fate, forced to hide even while alive, hoping that some day his child would finish his unfinished work and restore his life. If they had searched for my father, how far had they succeeded?

From Girish Park I went straight home. I left the book in my room and went to ask my mother about my father's family. After a little hesitation she told me which family he belonged to. The name was not unfamiliar— a girl from that family had studied with me; in light of this revelation, she would in all likelihood be my cousin. Our relations had never been more than a polite acquaintance, so neither she nor my mother knew much, but what was unknown could be discovered. With that thought I set off to see them.

They lived in Shobha Bazar, not far away, and I reached there quickly. Their residence was a great mansion, a symbol of their wealth. Seeing it, a strange notion rose in me— I too might be entitled to this house by birthright— but would they accept me? More than acceptance, would they show me any pity once they learned the truth?

I stopped the car by the gate and signaled the guard.

"Is Dona madam home?" I asked directly— the girl who had once studied with me and who might be my cousin.

"Yes, sir. She should be at home," the guard replied politely— perhaps the car's presence had softened him.

"I need to meet her—she studies with me." For the moment, that excuse seemed sufficient.

"You may go in; your message will reach her." He opened the gate and went to inform the household.

A woman appeared on the veranda almost immediately and bowed with folded hands, welcoming me. "Please come in— memsahib will be out shortly."

She led me to a well-appointed sitting room and left me there to wait.

Within three- or four-minutes Dona entered, draped in silk, hair loose around her shoulders. Her face showed more surprise than pleasure at my arrival— I could tell this was no small astonishment for her. I rose and offered a formal smile.

"Hello, Soumitra— sit," she said, a little awkwardly.

"Hello, Dona— how are you?" I asked.

"Fine. I missed Ranjana ma'am's class yesterday and didn't go to college today either... did she send you here?" she asked, embarrassed.

"No, I haven't been to college since yesterday," I lied casually. "Actually, I'm here on some business."

I hoped the informality would calm her.

"Business?" she said, puzzled.

"Yes. First, could you tell me about your family? Who lives in this house? I mean, who are your relatives?" My heart raced as I asked— this was not just curiosity about their household but a step toward learning about my own origin.

"Why do you ask?" she eyed me suspiciously.

"Come on, tell me. I'm not here to rob the place." I smiled, trying to ease her.

"My grandfather is here, my mother, my father, a sister, a 'bade papa' (elder uncle) and 'badi mummy' (elder aunt), and their two sons who study in England," she said, glaring as if I'd done something improper.

"Did your grandfather have only two sons?" I pursued.

"Why are you asking this?" she blurted.

"Just tell me. If your grandfather had another son, that would matter." I chose my words carefully.

"He had three sons and a daughter. Aunt lives in Dhaka; the youngest son— our youngest chachu— no one among us has seen him. People say he left before my father and elder uncle married, and he never returned." She hesitated, and my breath quickened. The missing chachu— that must be my father.

"Who can tell me more? Is your grandfather in a state to talk? I think he might be able to answer."

"If you must ask about him, you should speak to Dadu. But he seldom meets visitors."

"Then take me to him. If he doesn't want to meet, I'll leave." I pleaded.

She hesitated, then agreed, and we walked through corridors into a large chamber where an elderly man lay on a cushioned bed. A blanket covered him; his shirt was disordered. His eyes were closed, and his chest rose and fell faintly.

"Dadu," Dona called softly. He opened his eyes and stared at us, bewildered.

"Who is it?" he croaked.

"It's Dona, Dadu. This is Soumitra. He studied with me. He says he knows something about our missing chachu and wishes to speak to you," she explained, coming close.

The old man cast a hollow, stunned look at me and muttered that such matters were best known by the friends of that man, not by him— "What do you have to talk to me about? His friends knew more about him than I did. If you have any questions, ask her father. I have nothing to tell you." he grumbled, refusing to speak.

"Dona, could you leave us for a moment? I need to speak with Dadu alone." I moved closer.

"What? I was just saying I don't want to be bothered. Go away. I've just had a coughing fit; it might return," he snapped, turning his face away.

"Dadu— look at me once," I begged.

"What— what's so special in you?" he barked, then blinked as if something in me changed him.

"Without glasses you can't see me properly. Put on your spectacles and look."

He rummaged and found his glasses, slipping them on. When he saw me, he was visibly shaken.

"Whatever you felt, Grandpa, I just want to talk about that — if you'll allow me." I said, folding my hands.

"Dona— you may go now," he said, and Donna looked at me with stern astonishment—what kind of magic was it in my face that Dadu had melted the moment he saw me. I asked her, with a quiet helplessness, to let it be and go. She pulled a face in protest, but eventually turned and left.

I had the sense that something in my face— perhaps a resemblance he had been waiting for— had softened the old man. I stood there, palms together, and prepared to speak.

"Sit," he said, pointing to a small wooden stool beside the bed.

I pulled it closer and sat near him. He kept studying me intently; then, as I came within reach, he raised a trembling hand and touched my face.

"You're Saumik's son?" he asked, his voice cracking.

"Yes," I replied quietly. There was no point in hiding it.

"How is he? Is he… all right?" His voice broke again, eyes misting with sudden tears.

"I don't know," I said softly— "There's much I can tell you, and perhaps much you can tell me. But please, gather your strength first and listen to me. Then, if you wish, you can speak. Because just as you want to know about your son, I want to know about my father."

He nodded faintly and clasped my hand. There was a warmth in his touch— frail, yet filled with belonging— that softened something within me.

Then I told him everything: the mysterious meeting with Saavri, the diary, the messenger's words, and all that had happened from yesterday until now. His face kept shifting between hope and despair— like a man hearing news from a world he'd buried long ago.

"So, he's alive… but no one knows where, or how." His voice trembled when I finished.

"Yes. That girl told me no more than that. She said everything else lies within my father's diary."

"You should have read it first."

"I will. But when I realized his family— my family— still lived in this city, I couldn't stop myself from asking why you all abandoned him. Why didn't anyone try to find him? Why didn't anyone care that his son— I— was growing up in another man's house, just a few miles away?"

"How could we have known?" he said, his tone turning sharp with pain. "All we ever learned was that he left for Assam with some of his reckless friends after returning from Africa, and then… nothing. Not a word. We never even knew he had married— or had a son. William knew us— he came here once or twice. If he knew the truth, he could have told me. But even he stayed silent."

"My father told him to. He instructed that until I turned twenty, no one— not even I— should know who I really was."

"But why? Why hide it from us?" His face tightened, a flicker of old anger in his eyes.

"There must have been a reason," I said quietly. "Maybe that answer is inside the diary."

He leaned back against the pillow, eyes closing for a long moment, struggling to steady himself.

"At first," he began, "he was just like my other children— cheerful, intelligent, full of life. We were wealthy, content. Then an Englishman entered his life— a professor, eccentric, obsessed with the study of 'evil powers.' Against my wishes, Saumik began visiting him, helping in his strange experiments. Slowly, he changed. His interests, his ways, his nights— everything became dark. He stopped meeting people. The only friend he still kept was William.

He'd spend nights away from home, pursuing those demonic experiments. When that professor went to Spain for a while, we thought it would end. But by then, Saumik had found others like him— and soon after, he left for Africa with them. Seven months he was gone, wandering through God knows where. Occasionally, a letter would arrive— just enough to say he was alive.

When he returned, he was half-insane. His body broken, his eyes haunted. We tried to help him, to bring him back to sanity— but his mind was somewhere else entirely. And then, one day, he spoke of Assam. Said he must go there. Didn't say why, didn't say where exactly. Just 'Assam.' One morning he left— and that night, he never returned.

A friend of his told us later that he had said those were his last goodbyes. For a month afterward, we received two letters — the last saying he was in the lower region of Assam and heading deeper into the forests where communication was impossible. After that— silence.

Three years passed. Then we tried to find him. Traced his path up to the regions near Manas. But you know what those jungles are like— vast, unforgiving. We searched every village we could reach. No one had seen him. Eventually, we accepted what we feared— that the jungle had claimed him. That he was gone.

And now, after all these years, I learn he's alive— somehow— and has a grown son who's been living like a stranger in our own city." The old man's voice cracked with bitterness.

"There must have been a reason, Dadu," I said gently— "If he left me with his friend instead of here, perhaps it was to protect me— to hide who I was."

He looked at me for a long moment— "Hmm… and what will you do now?"

"First, I'll read that diary. Find out what really happened to him. After that, I'll decide what must be done."

He sighed— "When will you come again?"

"Tomorrow," I said— "By then, I'll have finished reading it. Then we'll decide together what to do next."

"May I tell the others about this?" he asked hesitantly.

"Not yet," I said— "Once I return tomorrow, you may. By then I'll know whether my father wanted my identity revealed— or still hidden."

He nodded slowly, accepting.

I rose and took his blessings before leaving. Outside, Dona was waiting, curiosity gleaming in her eyes. She wanted to know what magic in my face had made her grandfather change so completely— but I avoided the topic, promising to explain tomorrow."

Just then, a faint sound interrupted the story. Soumitra Babu stopped speaking.

Debu followed his gaze— the door had opened, and Bhagatram entered carrying a tray of tea. He set it down carefully on the side table and slid it toward Debu. The tray held cups, biscuits, and a small plate of savouries.

"Go on, have your tea, Debashish," said Soumitra Babu. "Bhagatram makes excellent tea."

"You won't have any?" Debu asked politely.

"My health doesn't permit much anymore," he said with a sigh. "I eat only for the sake of it— and even that with restrictions."

Debu smiled sympathetically, took the cup, and sipped.

"Bhagatram," Soumitra said, turning to his attendant, "make lunch for Debashish today. He'll have to stay till night — until I finish my story. Give him a simple meal this afternoon— lentils, vegetables— and later, get some fish from the market. Tonight, he must taste proper hospitality. What say you, Debashish? Any preferences or restrictions?"

"None, Sir," Debu said warmly, "Whatever you offer, I'll happily eat."

Soumitra nodded, and Bhagatram left quietly.

"By the way," Debu said after a moment, "when you found your father's real family, why didn't you stay with them? Living alone here with only a servant… it must get lonely."

"There were reasons," Soumitra replied, his tone calm but distant— "You'll understand them soon enough. I couldn't have adjusted there. The parents I truly knew were William and Irene— and they're long gone now. I had two sons, but their lives have always been shadowed by the same danger that haunted mine— the reason my father hid my identity. Just as he entrusted me to his friend, I entrusted my children to my cousin's son in England. They grew up away from me, and the bond never became what it should have been. They want me to live with them, but I can't. And you'll understand why— later."

"And your wife?"

"She was never really gone— nor truly with me. She's… a curse that clings still. Her only kindness was giving me two sons."

"You mean she left you? Then why didn't you remarry?"

"I did," he said bitterly— "Twice. Both my later wives met the same fate. They changed— transformed— before my eyes, and by the time I realized, they were dead. The whole of Calcutta came to know what happens to women who marry me. After that, no one was willing."

"What happened to them?"

"That too," he said, "—is part of this story. You'll understand in time and with it, the reason I sent my children away."

Debu leaned forward— "All right. Then continue. When you returned from your grandfather's house, did you begin reading the diary?"

Soumitra nodded slowly. He reclined against the headrest again, eyes drifting toward the wall of photographs, as though slipping back into another lifetime. His voice, when it returned, had the hush of memory.

"With every passing moment, my curiosity grew stronger. What was my father's story? From what I'd heard, he seemed like a man out of legend— extraordinary, terrifying, and surrounded by mysteries.

When I reached home, my mother was anxious— she wanted to know how my father's family had treated me. I told her briefly that only my grandfather knew the truth, and it was from him that I learned more about my father. She was relieved— not because of what I'd learned, but because I hadn't decided to leave her and Father to go live with them. That was her greatest fear— that once I knew the truth, I would abandon them.

I assured her that I wouldn't. I didn't want to leave— only to understand. After lunch, I locked myself in my room and opened that diary.

And what I'll tell you now," he said, his voice dropping to a whisper— "are my father's words— written seventy years ago. I can't repeat them verbatim, but what I remember— what has burned itself into my memory— I will tell you now."

He paused, eyes distant, then spoke again, slowly, almost reverently.

"He had written…

••

Chapter 4

Today's date is 7 March 1928. It is two in the night, and I— Saumik Banerjee— put pen to the first blank page of this book. Today was my birthday— no, the next day has already begun; yesterday was my birthday. From Governor Francis Stanley I received this book as a gift, its blank pages bound so that its rightful owner might write whatever he pleases. A novelist might fill it with fiction, a poet might arrange verses, a traveler might record journeys— I am none of these, so I will use it as a diary. From this day onward this diary will stay with me. Whatever of my life is worth preserving, I shall etch upon these pages, and for that purpose I begin today.

ooo

The philosophies that bind my life leave little room for the ordinary man. That is why those tied to my childhood have slowly drifted away, and now only three remain who truly care for me and do not call me mad. One is my friend William; one is Professor Frederick— my teacher— and one is Dr. Deepdas. He is neither a mere mentor nor merely a friend, but an honest man who guides me. He knows many languages and has assembled a vast library in his home, with books ranging from China to Baghdad, from India to England. Much of his time is spent learning Arabic and Chinese; like a skilled raconteur, he translates those books into Bengali for me, opening doors to other tongues and other worlds.

Yes— the centre of my fascination remains that dark world which most take me as mad for pursuing. My father calls me "the eccentric" instead of my name. At first it wounded me, but habit has dulled the sting. It is not that all of Calcutta have become scientific skeptics who deny spirits and ghosts; they believe in such things as readily as they believe in God. Yet with God they wish to approach— they do not fear Him; with these occult powers they are frightened and try every means to avoid them.

I do not fear them. I know these mysterious forces can harm me, yet I want to reach them. For two years Professor Frederick and I have been conducting research and experiments on how to contact them and how to master them, but so far we have no conclusive success to speak of. We have not yet seen a single ghost or spirit, but that does not mean they do not exist. They do, and mastery over them is possible— one day I will prove it.

ooo

Days passed as I filled the blank pages of this diary, but success eluded me. Yet I am not despondent. Today a new hope has arisen. I met a sanyasi who told me of a dark goddess named Agashi— she hunts once a month, preying on humans. She has no age, no fixed face. No binding can hold her; she must be vanquished, not merely bound. If controlled, she grants wealth and many powers, and bestows a kind of immortality. But the price of mastery is steep. She resembles a yakshini in some respects, yet differs in fundamental ways.

Professor Frederick and I have attempted many rituals, most of them fruitless. I shall list some: in tantric practice there are six main rites— shanti (peace), vashikaran (enchantment), stambhan (paralysis), vidveshan (discord), uchchatan (banishment), and maran (killing). Beyond these, certain texts describe nine experiments: maran, mohan (captivation), stambhan, vidveshan, uchchatan, vashikaran, attraction, yakshini sadhana, and rasayan kriya. Various deities are then invoked for these rites. Aghoris employ Shiva sadhana, corpse rites, and cremation-ground rituals. Many practice bhairav sadhana, naga sadhana, paishachini sadhana, yakshini sadhana, or rudra sadhana. We attempted some failed experiments within paishachini, bhairav and yogini practices, and we intend in the near future to attempt yakshini sadhana.

According to tantrik lore, a yakshini devoted to carnal pleasure, if pleased by the practitioner, grants twenty-five gold coins. A "sau-sundari" yakshini grants wealth and longevity; an "anuragini" grants a thousand gold coins; a "jalavasini" grants gems; "vatavasini" grants jewelry and garments. Tantric manuals provide elaborate instructions for yakshini and yaksha worship. But the power I seek is different — not found in scriptures or puranas. She is like a yakshini yet far stronger; the singular thing she can grant is immortality — something given to a few mythic heroes, but not to any living person of our age.

Agashi cannot be bound by ordinary rites; she must be defeated. That defeat— call it a sadhana— is nearly impossible. For it, one must already possess certain powers that can blunt Agashi's influence. Where she might be found, the sanyasi could not give a precise location, but he named regions: Barpeta and Bongaigaon in Assam, and the southern forests near Bhutan, along the banks of the Bekhy river— go there and you may learn more. I have abandoned the purely yakshini rites and resolved to conquer Agashi; from tomorrow I will direct all my efforts toward that end.

ooo

Ten days have now passed since that meeting with the sanyasi, and in the meantime, I have found four men who, like me, desire mastery over such forces. Their names are Smith, Olanga, Carter, and Sahdev. They already belong to a group, and now I have become part of it. Among them, Sahdev is an old zamindar of Cooch Behar who spends his wealth on this passion— he travels the world and arrived in Calcutta only last month. Sahdev is Bengali; Smith and Carter are Italian; Olanga is African. The first part of their lives was spent in study, so there is no doubt they are men of learning.

I told them of Agashi, and they too grew eager to conquer her. But this is plainly a life-and-death venture. It is better to gather information first. They intend to go to Assam. I cannot leave now— my own trials are ongoing— but these four plan to go. The region once used by the royal family of Cooch Behar and by the Gauripur kings as a hunting ground has since been declared a forest reserve by the British and, I hear, is now or soon will be a game sanctuary. Sahdev has connections with the Cooch Behar royals and can make use of them. They hope to depart tomorrow and return with every scrap of intelligence about Agashi.

○○○

A month later they returned alive and intact. They had not gone to Bhutan's high ranges nor penetrated the heart of the forests where Agashi's domain truly lay; rather, they reached as deep as was safely possible and gathered what they could, then came back satisfied. Their account resembled tales of Perseus and Medusa— that to slay the kraken Perseus needed Medusa's head, for one glance would turn the monster to stone. Agashi commanded many occult powers and an entire nocturnal army under her sway.

The local tribes revered her as a goddess. Once a month she chose a human prey— not from among her own people but a stranger— and could assume any form. Her favourite weapon was a bewitching multiform beauty that would hypnotize its victim; in the embrace she would drain the prey's life-force. After that, the weakened prey would be torn apart by her night-creatures and devoured.

To neutralize such an assault, one must attain absolute control over the senses and render the body almost like adamant. How to make the body like thunderbolt? We learned that those who seek to subdue such power must undertake an odd tapasya— an ordeal not found within Indian lore, but known to the Malawian Kasungu forests of eastern Africa.

Olanga spoke of a ritual called ariki. It is performed by a tribe living in Kasungu; they begin an observance twenty-four hours before a lunar eclipse, and, using a trident that reflects the moon's returning rays, they draw those rays upon the body. This trident is their sacred gift from the gods, their dearest treasure, and the ritual is performed only by their highest witches. It grants powers enabling them to protect their group from calamities and to foresee ways to survive scarcity of food and water.

We resolved to go to Africa and perform that ritual, come what may. My father will provide no assistance; Sahdev will fund the mission. I have spoken to Professor Frederick and Dr. Deepdas about this. The professor knows little of the matter but wishes me to undertake the mission; Dr. Das has heard of the ariki practitioners and warns that they are violent — the local name for them is "Angozha," formidable hunters.

Those who roam the Kasungu forests feed mostly on animal prey, but if a human falls into their hands they do not release him. They are not kindly; they are ferocious. One must approach them with extreme caution.

None of us fully understand how to perform such a dangerous tribal rite when they will not cooperate, but the thought grips us: we must somehow reach them. Whatever follows, we have resolved to bear it. A way will appear.

We shall depart for Africa soon.

ooo

After nearly two months of travel, we have reached Africa — by sea from Calcutta to Bombay and onward to southeastern Africa, landing in Mozambique, where we first made camp at Pemba. The Portuguese rule this place; most people speak Portuguese, which Smith and Carter manage well enough, while the local populace speaks Chichewa, which Olanga understands, so we have not run into trouble yet. From Pemba we made a long, tedious overland journey and reached Lichinga. There Olanga, using his African roots, found a guide who will take us on to Kasungu— for which Sahdev is paying him handsomely.

Tonight, we are enjoying our last evening with the Bantu girls— tomorrow we will press westward and by evening reach the eastern shore of Lake Malawi, where we will camp and arrange passage across the lake so we can get to Agostino. After that we may have to proceed via Ankotakhota to Kasungu, a journey that promises to be very difficult. We have not told our guide our true purpose; we told him we are explorers wanting only to learn about the Angozha people. We convinced him we could handle them, though he does not know we carry firearms that might be used on this expedition. In any case, I'm about to join their festivities— I too deserve a little merriment.

ooo

Four days have passed since we left Lichinga and crossed Lake Malawi; we are now within Malawi's borders. We are not certain of our exact location, but we know we are in the Ankotakhota region on the road to Kasungu. We have endured many hardships. The lake crossing took a full day, and we reached Agostino only after sunset and had to camp on the shore. The boatman who took us this far stayed with us and planned to return in the morning. That night the weather turned foul and we spent it awake, soaked by the rain; by morning Sahdev developed a fever so high we could not continue.

We decided to remain there for a day while the boatman departed, leaving us without a practical return option. We were now entirely at the mercy of Providence. If any one of us fell ill further, or if Sahdev's condition worsened, we could neither take him back to Lichinga nor reach any settled population in time. We carried only a small stock of medicines as a precaution, so for now we survive on those. Over two days his fever abated but did not fully vanish.

After a day's pause we resumed toward Kasungu at first light. With our guide Chakwera, there are six of us and eight horses. Some gear we carry on our own backs; the rest is loaded onto two of the horses to ease travel through the forest. The trouble is these horses are not very docile, and they cause us much difficulty at times.

Today a baboon attacked us— no one was seriously hurt, but the horses panicked and it took a long while to bring them under control. In the chaos we all suffered minor injuries; Carter hurt his leg badly. Walking would have been hard, but since we still have horses, Carter's injury is not yet a crippling obstacle.

The others seem seasoned to such hardships and are less fazed than I am. Last night by Lake Malawi was tolerable compared with the previous night when mosquitoes and other biting insects tormented us severely. Tonight remains to be seen how it will pass. By dusk we reached a small village called Banga and reassured the villagers that we posed no danger; we camped at the village boundary.

Near our camp some wandering Chila people performed a traditional dance. Most locals we've met speak Chichewa, which our guide understands, so we have avoided unpleasantness. Chakwera says the Angozha do not speak Chichewa; their tongue is different, one he only partly knows. He told us not all Angozha are violent or man-eating; it is principally the ariki practitioners among them who are dangerous.

The ariki move within a radius of a hundred kilometres and live without a fixed abode; contact with ordinary Angozha makes it possible for guides like ours to learn something of their language. Today, then, we take this small respite among Chila dancers— Carter still lies feverish in the camp while I sit near him and write these lines. I will join the dancers shortly.

ooo

After enduring the trials of the road, we finally reached Kasungu, but the Angozha we sought were not there. The place where we had expected to find their encampment was deserted— they had moved on— and for two days we wandered in search of them to no avail. Today, however, a glimmer of hope returned.

It has been a week since we left Banga; the route has been cruel, and we have suffered nearly every hardship. We endured animal attacks, and at one place monkeys stole much of our food. In the panic one horse's leg broke and we had to leave it. We redistributed its load among the rest.

Sahdev recovered, but my own strength is failing. I am not cut out for this life. Food is scarce, sleep fragmented; insects bite through the night. We fall into exhausted dozes only to rise before dawn and move on.

Our horses can run like vehicles when the terrain allows, but often there is no ground suitable for galloping. We cover what we can, but most of the time we simply walk. It took five days to go from Banga to Kasungu, and for two days since then we have been tracking the ariki Angozha through the forest. We did encounter two other Angozha bands, but they were not the ariki practitioners we sought; those meetings were uneasy, but Chakwera handled them deftly.

Ordinary Angozha are not as ferocious as the ariki, yet they are reserved and keep strangers at a distance. That raises the crucial question: how will the people we came to meet tolerate us?

Another problem is that we lacked full preparation. With more training and supplies we might have accomplished the mission regardless, but as it stands, we are at the mercy of God and gamble on fortune. The ariki ritual must be performed at the time of a lunar eclipse— one visible from this part of the world, and that eclipse will occur this month. The next such eclipse is a year away; we cannot wait.

It puzzles me how these so-called "primitive" forest people, far removed from civilized calculation, know the precise timing of eclipses well enough to begin rituals the day before.

After two days of failure today brought some success: as we advanced toward Kavu we met two hunting Angozha who reported seeing ariki Angozha in Kavu; perhaps that is where they have camped. We decided to head there tomorrow. Whether we will reach it safely— that remains uncertain. Everyone's condition is poor, and my own worst among them.

Dense forests may hide other tribes that are man-eaters; they strike from concealment with poisoned arrows that either kill or leave the victim dying.

Besides human danger, wild beasts hostile to human intrusion— especially to people like us from the modern world— lurk constantly. To survive we must remain vigilant. At night three of us keep watch with weapons while three sleep; we keep the fire burning throughout. Chakwera was surprised and angered by our arms at first, but once we explained the forest's realities and that our weapons are for defence only, not for murder, he accepted it with some irritation.

If the night passes safely we shall depart at dawn for Kavu. This region once formed part of British-protected Rhodesia, so perhaps official trouble will be limited— our real peril is our ability to keep ourselves alive in the jungle, which is by no means easy.

ooo

Four more days have passed, and so much has happened that my hands tremble as I write, yet I put pen to paper hoping that if I do not survive, whoever finds this diary will know what befell us.

The night I last wrote about passed without incident, and for a while it seemed we might achieve our aim that very day. Instead, we spent the whole day wandering the forest, wrestling with dangers, and scored no real success— indeed, we suffered a grave loss. A pride of lions surprised us; the horses bolted, and though we recovered four of them with great difficulty, three were lost along with a large portion of our equipment.

Food was not the only worry— one can forage in the jungle— but our camp kit was gone, and suddenly we were reduced to the same precarious condition as the natives.

We decided it would be safer to spend the night in some sheltered hollow rather than out in the open. Searching for a secure place, we found a large cave. Geographically we were on Kasungu's western edge, not far from Kavu, where the forest thins and danger lessens.

The cave showed clear signs of regular human use. In such a remote wood, who else but the Angozha would gather here? Encouraged, we made camp and tethered the horses deep inside a dense thicket so that any wild animals would not see them.

Two things unnerved us— first, a foul, unsettling smell hung in the place; second, deep within the cave stood a grisly idol, and before it a low altar of piled stones stained with dark blood.

Chakwera guessed this was an Angozha sacrificial site, used for rites in which offerings were made. Whether they sacrificed animals or humans we could not say. Fear gripped us, yet Chakwera reassured in his blunt way: in such deep forests they would usually find animals, not men, to offer.

If they performed rituals here, they would at least return — when they did. We smoothed our minds and decided to sleep in hiding, armed and ready.

We rationed whatever food remained and waited. After perhaps an hour many sounds and faint lights approached. We went quiet and hid; yes, now we had our weapons ready. Four pistols belonged to Carter, Smith, Olanga, and Sahdev; Chakwera and I were unarmed. Our protection rested on those four.

A filthy, savage throng entered— men, women, old, young, children. They looked feral; their bodies were scarcely clothed, painted with a reddish earth, their skin incised with carved figures. Their noses and lips were oddly pierced and decorated. Some carried spears, some bows, some trumpets; the women held fat-torches, fanning smoke and light. At the front strode an ancient man, heavily scarred as a show of ornament.

Behind him two brawny youths dragged a wild boar whose muzzle was bound. We counted nearly seventy of them.

They settled in the cave's inner recess before the idol, lit a fire, and laid the hog upon the altar. The old leader mumbled, then others rose, hands raised, chanting in unison before kneeling and bowing their foreheads as in prayer. They repeated the ritual again and again. The leader took up a cleaver and, intoning a harsh chant, struck the boar's throat — the poor creature's head was not fully severed; a part remained attached as its body convulsed and blood streamed down over the stones.

We were six men, only I a Brahmin by birth, but we all ate meat; yet nothing prepared us for that sight. As the boar's throat was cut they exploded into wild rejoicing and danced in grotesque celebration. The leader collapsed in a stupor before the idol.

They skinned the animal while it still writhed, cut it into pieces and roasted the choicest parts upon the fire. The smell of burning flesh filled the cave.

They ate ravenously. They were so absorbed in the feast that they did not notice anything beyond their own revelry. The spectacle lasted an hour and a half. Afterwards they doused the fire and returned in slow, lazy procession, as if leaving a dinner party. Silence fell over the cave.

Chakwera said they likely only performed such large rites when the hunt yielded a prize; otherwise they survived on smaller kills or raw fare. We slept fitfully in shifts. The important thing was that our horses were not seen by the Angozha.

We resolved, without telling Chakwera, to seize the leader — our belief being that our purpose could be advanced only by questioning him. Chakwera would have argued against it, so we chose secrecy. Fate, however, betrayed us. Before we could approach, their eyes found us, and arrows and small poisoned darts rained from everywhere.

We were struck before we could react. Arrows grazed the others; one dart pierced Smith's eye, lodging into his brain— he fell dead at once. We drew our weapons but the poisons in those darts took hold faster; we began to swoon. I thought later why they had not given warning, why they had not tried to drive us off; their intent became clear only then— we were prey.

I blacked out. When I came to, we were confined in a small cage-like hut built of wood so tightly that with bare hands and feet freedom was impossible. It was not a hut but a pen— they had placed us there as their meat. Smith was already dead. The remaining five of us were injured and needed medical care, yet who would provide medicine where we were kept as dinners?

The place where they had trapped us was a clearing amid dense trees. Around it stood thatched huts made of branches, vines and grass— a small village. Near them was a large clay oven.

Perhaps during transport, they had killed Smith; in the evening they stoked that oven and slowly roasted Smith's body inside it so that it would be cooked through without burning outright. From our barred windows we watched the horror of his roasting, and our souls trembled. I passed out.

I did not see it myself, but the others said that when Smith's meat was ready, the tribe divided it and ate it much like they had the boar. They finished before dusk and returned to their huts. We lay shivering.

Yet we noticed one small child among them who did not seem to share the others' appetite; when she looked at us there was pity, not hunger in her eyes. For a moment hope stirred: perhaps she might help.

During the night that child slipped to our window and gave us water. Chakwera could not fully converse with her, but he managed to win a small compassion in the child's heart. She dared supply us with water, but she was small, and we feared she could not do more.

The next day they did not go hunting, staying near our cage; they seemed content to keep us alive for some purpose.

At noon they fed us strange fruits that quenched thirst and kept starvation at bay. In the evening, they dragged us, bound and groaning, back to the same cave where we had first found them. We felt them preparing to sacrifice us. I staggered half-conscious, expecting death; there was no reprieve.

In the cave they repeated the savage pageant we had witnessed earlier. We did not know who would be chosen until they dragged Carter down. Helplessly he thrashed and screamed; in unconsciousness the leader slit his throat and Carter was roasted and eaten.

My fingers tremble so much as I write that the ink shakes on the paper. I record this, so others may know what happened to us.

That night we were maddened with fear. The child again brought us water. From Chakwera's broken speech we gathered that perhaps they would spare him— not us— and that he might be used to pass messages between their world and ours, bait for future hunts. The night crawled by; our hearts lurched at every sound, each imagining this could be our last hour.

The next day followed the same grim procession. It marked the end for Sahdev. We watched as he was offered and consumed. None of us slept that night; Chakwera all but said aloud that today it might be my turn, and indeed I believed the sun might not rise for me.

At dawn I begged in frantic supplication— that they allow me one thing: to retrieve my belongings, my diary, and a pen so I could write before death. Chakwera intervened and moved the leader; my plea moved him.

He gave me this diary and a pen. With quivering hands I write, convinced that tonight may be my last. Memory floods me— every error that led me to this bloody route— and I now understand how grievous a mistake it was to begin such a perilous journey unprepared. I may pay for it with my life.

I end here for now, believing these may be my final written words.

ooo

If I am writing this, it means I am alive— and my being alive feels less like chance than a miracle. Fate had not written death for me, so it passed me by. I am a believer, and my faith in God has only hardened. I do not know why, but after surviving by a near-impossible turn in Africa, I feel certain I will find success in Assam as well.

When I last wrote, the pressure on my skull had knocked me unconscious. In the evening, when I came to, they had bound the three of us to bamboo poles and were carrying us on their shoulders toward the same cave that had been our destination.

We were in a dreadful state— we wanted to scream, but terror had strangled our voices. We had no strength to struggle; our minds felt numb. All we could do was weep like madmen, and that is what we did.

When they resumed their grotesque ritual in the cave, we realized that I was not the chosen prey this time— Olanga was. They had tied him tightly so he could not move; before he understood what was happening, he tried to struggle and fainted in agony.

I felt a grotesque relief at not being chosen— strange and shameful on any human scale, yet by then what did shame mean to me? They flung me and Chakwera aside as if we were of no consequence.

While the elders offered thanks to their dark goddess and resumed their singing and dancing, the little girl who had shown us pity slipped away from the crowd and came to us. Chakwera, fighting his panic, tried to talk to her.

My relief at surviving did nothing to steady me; I could not shake the image of Olanga being roasted and eaten a short distance from where I lay— Olanga, who had journeyed with us from Calcutta to Nyasaland, who had shared every hardship and joy. Memories of him passed through my mind like film, and I wept.

When their grisly feast finally ended, they returned us to the same penlike hut. Chakwera told me the little girl had whispered that tomorrow the lunar eclipse would begin and the ariki ritual would already commence. Because I was among the two survivors who were stronger and more handsome, they had reserved me as the main offering; that was why Olanga had been chosen for tonight's banquet.

The irony was bitter— the very ritual I had hoped would grant protection against Agashi was to demand my sacrifice. The thought of dying before my time filled me with sobbing despair; I wept like a coward. Chakwera could only pity me.

Shortly thereafter torches and fires were lit. Beside our hut lay a small clearing that they used for dances and rites. From our barred window we could see them preparing an altar: wood piled and set alight, aromatic smoke drifting up, a canopy of four bamboo poles stretched above so the open sky could not be seen.

The leader's regalia had been increased; the shaman looked like a bridegroom— he had wrapped an animal skin around his waist and donned a crown of flowers. Near the altar they set a wooden block with a notch carved for a throat— the sight made my flesh crawl. They planted a metal idol shaped like a monkey before the altar, and behind it on a particular angle they stuck a double-handled trident so that the idol stood in its shadow.

Chakwera thought— as indeed it proved— that the idol represented some goddess.

The shaman struck an instrument; the leader sacrificed a rabbit and daubed the shaman with its blood. The shaman sat before the altar like a priest and began intoning mantras while the crowd swayed, repeating his words at intervals. Thus, the rite began— a ritual that would end only after my sacrifice and the eclipse had passed.

All night they performed their rites. Sleep was impossible for me. Their ceremonial dances, their shouts of victory, the way they stoked and subdued the sacrificial fire, the strange things they added to the flames— every three or four hours a rabbit, a chicken, a kid would be offered.

The shaman did not perform alone; two others took turns acting as officiant— perhaps his sons or disciples— so that the work was shared and rest was possible. The others participated in shifts as well. For me it was a macabre spectacle of my approaching death, and I watched with hollow eyes and a heart that felt like it was sinking. Three times during the night the little girl came to us with water; her pity felt like the last ember of hope.

Out of some sudden resolution I decided: if I must die, I would not go quietly alone. If I could, I would try to take some of them with me. It was a desperate thought, born of equal parts despair and resolve. The remaining hours passed in the frantic scheming of how I might resist.

At dawn, when most were exhausted and slumbering, the little girl slipped away— perhaps to relieve herself. I signaled her and roused Chakwera. Sleep-fogged, he woke with difficulty, but by luck he managed to explain to her, and she understood.

He convinced her to fetch my shaving kit from my belongings, telling her I intended to purify myself before offering my beard to the goddess. In any other circumstances she might have balked, but exhaustion made everyone careless; she brought the kit.

I shaved with the water in a bamboo basin and hid the blade in the folds of the decorations tied to my body. Then I pretended to sleep, convincing them I had succumbed to the ritual's effect. They assumed I was docile and left me in the hut. Chakwera watched me with bewilderment at the sudden change in my spirits.

I sat in meditation, preparing for the coming moment. Perhaps I could kill two or three of them and still die; I accepted that death might be my end. The thought of fighting, of grasping at life, steadied me— the adrenaline that had numbed me since Smith and Carter's deaths was easing.

Night fell and their revel grew louder. The small hourly sacrifices now occurred every hour; drums beat and the shaman chanted as if possessed. When darkness came, they brought me out into the clearing.

They bound my hands behind me, smeared my forehead with the blood of a plumed rooster, and forced me down so my head was thrust forward on the altar, ready for the cleaver.

My heart hammered in my throat as if it would burst— all the practice of my intent seemed mockery when the moment arrived. The shaman danced and his two aides stood on either side of me, holding me down.

Then the moon's shadow began to fall. As the eclipse deepened, the whole ceremony stilled; fires were damped, and lights went out. The crowd lay prostrate, faces turned to the idol.

In those moments I worked my fingers until they found the blades hidden at my wrists and cut the cord binding my arm. I was almost ready. As the moon began to reemerge, the shaman raised the cleaver.

In the instant my bindings fell away, I grabbed the nearest youth by the arm and shoved him— the momentum carried him forward and, disastrously for him, beneath the swinging cleaver. The shaman's blade severed him up to his neck; he howled and staggered as blood gushed.

The suddenness froze them all for a breath; in that single stunned moment I wrenched the cleaver from the shaman's hand. He was old and weakened; the shock robbed him of any immediate resistance. I pulled the blade and drove it at the other youth who had been holding me. The cleaver bit into his belly; he crumpled, gushing blood. I struck again, and his neck was nearly severed. Blood sprayed and splashed my face until I was stained.

Holding the cleaver, I rose. The moonlight, now slipping from behind the earth's shadow, struck the trident behind the idol and reflected like a shower of light.

Those rays washed over me. The shaman collapsed before me, trembling, and all the Angozha fell to their knees, prostrating themselves as if I were their god. I stood, naked and blood-smeared, cleaver raised, two of their men dead at my feet.

In that moment a strange memory came to me— the image of Lord Parashuram.

It felt as if the rays passing through the trident had suddenly turned molten, burning through my skin and flooding my body with feverish heat. My hands trembled, the cleaver slipped from my grip and hung loose by my side. When I tried to move away from the trident's shadow, my legs refused to obey— they were fixed to the ground like roots.

I bent my knees to steady myself, but the body could no longer bear its own weight and collapsed to the earth. A sharp, stinging vibration filled my skull; darkness swam over my eyes, and in that whirl— the corpses, the shaman, the chanting tribe— all vanished into a consuming void. I tried to stay conscious but failed, and before I could think further, my senses drowned and I fell senseless to the ground. By the time I would wake again, the moon had completely emerged from the Earth's shadow.

When I opened my eyes, the scene had changed beyond recognition. My status had changed— I was now their Ojha, their seer, their protector— the one destined to guide them, save them from dangers, and divine food and water for their survival.

The former Ojha had become my disciple. In their world, there was no deceit or competition as in ours; what they believed became their truth. Even though one of the two young men I had slain was that Ojha's son, the man now bowed to me with complete surrender.

At last, I could breathe. My life was safe. Chakwera told me that the two men who had died the night before were later offered as a ritual oblation— cooked and consumed— The sacrifice had been made in my place. But now, at least, I was no longer in danger of being part of such a feast.

Yet the future was uncertain. These were cannibal tribes — nara-bhakshi log, who believed in consuming human offerings. How long could they remain loyal to a leader who refused to share their ways? How long before their faith turned to suspicion and they chose another Ojha? I had to escape soon; besides, my purpose here was complete.

I had received what I came for— the 'ariki snan', the sacred lunar bathing— though I felt no change in my body, no hint that it had turned to the steel of legends. Still, if this was the traditional ariki chandra-snaan, then perhaps I had received its effect by fate alone. Now it was time to leave— even if that required lies or deception. Against such people, deceit no longer felt sinful.

ooo

It has been three days since I became the Ojha of the Angozha, and I am ready to leave.

From the old shaman— now my disciple— I asked, "What powers have I truly gained from this ritual?"

He told me, "Now, no spirit, no demonic or otherworldly force can control you. For them, you are nearly invincible. You can see what lies unseen— the dangers around, the paths ahead, the fate yet to come. This is the gift of the Ariki."

He said that before my arrival, when he was still Ojha, he had seen a vision— a danger approaching from afar— and knew we were coming. That was why they had attacked us before we could defend ourselves. I had also asked how they always knew the exact time of a lunar eclipse without written calendars or calculations.

He claimed that seven days before each eclipse, the vision would come to him in trance.

His words sounded more like imagination than truth— yet one could not deny the eerie precision of their timing. How did they know we were coming? How did they anticipate the eclipse to the exact hour?

That first evening of my new role, I had meditated in the way he described, seeking the same visions. Despite repeated attempts, I saw nothing— and consoled myself thinking he was a liar.

The next day, I asked him to teach me how to see as he did. Through Chakwera's translation, he explained the method— a form of deep concentration, not unlike the meditations of our own rishis.

By then, I had assigned that little girl— the same one who had pitied and saved me— as my attendant. She saved my life, and perhaps this was my way of honoring her compassion.

That night, I tried again.

At first, blurred shapes. Then faint clarity. And finally, as the night deepened, the visions came— vivid, coherent, unmistakable. What I saw, however, was not good for the Angozha.

Because of their habits— their hunger for human flesh— they had recently killed and eaten an English survey team near Kavu. Their disappearance had reached the ears of British officers, who had dispatched a heavily armed unit into the forests. Within five days, that battalion would reach these tribes and wipe most of them out. Only a few would escape into the deeper jungles.

I felt no pity. I would not warn them. Their fate was the payment of the sins they had fed upon. That night, I chose my own path— a way out— and went to sleep.

By morning, I told my first lie to Chakwera.

I said, "Last night, in my vision, I saw all of you perish. Even you. But I can save you— only if you do exactly as I say."

Being a simple man of faith, and convinced of my powers, he fell to my feet, begging for life. I told him he must protect that little girl, Iyanka, as if she were his own daughter, and live among the civilized as a better man. He agreed instantly.

Then I gathered the rest of the tribe and told my second lie.

I said— "The people you killed near Kavu were British officers. The government has sent a full armed force to destroy you. They have guns you cannot fight. But I can stop them. I am the son of a great officer of their empire. If I go and speak to them, I can make them believe you are innocent."

Fear spread through their faces— then submission. They believed me.

I laid my final conditions— "Chakwera and Iyanka will come with me. Without Chakwera, I cannot speak your tongue. And Iyanka will prove to them that you are not savages."

They agreed, grateful for any hope of survival.

Tomorrow, at sunrise, we depart. The plan is clear.

We will take all supplies in the name of this "mission."

At Kavu, Chakwera will take Iyanka and flee east, while I will move north through Chipata and Lilongwe to Quelimane — from there, I will sail back to India.

Everything is unfolding exactly as I wished.

Now I write under the fading lantern light, waiting for dawn.

Tomorrow's sunrise will not just be another morning — it will be my sunrise— the light of my freedom, the beginning of my return.

°°°

It has been more than three months since I left Kasungu, and now I am back in Calcutta. My appearance has become so disheveled that people look at me as though I've lost my mind. Father scolded me harshly, tried to reason with me, but I have long crossed the threshold where reason can reach. The mission for which I left home— half of it I have accomplished, and the rest I cannot abandon midway. Whatever the consequence, I will go to Assam. I will face Agashi— and conquer her.

Even William finds my state troubling; he worries for me. Perhaps he is right. After all that I endured on my first journey— where mere survival felt like a miracle, and where I returned with powers that lifted me beyond ordinary human strength— perhaps madness was inevitable. My words, my wild appearance, my erratic behavior— they must all testify to a mind unhinged.

The belongings of my fallen companions had come into my possession at Kasungu, and the money Sahadev had carried for our expedition proved enough for me to travel back from Africa to Assam without begging for help. There was no one left dependent on Sahadev, no moral debt binding me to return what remained of his wealth. Without guilt, I decided to use it for my purpose.

At Kavu, I had sent Iyanka away with Chakwera, while I sought help from the British officers, using my father's name and his connection with the Government of India. They helped me travel safely to Chipata. From there, through Lilongwe and Quelimane, I journeyed with traders and travelers, until a British merchant vessel carried me across the ocean to India.

As for those cannibalistic Angozhas, I did the opposite of what I had promised them— I told the officers the truth, that they had killed and eaten my companions. But I made no further effort to bring punishment upon them. The vision I had seen in Kasungu was already destined; I merely let fate play its part.

I have always believed in harmony with nature— that forests belong to those who live within them, and that the so-called "civilized world" should not destroy them in the name of progress. But such tribes— nara-bhakshi, devourers of their own kind— cannot be allowed to thrive unchecked. I do not regret their fate.

In Lilongwe, I meditated again. My vision showed the prophecy fulfilled— the British troops had arrived, and most of the Angozha had perished. The few who survived had fled deep into the forests. Perhaps they would live, perhaps they would change.

The journey home was long, but life aboard the ship was almost pleasant. I made friends among sailors who had spent their lives at sea. They told me stories— tales from ports and oceans across the world— and I, in turn, filled pages with their words, in small chapters that broke the monotony of time. Yet my real story— my purpose— begins again today, as I sit here, ready for my Assam expedition. At dawn, I will leave without telling anyone.

I cannot risk it— Father will forbid me, and William will plead with me to stay. Only Dr. Deepdas and Professor Frederick know. They not only understand me, they have helped prepare for my departure.

ooo

Calcutta is behind me now— I am on my way to Assam. I have sent a message to a trusted acquaintance to inform my father only after I've gone too far to be stopped. By the time they know, I will already be in Dhaka. From there, the route is clear— train through Karimganj, Agartala, Lumding, then Guwahati— and from there, I will continue by motor vehicle. Dr. Deepdas has already arranged it.

The train clatters steadily over the tracks; through the window, the countryside rushes backward— fields, forests, scattered villages, brief flashes of faces by the stations. Most passengers are laborers, being taken by British officials to work in Assam. A few, like me, are men of better birth, traveling on personal errands. But among them, I doubt there is anyone with an errand like mine.

Now, Agashi fills my thoughts.

It was from Sahadev that I had first heard about her in depth— the mad monk had mentioned her only in fragments. She is the goddess of darkness and mountains, worshipped by the border tribes between Bhutan and Assam. Little is known of her beyond those forests. She commands a nocturnal army that moves only by night. She is more active during Dakshinayan than Uttarayan, and stronger under the waning moon than the waxing. In the regions touched by her shadow, the chances of an encounter rise.

Every new moon, she goes on a hunt.

Her prey— always men.

She entices them, draws them close, drains them of life, and feeds.

It is said that her victims are never found whole, that she leaves no trace of her presence except the silence of the jungle. From Dhubri to Tinsukia, there are tales of those taken by her— but none of anyone who has ever conquered her. Only one legend exists— that if a mortal ever overpowers her, she will surrender herself and her army to his will, bestow upon him gifts beyond imagination, and freeze his age forever. Immortality.

I do not crave immortality. That is not my goal.

What I desire is knowledge— to see, to understand, to measure the world of shadows that has haunted my thoughts since childhood. Are these entities truly real? Or are they only the echoes of ancient fear— myths woven by human minds to explain the unknown?

If they are real— what is their life like? What do they eat, where do they dwell, what laws govern their existence?

Is there a science behind their powers— something akin to psychic energy, perhaps a principle yet undiscovered?

Since childhood, I have only heard the tales— never witnessed them. No matter how hard I tried, I never experienced anything myself. But now, after Africa, after Ariki, after seeing visions of things that had not yet happened — I can no longer dismiss the supernatural as rumor. I have become part of it. I am no longer bound by the frailty of ordinary human perception.

And yet, one question torments me:

Will I truly meet Agashi?

The thought gnaws at me because— though I can still see visions of Calcutta, of Bengal, of all that unfolds politically and socially— there is no vision of her. My power falters before her name. Of my future— the one that entwines with hers— I see nothing. Only fragments: an obscure tribal ritual, two sacrifices, smoke rising in the dark. I do not know what they mean, nor if they are connected to her.

God alone knows what lies ahead.

The train keeps racing through the falling dusk, and I close my diary, as the first stars appear beyond the window glass.

ooo

I do not know exactly where I am, but I believe this is somewhere within what locals call the Manas Park region. After reaching Guwahati by train, I had contacted a man transporting government goods toward Nalbari, and through him, I managed to reach that small town. I stayed there for a day, and the next morning secured a paid lift in a vehicle bound for Narayanguri. That is how I arrived here— on the very edge of the forests where the plains begin to dissolve into hills.

These small places share a common hardship— there are no inns, no lodges, and people are reluctant to host a stranger, especially a Bengali, in their homes. Whatever the reason, I had to set up my own camp outside the populated area both nights, just as I had planned— for I knew, sooner or later, my true dwelling would be the jungle itself.

Beyond Narayanguri, there were no roads. It wasn't that human presence vanished altogether— tribes existed deep in these forests, stretching all the way to the Bhutan border— but they lived in isolation, detached from the so-called civilized world. Most were harmless, unlike the Angozhas of Africa, though even they could turn dangerous under certain circumstances. Still, I was mentally prepared to face anything that awaited me.

That was two nights ago— the night of amavasya, the new moon. The night most sacred to darkness. The night when, if ever, Agashi or her shadowy emissaries walked this world, I might encounter them.

I remember thinking— this is the night I've been waiting for.

Fear? None.

If I had escaped death's jaws once before in Africa, perhaps the same divine hand would protect me again. With that thought, I began my trek deeper into the forest, heading toward the Bhutanese frontier.

The day passed uneventfully.

I met three tribal hunters who neither feared nor threatened me. We could not communicate— their dialect was unfamiliar— yet they shared their food, and I ate with them beneath the great trees. Along the way, I saw elephants, rhinos, a water buffalo, a herd of barasingha, and a few sambar and cheetal. Once, a tiger crossed my path— another time, a leopard— and both times I dropped my pack and climbed a tree, clutching my gun close.

I could have fought them, yes. I carried a rifle, a pistol, and two hunting knives. But I had not come to kill. My purpose was elsewhere, and I would not waste a bullet that was meant for destiny.

By evening, the forest had swallowed the light. Dusk fell fast under the dense canopy. The moonless sky offered no grace. I built a small shelter from branches and leaves on a raised patch of land that overlooked a steep slope— far below, the faint roar of the Beki River reached my ears like a whisper from another world. I had gathered dry wood for a fire, but I would not light it until night fully descended— I did not wish to attract attention from anyone who might be searching for me.

Inside my small tent, I lay quietly, watching the glowing hands of my wristwatch crawl toward ten. I was about to light the fire when I heard it— faint but unmistakable— the sound of people struggling, of someone being dragged. My instincts sharpened instantly. I drew my pistol and stepped out into the darkness.

At first, I could see nothing. The night was pitch black, the air heavy. Slowly, my eyes adjusted. From the trail I had used earlier, I spotted shadows moving uphill— a group of people, carrying others against their will. The muffled sounds confirmed it— captives, perhaps two of them, gagged to silence their cries.

A chill ran down my spine. I did not know who they were or what they intended, but something primal told me what was coming.

A sacrifice.

A bali.

I followed them silently. The path ended at a high ridge overlooking the river valley. Under the starlight, I saw it clearly— a small stone temple stood there, its front open to the night. From my position, I could see the idol— though the features were hard to discern— and before it burned a small ritual fire.

There were about a dozen of them. Two people lay bound near the altar. The captives' muffled groans carried through the still air. Then the chanting began— rhythmic, low, and ancient. The sound of it scraped against my nerves.

I remembered what I had heard— that in Assam, the Deori priests of the Chutia clans were once known to offer human sacrifices to ward off famine or flood, to protect their lands from misfortune. Could these be their descendants? Or another sect entirely? It no longer mattered. What mattered was what I saw— two helpless lives, bound for slaughter.

And then— Africa came alive before my eyes.

Carter, Olangha, Sahadev— their blood, their terror— all of it surged back like a fevered vision.

This— this was the scene I had glimpsed in my visions.

And now, it stood before me, real, breathing, and about to unfold.

Before I could think, my body moved on its own.

I stepped into the clearing and shouted— a warning, a command, anything that might stop them. They turned, startled, their faces struck with the disbelief of seeing a ghost. The starlight gleamed on the pistol in my hand.

They didn't understand my words, but they understood threat. For a few moments they froze— then one of them, perhaps their priest, raised his blade again toward the captive's neck. I had no choice. I fired.

The shot cracked through the night like thunder. The man screamed, fell, and writhed on the ground. I hadn't meant to kill him— only to wound— but fate had other plans.

The rest backed away, whispering, hesitating. They had never seen such a weapon. They could sense its power— and their fear was almost tangible. I advanced cautiously, keeping my gun raised, and with my free hand pulled the hunting knife from my belt. I reached the captives— one man, one woman — and cut the ropes binding the first. His mouth gagged, his face streaked with dirt and terror. Once freed, he grabbed the knife and cut the girl's bonds.

When she stood, trembling, I gestured for them to run— go, now! They understood, and bolted into the dark path from which I had come.

Behind me, the wounded priest had gone still— his body lay limp, blood dark beneath him. I crouched to check, but before I could, something sharp flashed through the dark—

a thrown dagger— it grazed my arm and tore across my chest. A cry tore from my throat.

Pain exploded, blinding, but instinct took over. Two of them lunged toward me. I tried to fire again, but they struck before I could aim. The shot went wild. My pistol fell from my hand, and I was surrounded.

I fought like a man possessed— because I knew what losing meant. To be captured was to die— to become the sacrifice I had interrupted.

We grappled violently, slipping toward the cliff's edge. The slope was steep, a fall like tumbling from a seven-storey height. Twice, we teetered, and twice two of them lost footing, plunging into the abyss with fading screams.

The third time, it was me.

My heel slipped. The ground vanished beneath me.

And as I slid helplessly into the blackness, the roar of the river rose to greet me— a cold, furious lullaby.

In that brief eternity before impact, only one thought flashed across my mind: So this is where it ends.

Then the world dissolved into rushing water, pain, and silence.

I struck many stones as I fell; my body took blow after blow, and one impact to the skull numbed my mind completely. I do not even remember when my body hit the water. When breath began to choke me, some dullness broke and my limbs started flailing. The water was bitterly cold, but the knowledge that I was still alive overwhelmed that cold— the wound in my head burned and my eyes saw things my brain could not register.

I do not know where I landed, where those men went, or how far I paddled in the scramble for survival. All I recall is that, when my feet touched ground and my torso rose out of the river, I fumbled blindly across the water-smoothed stones to reach the bank. My whole body throbbed with pain; dizziness took over so fully that, collapsed on the river's edge, the effort to gulp air itself robbed me of consciousness.

When I came to, I was elsewhere. It took a long while to gather myself, to understand the situation, and to convince myself that I was still alive and no longer in immediate danger. Later I learned that I had been carried to the hut of two siblings, Tashi and Boyal, and that I had lain unconscious for a day and a half.

The events had taken place two nights before; after the sacrifice, the brother and sister had hidden nearby because they knew— even if I did not— that I might need them. They had seen me fall, searched the cliffs, and at last found me senseless and half-frozen. I was as close to death as a living man can be.

They carried me to their hut, a half-hour's walk away, and the only way to warm my freezing body was for Tashi to lie beside me and transmit heat. That held me together long enough for Boyal to dress my wounds and tend me through the night. By morning a fever had risen; it burned on for the whole day.

The siblings never left my side. To bring the fever down, Tashi kept washing me with wet cloths. The fever eased by nightfall, but my consciousness did not return until the next morning. When it did, relief showed on their faces. Their language differed from Assamese; I knew only enough Assamese to muddle through, but with patient effort they explained what had happened.

They told me their hamlet contained barely a dozen huts, a simple settlement whose people worship the Manasa goddess— they called themselves Nag, and in their eyes, they were Nagas. Ordinarily they do not venture far from their woods, but sometimes the need for game carries them outward.

Two nights ago, in such a foray, they had wandered into the path of a wandering Deori band who capture people for sacrifice. Had I not intervened, the siblings would have been taken. I had saved them; in saving them I had risked my life — and among their people saving another binds you forever. In their community, saving someone meant lifelong devotion. From that moment on, their life was entrusted to me, and I was its master.

It sounds noble said plainly, but the idea of owning other human lives felt abhorrent to me. I tried to explain, asked them not to think of it as servitude, but there was no changing their belief. So, I left them with their certainty.

I was not fit to travel. Amavasya had passed; according to local lore, Agashi and her army sleep through the moon's dark nadir and reawaken with the returning light. Their activity would begin again only as the moon returned, so I chose to stay and mend. My head had split— Boyal had bound it with a herbal poultice; a knife wound on my left arm, which ran down toward the chest, had been dressed as well.

Beyond those obvious injuries, my body bore bruises and lacerations across every part; I ached in every pore. One leg was so bad that I needed a staff to limp; even then the limb protested with every step.

When I recovered enough to speak, I sent Boyal back to the place where I had pitched my camp and where the struggle had happened.

He returned with all my gear— a small mercy— and, by luck, he found my fallen pistol too. Knowing I still had my things felt like a door reopening; I could still travel. That night they left a lamp burning beside my head, and it is by that light I write.

Their hut would hold four or five; Tashi sleeps by my feet — oddly, without the usual worldly ties she has offered herself to watch over me. Boyal sits apart, leaning against the wall.

Tashi and Boyal have no close kin. Their parents vanished when they were small; the village reared them collectively. Such disappearances are common in these forest settlements: people vanish and never return.

The old tales say Agashi's army sends pishachinis to take men and pishachas to take women. To protect themselves, people perform rites from animal offerings to human sacrifice; it is possible those two captives were to be given for such reasons.

Whether it is true or superstition, it does not alter my course— I will not leave these woods without finishing what I came to do.

Two days after leaving the siblings' village I set off again. The first day passed northward without incident; at nightfall I picked a safe place and camped. I saw birds and beasts by day but no humans or demons troubled me.

On the third day I reached an old royal hunting ground— once probably used by the Kooch Bihar or the Gauripur royals, now abandoned and maybe kept by British officers long ago. For now, it was empty and bleak, its rooms that perhaps once sheltered officers serviceable enough for a night.

I settled into one such room. The place had that uncanny desertion that makes the heart quicken: alone in a haunted hunting lodge with nothing alive but yourself; a man less made of courage than obsession might have fled. But I am not that man. Years of experiments with Professor Frederick have taught me to sit with fear, not to flee from it. I felt dread, but not surrender.

A large torch is with me; its beam cuts the night. By its light I write, so that each detail— every aberrant happening and passing thought— is recorded. I spent roughly sixteen days with Boyal and Tashi; during that time, I learned much of their tongue, enough to be of use here in the forest.

The full moon has passed and the moon's return has begun; staying on any longer where Agashi's influence could gather would be foolish. Tashi told me more of the goddess: her retinue includes shape-shifting pishachinis and wandering spectres.

They seldom show themselves in daylight, but they weave circumstances that cause humans to stray into Agashi's territory; once trapped, the pishachinis ensnare the prey with irresistible allure, keep them until the new moon, and then surrender them to Agashi who feeds and consumes, completing a ghastly cycle.

Has anyone ever bested her? Tashi had only second-hand talk of a Buddhist ascetic who did so; where that ascetic went afterward, no one knew. That, at least, suggested victory was not impossible, though how he achieved it remained mysterious.

For me that was enough: I would not expect a meeting with Agashi to be straightforward; my approach would likely be by way of one of her lieutenants.

One other thing must be noted. Tashi is young, and her body is arresting in ways that weaken a man's discipline. Staying so close to her, touching her repeatedly in the pretext of care, shook something in me. One night my restraint failed; she yielded to me willingly.

Boyal, too, became aware of this after the incident had taken place, yet there was no change in his behaviour. Where I was consumed by remorse after the act, those two—brother and sister— were pleased that I had considered Tashi worthy of such regard. What, for me, was a source of shame, an immoral and improper deed, was for them a matter of good fortune. Perhaps this was their social structure, where such an act was not a reason for anger or rejection.

This all happened two days before I was to leave that place. And when, instead of resistance or objection, I saw their willing acceptance, the very next day my mind, in moments of solitude, turned dishonest of its own accord, and I repeated the act that I myself regarded as my mistake and my weakness. Only after it was done did I resolve that at first light I would depart on my journey. If I stayed here any longer, I would continue to break before her beauty and her surrender, and keep using her body in this immoral way—one that could even result in her conceiving.

ooo

As I had just finished writing these lines, I heard a small laugh— so soft it could have been wind. My spine stiffened. The hut was silent; I remembered I had barred the door against animals, yet now the door stood open and a shadow stood in the threshold, watching me.

My hands trembled as I raised the torch. The figure stepped into the light and for a moment my breath stopped.

It was a girl. Her clothing was of the forest folk, but her beauty seemed of another order— an apsara walking in mortal garb. Tall, with heavy lashes and deep eyes that looked straight at me, her lips curved with a smile that could be called either tender or lethal.

She stood in the doorway as if she had always belonged there, watching me in a way that made my chest clench.

A quick thought leapt into my mind: a girl out here at this hour could not be ordinary— she must be one of Agashi's warriors. The idea made every hair on my body stand on end. Years of yearning and practice seemed to converge in that instant.

I had pushed myself into hunger after hunger to see such things, and now she stood before me. The shiver of fear I had felt a few seconds earlier was overwhelmed by a different, thrilling tremor— I was in the presence of a power not of this world. I steadied myself and, with a kind of tenderness, invited her inside.

I could not say what powers she possessed, but she could not read my thoughts; where she had perhaps expected to find me terrified or awed, my calm confused her. When she hesitated, I rose and, laying a hand on her shoulder, guided her to the bed and made her sit. She volunteered her name: Hirvi.

She lived nearby and often wandered here when sleep eluded her. The sight of a light tonight had drawn her; she had laughed because she thought it ridiculous that anyone would come and remain alone in such a place. I nodded as if I believed her. As for the question of fear, I told her I was no ordinary man but a spirit, and therefore had no reason to fear anyone. She did not believe me— of course, she could smell the man within me.

The only thing left was: what would she do next? Whatever habits she followed with others did not seem to produce the effect she expected in me, and that uncertainty troubled her. I asked what she intended to do— would she go home or pass the night here?

Her manner changed at once; hunger spread across her face. Without ceremony, she said she liked me and desired to make love— to take pleasure from me. The significance was clear. The Ariki ritual I had taken part in at Kasungu had gifted me a power I had used several times; perhaps in this forest it would be less potent, perhaps it would be mutable, but it was real.

This evening presented a golden chance for the other truth of that ritual to be tested: that no demonic or otherworldly force could act against me. If I remained undefeated in this encounter with a beauty such as Hirvi, then perhaps I could stand before Agashi as well. The only danger was if she turned out to be merely a village girl.

To test myself I accepted her invitation. There, on that bed, we came together.

At first, she lavished delights upon me as though she were the sovereign of youth itself. The body rejoiced; the mind rejoiced— an unbroken torrent of pleasure carried me along. At the peak, where rapture cresting would have signalled total surrender, a jolt struck my consciousness.

If I allowed myself to be carried over that brink by emotional tide, that would have been my undoing. What she wanted— and would have had, easily, if I had given in— was to take me as any lover takes a willing body. If I were to crumble into the lap of a mere concubine, the dream of mastering Agashi would be over.

The thought altered everything. The surge of bliss stopped as if someone had wrenched the current from me. I opened my eyes and saw the change.

It was as if the warm skin under my hands had become something rotten; I kept the torch burning in its place so I could watch. Her eyes, half-closed in delight, opened and her face trembled. Her beautiful, taut body seemed to slacken as if her skin were shrinking away from a skeleton; the erotic moans that had escaped her lips turned into pained gasps. Before my eyes, the contours of her body withered, taking on the look of a two-hundred-year-old crone draped in sagging flesh.

Her face went the colour of old paper; her teeth became crooked and sharp. Her eyes sank into black rims; the skin around them turned ashen. She writhed now as if the pleasures had become torment, and what I felt was the sense of stabbing into filth. When her endurance broke she tried to push me away, but I caught her hands— now fitted with dagger-like nails.

She could tear me; I had to keep those talons away. I stopped then, watching with the calm of a victor as she raged with black glare.

She wanted to know who I was and how I had controlled myself on that slippery slope. I told her I was a yogi and that I had mastery over my senses. Because I already knew something of her true nature, I intended to play the game of desire on my terms.

She swore she had no guile; she only wanted pleasure, and if I had not restrained myself, she would have granted me that natural rapture any man would expect. It was clear: their work was to ensnare prey, feed them to Agashi at the appointed hour. Until she took me to Agashi she posed no imminent threat; for now, then, I might as well test my power by enjoying what she offered.

But my real goal was to see whether, faced with such seduction, I would remain sovereign.

What occurred had to be confessed: despite her fragile-looking frame, she had uncanny strength. I realised she was no ordinary girl, and I doubt a common man could control her. Part of my steadiness came from my physical and mental training; part came from that other, acquired, almost divine element within me.

Still, I could not keep her with me in the bed, so I dragged her, naked and heavy with the residue of the encounter, out of the room.

My plan was to lock her in one of the hunting-lodge rooms. I knew it was foolish to assume she could be contained— the powers she owned made containment a fantasy— but I only wanted to remove her from my head. With that thought I forced her into a room and shut the door.

I went back to my chamber, dressed, and thought over the events until sleep finally stole me.

I drifted back to sleep, and in the dream the sequence of union with an unparalleled beauty resumed. It felt as though a lava long held at the brink— quivering, denied release— could no longer be contained, and finally flowed free. Despite sleep, an uncanny fulfilment coursed through me, after which the sleep itself seemed to deepen further.

At dawn I woke to find my clothes off and Hirvi lying beside me as she had been when I first saw her— dishevelled hair around her face, amused by some secret victory. She must have sensed my gaze and opened her eyes. Pride and triumph played across her features: she had taken, and I had been taken.

The thought that I had been defeated at such a test filled me with cold dread— if I could be overthrown in this way, how would I stand before Agashi? The thought poured sweat on my skin even in that chill place.

She did not understand why I trembled so. When I asked her what she wanted, she said simply that she liked me and wanted to stay for a few days. I understood her meaning: she would wander with me until that final surrender to Agashi.

I was left in confusion; my defeat at her hands was a warning. I needed to reconsider my plan. After some thinking I concluded that I should accept her company. There was no point in trying to return empty-handed now. Better to approach Agashi by the hand of one of her own agents than to wander lost through the jungle searching her without hope. With Hirvi at my side, the path to Agashi would be open, though certainly fraught.

That night's lesson had been salutary: my weakness had been revealed before the final exam. If I was to live to face Agashi and not be consumed, I must control not only waking senses but the unconscious too. Control must remain intact even in sleep— or the enemy will have me.

When I returned, Hirvi was dressed. I told her I would take her with me, and she brightened as though a test had been passed. I could see why. Once the matter was settled, I sat down and wrote these remaining words, to keep record of the mistake and the learning that followed.

ooo

The day I had been wandering the jungle for finally drew near… today is Chaturdashi and from five o'clock tomorrow evening the new moon will begin. What tomorrow will bring — who knows in what state I will be— so today I set down everything that has happened since I left that hunting lodge and reached the place where I now sit.

About ten days have passed as we drifted through these woods, and in that time, we climbed toward the Bhutan border and higher ground. We hunted; we struggled with many dangers. I cannot say for certain that what threatened me threatened her too, but she admitted one thing plainly: her powers are almost null in daylight, while at sunset they awaken as though a starving creature had been fed to the brim.

By day she behaves like any ordinary person if she is outside, or else lies dormant in the darkness of her own world. This was precisely what I had come to learn; for this I had altered the course of my life. She speaks a little, wants to speak more, and then stops as if some terror sits on her lips.

Sometimes she gives a fragment of the past that increases my understanding, but she refuses to say who she once was, where she came from, why— if she had been human before becoming a pishachini— she did not find release and instead remained a pishachini. On that question she clamps her mouth shut.

Had she told me, my knowledge would have blossomed unexpectedly— but alas, she avoids that topic.

Yes, almost every night she makes love to me. I do not refuse myself, but I keep perfect control: if I ejaculate it will be at my will and at my chosen moment.

This practice sharpens me and gives me a final chance before the exam. Even in sleep I stay vigilant— if a beautiful woman appears, it could be an illusion, and my subconscious must be alert enough to stop the dream from dragging me into sleep-paralysis. Breaking that paralysis afterward drains me of all strength. To practice restraint during waking lovemaking is one thing; to restrain myself in sleep is far harder.

I manage it somehow. When I wake, she looks defeated and irritated with me.

Ten days went this way. Five of those days were ordinary; in the other five incidents occurred worth writing down, events that have taken a firm place in my memory.

The day after we left the hunting lodge, we were harried by a horned rhinoceros whose mood— who knows why— had turned belligerent. It declared us its enemy and chased us for hours. We barely escaped; exhausted and beaten by running, we camped on the spot.

That night I tried to rouse her desire, but like a well-polished pot she remained slick and impenetrable; after a satiating coupling I slept.

The next day was normal, but at night we reached a deserted village: ruins half-collapsed, yet usable as shelter for one night. We took refuge in a sturdier hut. The exhaustion of the day made me think rest a wiser choice than denial of desire, but that night she penetrated my dreams. I woke to a struggle with sleep-paralysis only to see her at my bedside, picking at a pigeon and eating it raw. She did not look resentful this time; it felt deliberate, as if she had purposely woken me.

After she had eaten, she told me to come outside. What I saw there removed the breath from my lungs.

The village that had looked deserted by day was now full — not with living people but with the dead, as if tombs had spat them up. The moon shone pale and they were visible: sprawled before the huts, clinging to thatched roofs, dragging themselves through rotting lanes.

They crawled; their faces were hideous; bodies decomposing; eyes glazed; slobber ran from slack lips. In some places they formed circles around half-dead animals— sambhar, chital— and tore at them with withered hands. Some animals still cried; yet the dead were tearing and eating them. They fought among themselves for pieces; a stench rose that could unhinge any stomach.

My hair stood on end.

This sight exceeded my imagination. For two days I had walked with a pishachini at my side, but these revenants were now living within whatever image I had of ghosts and demons. She— Hirvi— laughed, a brittle, high peal, and the dead turned as if drawn by that laughter.

Her laughter was an affront to me, but what mattered more was that it summoned those risen corpses and they started to move toward us as if I were the quarry. Seeing them come, I felt my wits go slack.

I could not face them alone. What use were the weapons in my hands against those already dead? If they ate animals, why not me? I thought my last hour had come. I had trained for Agashi, but here the exam paper bore other monsters.

I wanted to run but my legs felt stone-bound. I looked at Hirvi in a hopeless plea.

She changed immediately.

Her body enlarged. In my sight she became a monstrous bat: hands stretched into huge wings, her face radiating a strange heat; her eyes flamed like coals. The dead in front of her froze, and fear spread across those blank faces.

Hirvi swelled until she belittled me— she could have picked me up in a single talon and flown away. She opened her mouth and a bifurcated, writhing tongue like a serpent appeared; when she hissed, my heart trembled like a small bird.

For a moment I thought the world would end there.

Her hiss rolled through the jungle like a single, terrible note— loud enough, I felt, to carry for miles. I felt my ear-drums vibrate.

The sound made all those corpses recoil with a howl of terror; they staggered back and began to slip away. It was as if I were their quarry and they had been poised to close in on me, but Hirvi had warned them off: this is my prey— stay from my prey. They accepted her claim and abandoned theirs.

I watched them, read their postures… and had no idea when she reverted to the shape she had worn when she lay beside me. I only knew it had happened when her mocking laughter brushed my ears. I turned to see her laughing at me.

No doubt my slackened face at that moment— the mingling of defeat, weakness and the fear that hollowed my core— must have given me away; my boast of victory over her after our first encounter was exposed as a fraud. Shamed, I went back inside and tried to sleep, but sleep would not come. There it was again: another of my weaknesses, another of their strengths revealed.

If I was such an easy quarry, what then of the oaths the Angozha ojha had made— that the Ariki ritual had granted me a protective armor against such demonic powers? Where was that armor?

Perhaps I had misunderstood how I was meant to confront them. What had happened, however, was useful: it forced me to think. At least now I could focus on how to break the faults inside me.

The next day and night passed without incident— we drifted like two people on a picnic through the woods. Then another notable episode happened.

The day was like any other; we had shot two peacocks for food. I cleaned and roasted mine; she ate hers raw and with the same nauseating ease. At times I felt sick thinking that at night I kissed that mouth. Yet at bedtime she was still the same mesmerizing, immaculate beauty, redolent of scents that disarmed the mind.

It surprised me that her teeth could tear raw flesh and her stomach digest it so cleanly. But their bodies are different; argument is useless.

That night we came upon a ruined temple hidden among dense trees— a great structure, perhaps three or four centuries old. Whatever god had once been enshrined there was gone; the roof had half caved in, the walls crumbling. The architecture suggested Buddhism, though there was no sign of recent visitors.

We camped within its broken shadow. Once more we consummated in a controlled, satisfying way and fell asleep. At some ungodly hour I woke to strange activity: she was missing. Silence and darkness, only the soft whip-crack of rustling sounds.

White gleams moved and vanished; there were whispers, words I did not know. Fear rose quickly, but I steadied myself — that very weakness I had to master. Fear feeds those monstrous powers; the more you fear, the stronger they become. Perhaps that was the principle the Professor and Das babu had always told me: you must not be afraid. It was time to test it.

I closed my mind and concentrated, returning inward. The intrusions continued like wind— touches that lifted and dropped me— sometimes a cruel sound like a throat being slit. Such noises could terrify an ordinary man, but I resolved to receive them and give them no purchase.

I promised myself I would not open my eyes, would not attend to those things. I tried to carry my mind to a place of daily normality: imagine you are at Howrah station, a crush of moving bodies all around, and you are simply an indifferent man lost in his own world. If the mind is restless, a contrivance will do; it need only be strong enough to keep the tremors from opening you.

Slowly the din dissolved. Everything outside grew still. The torch lay where it had fallen. I picked it up, extinguished it, and lay back down. If I had let my thoughts run, the fear would have devoured me; instead, I set them aside and slept. When morning came, she was back beside me. I did not ask where she had gone; no need was felt. We prepared and moved on.

The next day a new episode unfolded: while hunting a peacock, several sambhars fled and a leopard surged in— our presence had disturbed it. The cat struck so suddenly I could not react: it latched onto me. I felt claws rake my flesh; its jaws nearly clamped my throat. Hirvi moved with the same speed she showed in every danger: she seized the leopard's haunch, pulled it away.

Its iron claws shredded my clothes, but I staggered free. Hirvi yanked the beast backwards; when it recovered it snarled and lunged at her, but I steadied, fired, and the bullet struck the upper part of its hind leg. The creature collapsed. Hirvi retreated, feeling the fresh wound, and the leopard subsided, sullen and hurt.

I pitied the cat— a hunting animal maimed is a sentence to starvation— but when survival is on the line, priorities shift. We could do nothing more. My body bore the scratches; I had salves and she knew herbs to apply. That too surprised me: she is a creature of the dark, and yet she knew the cures of the earth.

A further incident happened two nights ago. We had no proper shelter, so we made a rudimentary camp of branches and leaves and kept a fire alight. At midnight a group of golden cats attacked— larger than normal, hunters of the area. Their target was not me but Hirvi; maybe they could scent her.

The struggle forced us from the camp: she fended a few with speed, but when she could not shake them off, her body shifted— she became like them, a huge feline.

Five big cats faced us now: Hirvi and four others that wanted to tear her apart. Their awful growls split the jungle stillness; they had turned the little clearing into an arena. I felt invisible to them, irrelevant; they fought as if I were not there. Hirvi fought bravely, but four on one takes its toll: she began to bleed.

Then they closed on her and, for a moment, I was struck numb. When the leopard had nearly bitten my throat, I might have died, and it was she who saved me; now I had the chance to repay that debt.

I shouted, a thunderous command, and the cats' intensity broke. Their grip slackened; Hirvi slipped free. I grabbed a burning stick from the fire and attacked. Not that my attack alone sent them away— no— they tried to leap at me too, but I fought with limbs and raw will. Hirvi aided me: wherever I faltered she sprang and tore at an assailant's flank. Gradually our onslaught made them retreat. One sign from one of them, and they melted into the darkness.

I checked Hirvi— she lay utterly spent. When she returned to human form, deep wounds lined her body. I offered medicine; she refused and told me to sleep. Even after such events we sleep, because habit steels the nerves. When I woke, she was whole; the injuries had vanished as if never made. I felt stunned but said nothing. We rose and continued.

Today we came upon an ancient temple— perhaps of the tenth or eleventh century. Its identity was unclear: not a single image or lingam remained to mark it as Hindu, Jain, or Buddhist. From the outside it looked temple-like and Hirvi agreed it was.

Oddly, there was an old ascetic living there— a priest of some sort. He is a riddle: he speaks little, perhaps refuses to speak, though he is not deaf. He neither responds to our questions nor shows any particular interest. He is garbed in saffron; his head bent and his body oddly sculpted. At times he seems very old; at others he appears suddenly young. I cannot guess his real age, and he will say nothing.

We have shelter for tonight. He neither refused nor accepted in any clear way, but he did not oppose our presence. We set camp.

I ate a little from our rations in respect for the temple; when darkness fell Hirvi slipped off into the woods and I, with my torch, began to write these moments down. My mind tells me: one more night of quiet. Tomorrow— who knows. The showdown with Agashi is certain— but whether I shall triumph or fail is still unknown.

I know the cost of failure; the cost of victory I cannot imagine.

ooo

Tonight is Amavasya— the night that will decide the fate of this daring act of mine, or rather, my future itself.

I am still in the same temple where I was yesterday. Properly I should have moved on, but a strange thing happened: when I woke in the morning, I had a high fever and my body ached as though it had laboured through a thousand nights— whereas I remember distinctly that Hirvi did not intrude into my dream that night.

Whether this condition was natural or whether Agashi's power had a hand in it I could not say; what was certain was that I was not in a travelling state, so leaving that relatively safe place to go on was out of the question.

Hirvi had not returned by the time I slept, but when I opened my eyes in the morning she lay at my side, senseless and sleeping. I tried again to speak with the mysterious monk, but his manner had not changed.

I had some medicines, so I took them, but the pills worked no miracle; the fever would not break and the pain lingered, and by the time the shadows lengthened toward afternoon the sun already leaned toward the western hill. In that condition, to depart then felt wrong— instead I resolved to stay and steel myself mentally to face Agashi where I was.

By mid-afternoon the fever still burned and the tiger-scratch aches remained as they were, but gradually, as the light dimmed, a little relief began to come.

In an hour the Amavasya hour will begin; before that I write this down— perhaps my last words. During the day Hirvi had gone off somewhere; the monk was unseen too. Now both are present again, sitting on the main terrace; the monk has sunk into meditation, eyes closed, while Hirvi sits with her legs dangling and keeps looking at me in odd ways I cannot fully read.

I guess she is attached to me somehow and perhaps worried for whatever may be my ending. I will stop writing and attempt meditation now, so that before facing Agashi I might be strong enough not to break before served fear.

ooo

How many months have passed since that accursed new-moon night which altered my life beyond repair— only today have I managed, somehow, to steady myself enough to begin writing again. If I am writing at all, it can only mean that I have survived; that I have crossed that night which, for me, was a verdict between life and death. Yet my survival does not, in any sense, mean that I emerged victorious against Agashi. On the contrary, something occurred that night which neither of us had foreseen, and we both won even as we lost, and lost even as we won. But that truth is not so simple that it can be grasped merely from these lines. I now belong neither to the living nor to the dead. The meanings of the world have shifted entirely for me; it is no longer what it once was when I was human. Yes— I am no longer human.

Now that I have sat down to write, I will inevitably return to that night when it all unfolded— when my attempt to make contact with that unknown world of darkness turned into torment for me.

Many months have passed since then, yet that night still rises before my eyes, alive and unbidden. Before the new moon set in, I had seated myself in a posture of meditation. I saw the monk and Hirvi one last time, then closed my eyes, and my mind began to fix itself upon a black point positioned between the two eyes. This art of concentration was not new to me, though I had never practiced it with any great discipline. External disturbances kept pulling me back from that void, even though success lay precisely in severing all contact with the outer world.

To draw the mind out of thought and bring it to stillness is an exceedingly arduous task, one that demands a severe and exacting discipline. Since I could not, all at once, bring myself to rest upon that single point, I guided the mind along another, more controlled path— one where, as it wandered, it would lose itself so completely that all connection with the outer world would dissolve, and every interruption, every obstruction, would be rendered powerless. It was like cutting oneself off from the external world and constructing an inner one instead— entirely shaped by my imagination.

In those moments I fashioned a magical world of my own — a beautiful place where the mountains were alive, waterfalls cascaded, trees swayed, multicoloured clouds drifted, the air carried fragrance, flowers floated, and everywhere a tinted mist lay spread, coiling around the feet. Before me was a tranquil lake, gathering the water of the waterfall into its embrace. Pairs of swans and ducks moved about upon it. Along one edge, masses of flowers had bloomed and slipped from the bank into the water. There, too, was a small boat, and seated in it was Tashi, smiling, watching me, beckoning me to come closer.

Though I had lived my life at a level where association with girls, friendship with them, had not been forbidden— even within a backward society bound by rigid conventions — yet a different sort of inclination and obsession of mine had kept the girls around me from drawing near. That was why, before Tashi, no one had come so close to me. Tashi was not my deliberate choice; she was merely a fortunate coincidence. But since she was the first woman to enter my life, the first to make me a complete man, she secured a distinct place in my mind and heart. Thereafter, whenever in moments of leisure or in a desire for romance I imagined a woman at all, that woman's face was invariably Tashi's.

That day, too, it was she— calling me to come with her. She sat at one end of the boat, holding the oar; at the other end lay flowers still attached to their branches, and I went and sat there. The fragrance of the flowers filled and sweetened the mind. Smiling, Tashi began to row, and the boat slipped away from the shore and moved forward. There was no sun — no moon— only a light spread everywhere, without any visible source. Slowly she began to sing— the same songs she had sung to me when we were together, folk songs of the Nagas, in the Assamese tongue. She sang the very ones that poured sweetness into my ears. It felt as though there was no one else in the world— only the two of us. She was Shatarupa; I was Manu. She was Eve; I was Adam, and we were still in paradise. This was our world— this was everything.

The boat continued to glide ahead at a gentle pace, her song steeping the air with sweetness. I remained half-intoxicated, lost in the overwhelming blend of her beauty and her voice. The lake was vast— like Dal itself— and at its centre stood a garden, like four chinars gathered together, which was our Garden of Eden. We lived there— there were trees bearing sweet fruit that fed us. Flowers lay scattered everywhere, keeping us fragrant at every moment, and countless birds nested there, singing to us morning and evening. That day she was singing and I was listening— circling that Eden again and again, she went on singing for who knows how long, and I went on listening.

There was no measure to my intoxication. I wished time would halt here and that this sequence would never end— but such things never happen. Everything that begins must come to a close. This, too, ended, and the boat came to rest at the edge of the Garden of Eden.

We stepped ashore. She slipped her arms around my neck, and we began to wander through that valley of flowers. She was humming now, yet it pleased me just as deeply. Her closeness, her touch, the warmth rising from her body gave me a pleasure of an altogether different kind. Never before had she seemed so beautiful— never before had the friction of her body felt so arousing. The heat within me kept mounting, and the desire to lose myself entirely in her presence grew steadily stronger.

When we reached that part of the garden where the ground lay so thickly strewn with flowers that it felt as though a bed had been laid out for us, I stretched myself there, and she sat beside me. Her smile grew ever more alluring, urging me to kiss those lips. I released the restraint I had imposed upon myself and gathered her into my arms. She hid her face against my chest; I lifted it toward mine and mingled my burning breath with her warm breaths. I drew her trembling lips into mine and felt the honey that flowed from them seep into my very soul. Then— who knows when— the sequence paused, when the rhythm broke and she stirred, slipping free. Restlessly, I caught hold of her again.

For reasons I cannot say, the choli and ghagra clinging to her body now felt like barriers, just as the kurta and dhoti upon my own body felt like a burden. I could not stop myself from undoing those obstructions; my trembling hands moved impatiently to remove them. She did not resist and surrendered herself as she always did— as though a handmaiden had offered herself before her deity. There was compliance in every gesture, surrender in every movement. Half-maddened, I kissed her as I freed her from her clothes, and her uneven breathing bore witness to her arousal.

Within moments we were unclothed. With eyes like a doe and an expression of utter abandon, she looked at me, and I gazed upon that peerless beauty like a thirsty traveller before a well that could quench not only the thirst of the body but of the soul as well. Never before had she seemed so exquisite; today every part of her body was so captivating that a lifetime would be required to love each one of them fully. There was a magic in those limbs that drew me toward her as iron is drawn to a magnet. A light seemed to break forth from her body, a warmth to emanate that was melting me. She lifted her marble-like arms and gathered me into her embrace. At the moment I entered her, the intoxicating sigh that escaped her lips poured sweetness into my ears. We became two bodies and a single life. This lake bore witness to that union; this garden bore witness to it as well.

The pleasure of slipping along that slick, pleasure-laden path was boundless— otherworldly, beyond description. A narcotic current seemed to race unhindered through every vein, scattering sparks as it went; fireworks burst within the mind. My eyes felt sealed by the excess of intoxication, and the body moved only in a rhythmic sequence of driving motion. It did not seem possible to apply any brake to this headlong rush, and I longed, as quickly as I could, to disgorge the restless lava churning within me and reach the summit of climax— where there was an otherworldly release, where there was deliverance.

Climax— deliverance. Those two words scraped violently against my subconscious, and in an instant it was as though the current of pleasure had been dammed. Eyes closed by intoxication flew open; the passion surging through the channels of the mind came to a halt.

Now, beneath my body, answering my thrusts with languorous cries, was not the beauty who had beckoned me to wander with her in the boat. She was not Tashi. Nor was it that she had suddenly changed; she was the same one with whom this enchanted union had begun— and yet she was not Tashi. When she had taken me with her into the boat, she had been Tashi. My mind, ensnared by the spell and intoxication of her magic, had failed to notice how, little by little, she was growing more beautiful— transforming from a mere beauty into an apsara. Each limb had taken on a finer lustre, shaping itself further, as though a sculptor had worked a statue again and again, raising it step by step to the highest pinnacle of beauty, while the eyes that watched without pause failed to register the change, until the figure became something altogether different.

As I looked upon her devastatingly beautiful face, my mind reeled— she was no less than Menaka, Rambha, or Urvashi. Yet what was enough to wake me was this: she was not Tashi.

In preparation for confronting her, I had been meditating — but she entered my mind directly, dislodged me from the real world, and drew me into that realm of illusion where the world I had fashioned for myself with Tashi was not only seized and set in motion according to her will, but where she herself gradually took Tashi's place. There was no Tashi now; there was only Agashi.

The hesitation that rose within my body alerted her as well to the shift in my inner state, and she opened her eyes and looked at me.

One detail here is worth noting. When, in a similar state, I had regained control and restrained myself while with Hirvi, not only had the sensation of arousal altered, but she herself had begun to change. Here, neither of those things occurred. Though my inner emotions had shifted, the physical response remained unchanged, and she stayed exactly as she had been — an apsara engaged with me. She made no attempt to alter herself or her intent. Instead, despite my awakening, she continued to cling to me, responding aggressively to my weakening thrusts, as though she were prepared for nothing other than culmination, willing to consent to nothing short of it.

The question was: what option did I now have? What she desired was something I could not give— for me, that would have been death set firmly within the frame of defeat. I was not in the real world but trapped within a world of my own making, a world that had now come under her dominion. As these thoughts took hold, my arousal began to cool, and I tried to pull myself out of that imagined realm. Yet no matter how fiercely I strained, I could not extract my mind from that state. Earlier, whenever such moments had arisen, attempts to break the sequence had led me into sleep paralysis— but that night even that did not occur. No matter what I did, I could not sever the chain.

I remained caught in my own creation like a helpless insect, with no other exit in sight. Here— at this very turn— resisting Agashi, holding myself back, and denying her the culmination she sought became my discipline. This was the final battle against her. I could not leave this world, but I could prevent myself from release. The change in my inner state extinguished my desire, and as my fervour cooled, the slackness and lifelessness that overtook my body began to frustrate her. Even so, she persisted relentlessly. She shifted roles— placing me where she had been, and assuming my position herself.

I had assumed that she would grow irritated, alter herself, and appear in her true form— but nothing of the sort happened. Even the first signs of vexation that surfaced when

I grew cold gradually faded, and she once again appeared just as absorbed and willing in the act as before. It made no difference to her that I had recognised her and understood her game. When all possibilities of union had ended because of my withdrawal, she separated from me and lay beside me, looking at me with affection. There was still no trace of defeat or frustration on her face; she appeared as content and radiant as she had been earlier.

I told her that I had identified her and that, under no circumstances, would I fulfil her desire. This had no effect on her at all; instead, she began to laugh. She said that I was mistaken in thinking she was Agashi— that she was, in fact, Sainvani, the goddess who had bestowed these powers upon me through the trident after the Ariki ritual. Today was my trial, she said; today I needed protection the most, and that was why she had come. In the outer world, Agashi stood ready with her forces to hunt me down, but she would remain unsuccessful so long as I did not awaken. Her purpose in keeping me here until the night had passed was precisely that. If I were to wake and step outside, I would be killed, for I was in no position to confront Agashi's powers in any way. As for seeking union with me, she said she did so because I had appealed to her as a male; after a fulfilling union she intended to endow me with further powers— powers that could truly aid me against Agashi, so that if not on this new-moon night, then on the next, I might meet her on equal terms.

I was plunged into a terrible dilemma over what the truth might be. I asked her to let me leave this illusion, but she replied that I could return only by relinquishing the powers she had given me— because here I was rejecting her help and insulting her by doing so. I need not grant her union if I did not wish to, she said, but I should not insist on leaving. If I valued my safety, I ought to remain here until the sun rose. My confusion deepened further: if she herself was freeing me from the lure of union, how could she be Agashi— when Agashi's very rule of the hunt was to drain all of her prey's power through union? One more thing forced me to consider her side: if she were like Hirvi, then why had her form or demeanour not changed the moment I became aware? How could she remain so calm despite failing in her aim?

I found no clear thread to seize and hold on to, yet my mind settled on one thing— that if she was no longer demanding union, then it was possible to spend time here with her. If there were any great obstruction awaiting me in the outer world, it would break my inertia on its own; otherwise, what harm was there in remaining here until morning?

At last, I gave my consent, and we began once more to wander through that Garden of Eden as before. Earlier our bodies had been clothed; now we were bare. And what need was there for garments— who was there to look upon us? She began to sing to me again— songs of tryst, heavy with intoxication, meant to draw my altered bearing back into that very current where the unbroken flow had faltered and come to rest. I asked her how it was that she, a goddess of Africa, knew my language, or Tashi's. She replied that she possessed no language of her own; whatever language her devotee or seeker spoke, she absorbed it. Nothing within my mind was hidden from her. She could read me like an open book and converse with me in any tongue I knew.

Whatever the truth— whether she was Agashi or Sainvani — she was certainly not human. And if she was offering me, in this manner, the chance to speak with her as a companion, then why should I not try to understand her? With that thought, I repeatedly interrupted her songs, probing her to speak of herself or of her world. Yet her answer remained the same: a human being is granted only as much knowledge as he can bear. There are many things it is not right for humans to know. Still, she did speak at length of Africa, and these accounts weakened my suspicion that, despite her explanation, she might yet be Agashi.

As time passed, I grew more at ease. My doubts continued to fade. Though I was trapped within a realm of imagination, I was aware that well past midnight must have gone by, and by all logic I should have felt sleep— but when I searched my mind, there was no trace of it. Instead, the intoxication of Sainvani's nearness began once more to take hold, rich and enveloping, and the mind grew eager again to plunge into the depths of that pleasant, slippery descent.

We walked along the edges of the lake, wandered through the garden; sometimes we sat upon ground carpeted with flowers, sometimes we lay down, and time slipped past of its own accord. Where we were, there was no such thing as day or night— only a suspended moment. Yet I sensed that outside, morning must have arrived, and that the new-moon night which was to have become my death had passed. With that, a greater carefreeness settled within me, and the body grew eager to reclaim the pleasure that had earlier been left incomplete— and it was as though she read my thoughts. Smiling, she took my hand and led me back to that same bed where the story of our tryst had been left unfinished. Once again we merged into one another, and that incomplete sequence of friction moved steadily toward its fulfilment.

We were both filled with pleasure and sought to reach our culmination through a shared, rhythmic motion of the body. It felt as though neither of us retained any awareness, as though we had surrendered entirely to one another and would not be released from that bond without reaching the end. If I was moving into her with restless urgency, she was answering with equal fervour, and our warm, scattered breaths tangled together. The sounds rising from our union seemed to steep the air itself in sweetness, until everything grew blurred by excess of sensation.

Yet even in those moments, drawing upon the discipline I had repeatedly exercised with Hirvi, I prolonged the course far beyond my natural limits. When I reached the brink, I felt the storm surge through my veins— and sensed, too, the tightening that took hold of her body. It seemed she was nearing her own peak, seeking to clutch me and draw me fully into herself. Driven by some sudden impulse, it occurred to me that while I might not be able to stop myself from being carried along in that moment, I could still withhold a part of myself from her. In doing so, my vow would remain intact—

that through this entire night I would not release myself in any woman's embrace, neither in waking life nor in the realm of dreams.

The instant this thought took hold, I withdrew from her body, and a cry escaped her.

Trembling, she tried to gather me back into herself, but it was no longer possible. In those moments I had no control over myself; with eyes tightly shut, I was carried away in the state of release, unmoored and flowing elsewhere. Her condition was no different— yet by some force of will she continued to struggle even then. When she realised she had failed, she pushed me away from her with a flash of anger and writhed in agitation. It took me a few moments to steady myself and pass beyond that state. When I looked at her again, she lay where she was, as though in torment, and with each surge something in her body seemed to alter, her face shifting from one instant to the next.

By "change," it was not merely her face that altered; her entire form transformed. Nor was it only she who changed — everything around her seemed to change along with her.

It felt as though the colourful, heavenlike world I had fashioned in my imagination— suspended somewhere between earth and sky— was now shedding all its beauty and colour, turning dark, crumbling into fragments, scattering as if it were made of sand, the sand breaking from its cohesion and dissolving into the wind. Everything began to lose its existence and fall downward, as though the whole of creation were collapsing. Flailing my arms and legs in a desperate attempt to steady myself, I too was falling— while she, writhing and transforming, fell alongside me— she whose true nature I could not tell anymore… Sainvani, or Agashi?

Even the light that had existed until then was losing its presence, and darkness, like a monstrous being, was devouring it.

When we came to rest, it felt as though we had reached the netherworld— a dark domain of a collapsing city. Everything that had been above had turned to smoke and lost its being; everything below formed a dead, urban structure of innumerable ruins, collapsing upon themselves, laden with enough terror to unmake the heart. It was certain that had I not spent so many days practising fear and resisting it, my heartbeat would have stopped at the sight alone.

Where my feet found purchase was the smoke-breathing, heated ground of a courtyard belonging to some palace-like structure in ruin. As far as the eye could see, whatever edifices stood there appeared centuries old, deserted, and visibly in the process of ending— my naked eyes could watch them break and fall, shattering into particles and becoming part of the surrounding darkness. Though the view was now limited by being grounded, while falling from above I had seen far and wide how the earth was venting lava in places, how pools of fire and molten rock had formed throughout. In those pools seemed to be people trapped— writhing, screaming, scorched as they tried to claw their way out. They were not alive; they were dead— striving somehow to cross the wall of fire that stood between them and the outer world, yet held back by some invisible force.

That darkness was broken only by the light born of the very fire that sustained visibility— there was no other source of illumination there. Where the two of us had fallen, a palace stood before us, half already collapsed, the rest crumbling before my very eyes. This was the dark world of my fantasy, given form and set before me in this manner… the one who had brought it into being stood before me, yet I was unable to grasp who she truly was.

The impact of falling from such a height struck the body exactly as it should have— but I do not know what force had entered me at that moment, for I was spared from breaking apart, though by all reason my bones should have shattered.

And she— who lay before me— was slowly stirring upon that same hot, steam-breathing ground. Her form had changed completely. Her height had grown to well over ten feet, her breadth expanded in the same proportion. Her face had become something strange— not human at all, but resembling a grotesque fusion of wolf and man. Long, pointed teeth showed through her open mouth, enough to send shivers through me at the sight. The hair upon her head seemed to have come alive, all of it in restless motion. The skin of her body had turned into something I could scarcely comprehend— less flesh and bone, more like a writhing mass of crawling creatures. In several places it did not even appear solid, instead giving the impression of smoke. Beyond this, numerous tentacle-like growths had sprouted from her body, their tips sharp like needles. Her eyes had grown enormous, blazing red, as though flames burned within them.

As terrifying as the surroundings were, she herself had become far more so. I had seen Hirvi in her demonic form, but this was vastly more dreadful. Now my heart bore witness: she could not be Sainvani— she was Agashi herself, and all this had unfolded as the consequence of my tearing myself away from her just before release. The question now was whether, in this state, I had lost— or whether she had.

It took me a few moments to steady myself. When I managed to rein in my fear, I looked around. The place where we stood was encircled by six figures kneeling on their knees — statues that looked like living humans, yet were so utterly motionless that they could only be called effigies. Two were men, four women— and upon recognising the faces of two of them, my astonishment knew no bounds. One was the monk I had encountered in the temple in the outer world where we had stayed; the other was Hirvi.

I was still struggling to gather my wits at the sight when movement ahead drew my gaze forward— where Agashi was now rising, drawing herself together. Her flame-laden eyes were fixed upon me, and the growl issuing from her opening and closing mouth was enough to make me tremble. When she stood fully upright, I seemed like a child before her. I tried to step back, but with swift force she lashed out, seized me by the throat, and dragged me toward her. With the sheer strength of her arm she lifted me into the air like a small child, raising me until my face was level with hers. Even so, I sensed that my weight was greater than she had expected, for the arm holding me aloft was beginning to tremble.

She then uttered a few words that I could not comprehend, yet it was clear enough that she was venting her fury at her own failure. What I could not grasp was this: if she had truly failed, then the victory should have been mine— and this entire spectacle should not have existed at all. But if it did exist, then it could only mean that since I, too, had reached release, the defeat was mine as well. That was why neither of us had won or lost completely. Which meant that the struggle for my survival had to be fought all over again.

My mind insisted that morning should have arrived by now— but if Agashi still held sway, then my mind was deceiving me.

The first principle of fighting her, or powers like hers, was mastery over fear— and it was here that I faltered again and again, granting them dominion over me. I closed my eyes for a moment and thought: if death is inevitable, then why not fight before dying— what worse fate could there be than this? Summoning what courage I could, I seized her wrists and tried to force them away from myself, then drove my head hard into her face. With a shriek, she flung me aside.

Where I landed, there was a wall— it collapsed under my weight. I was injured, but not so badly that I could not rise. As I struggled to my feet, reason returned: in sheer strength I could never match her. Why not try to escape? Even if my sense of time was failing me, enough time must surely have passed for the night to be waning— and if I could somehow survive until sunrise, Agashi would be powerless to harm me.

With this thought, I was just about to rise and run when my gaze fell upon the effigies. They were stretching, straightening themselves, coming alive. The eyes of the monk and of Hirvi— now living— met mine, but there was no trace of recognition in them. It was no longer difficult to understand— this was Agashi's army.

Even so, I tried to flee, but it was impossible to give those soldiers the slip. Nor did they seize me to deliver me to Agashi— instead, they set upon me themselves, striking, hounding, flinging me about, turning me into a football among them. The palace, already in ruins and collapsing, began to fall apart even faster. My body was taking innumerable blows and wounds, and they would not let me break free. It felt as though they meant to tear me to shreds.

Then— from nowhere, somehow— tearing through the sky wrapped in black ink, six Aghoris appeared, their bodies smeared in white ash, crying out "Har Har Mahadev." They fell directly among us and, even as they landed, steadied themselves and stood upright. At the sight of them, Agashi and her forces let out a terrifying roar. That alone was enough to scatter the focus of the powers hunting me and grant me a brief chance to recover. Badly injured, wounded, I somehow gathered myself and tried to flee from that place. For me, what mattered was not taking part in their battle, but surviving— enduring long enough for the sun to rise.

But was it really that easy? Not at all. Those soldiers of Agashi who had until then appeared in human form, upon seeing themselves confronted by the Aghoris, revealed their true bodies— the same forms Hirvi had shown me earlier in the settlement of the dead. Now the Aghoris seemed like children before them, yet this appeared to make no difference to the Aghoris themselves. With tridents clenched in their hands, chanting praises of Mahadev, they continued to attack relentlessly. Agashi's soldiers sought to break free of them and turn their attention toward me, while the Aghoris, at any cost, meant to keep them entangled— and so one remained locked with one, without pause. Agashi was left alone, which allowed her to focus on me, and at the very least I could attempt to evade a single adversary rather than seven.

We moved forward and back, emerging from the zone of shattered alleys and collapsing, lifeless house-frames, from among the ruins and the places where lava boiled or pooled. It was a vision of hell in every direction, yet there was one mercy— despite so much fire and molten rock, the heat was not so extreme as to scorch us outright. It was hot, but bearable. When at one point Agashi flung me with a kick into a basin of lava, I discovered that it was not so searing as to melt me— it burned enough for me to feel the searing pain, yet not enough to destroy me. The real danger came from the dead trapped within it, desperate to escape, who seized hold of me and tried to drag me down into the molten depths.

No matter how much strength I exerted, I could not free myself from their grip, and just as it seemed they would pull me under, another Aghori dropped down from above. He struck Agashi, who was advancing toward me, shoved her aside, seized me, and dragged me out.

The battle now spread through those streets and across the lava basins. From time to time, Agashi's soldiers would catch hold of me and hurl me far away, or fling the Aghoris —who were engaged with them— into those fiery pools. Yet helpless as I was before the dead, the Aghoris were not. They struck at them with their tridents and quickly tore free of their grasp. Agashi, too, became entangled with the newly arrived Aghori, which afforded me a little more reprieve. It was this same Aghori who signalled the direction in which I should run, and now, enduring blows and wounds to my body, I was struggling to flee in that very direction.

Every blow that reached me carved a wound into my body, and because of those wounds my entire form was drenched in blood— skin torn away in several places, flesh ripped open in others. It was sheer fortune that my bones had only been battered, not broken. That alone was why, even as I stumbled, fell, and limped, I kept running like a madman.

As I ran, I began to sense that the boiling lava and the pools formed from it were losing their presence in that direction, their numbers thinning. It also began to feel as though there was some invisible wall ahead, behind which light existed— and from where a faint glow was seeping through to this side. That glimmer became a source of hope for me, one that breathed new life into me despite my grievous injuries. All of us— fighting, colliding— were moving toward that very direction. Agashi and her forces were trying to stop me, while the seven Aghoris were trying to stop them. Nor was it only I who was being wounded; the Aghoris were as well, their ash-smeared bodies now streaked red with blood.

The Aghori who was trying to help me and confront Agashi suddenly lost his balance to one of her blows and went rolling far down the slope there, giving Agashi a brief chance to recover herself. Drawing herself together and letting out a piercing shriek, she suddenly swelled, and with a sharp sound two enormous wings burst forth from her back, spreading wide. They were so vast they resembled the wings of an aircraft. Before my would-be protector could regain his footing and climb back up, Agashi seized me in a long leap and attempted to take flight.

It felt as though my weight was far too great for her— though it should not have been— yet that was how it seemed. Within moments she staggered and crashed back to the ground with me. Even so, we had come far enough ahead of the others that they could no longer aid me, and she could hunt me at her leisure.

And that was precisely what she did. She lunged at me, clinging to me, and all her tentacles pierced into my body, tearing their way inside. Despite every attempt to restrain myself, a scream tore out of me. In the next moment she tore herself away, then lifted me with both hands. It felt as though I was too heavy for her to raise me above her face; so from that lesser height she hurled me down to the ground with all her might, and once again a scream burst from me.

This time, I felt several bones break.

Yet the cruelty did not end there, even as my mind throbbed so violently from pain that consciousness threatened to slip away at any moment. She picked up a stone lying nearby. As I lay on the ground like a crushed insect, I saw my death in that stone. She was about to smash it down upon my face. My Aghori protectors were still too far away to help me in time. She raised the stone high into the air.

At that instant, the invisible wall collapsed— the one behind which light seemed to have been imprisoned— and suddenly a fierce, blinding radiance spread in all directions.

Agashi screamed. The stone slipped from her hands and fell somewhere behind her, and the light seemed to pierce straight through her body. She collapsed onto me, trailing smoke, and clutched my body with crushing force. In those moments I felt her entering into my very being, and my mind filled with such overwhelming light that nothing else remained to be seen or thought— and everything was covered, as if by a brilliant white sheet. This was the end of that consciousness which had remained bound to me as a human being… no— this was the end of my being human itself.

That void of consciousness lasted a very long time— many months. During this interval, in the outer world, I existed merely like a statue sunk in deep meditation, one that had passed beyond all disturbance. I had been removed from the temple where I had endured that catastrophic night of meditation, and the Aghoris who moved me had taken me, by their own reckoning, to a secure cave. But for me, any sense of safety or danger had already ceased to matter. During this period of void, my state in the outer world resembled deep samadhi, while within it was like a coma— yet in the meantime my body had repaired itself.

When consciousness finally stirred, what I learned was this: there had been a group of seven Aghoris, whose leader was an Aghori named Asimanand— the very one who had struggled against Agashi to save me. The temple where we had been on that new-moon night was, in fact, Agashi's own temple, the central point of that entire region, where their gatherings on new-moon nights took place. On other days, they wandered elsewhere.

Asimanand possessed answers to all my questions, and as I spoke with him, I could not help thinking that had I met him earlier, I would not be in this condition today. The greatest reason for my incomplete victory— or my defeat— was simply this: I did not know how Agashi was to be confronted at all. What he explained to me, in essence, was this— she was a goddess of the dark world, one who did not truly exist anywhere in the outer world. The realm she inhabited could be reached only through the corridors of the human mind and imagination— and it was there, and only there, that one could face her.

Those who formed her army had a specific task— by the time of the new moon, they were to bring a male victim to that temple. Whether the victim was asleep or, like me, in a state of meditation, he would be drawn directly into that realm where Agashi dwelled.

She was immensely powerful, capable of reading the human mind as though it lay open before her eyes. She would then shape her world according to the desires of her prey and present herself in the form of the woman he longed for most. To the victim, it felt like a beautiful dream, one in which he was unable to exercise any control over himself. She would unite with him, and at the moment of his release, he did not merely discharge seed— he surrendered all his strength to Agashi in that very act. The power drained from the victim fed her, made her stronger, and it was this hunger for strength that had kept the cycle going for who knows how long. The members of her army could also enter her illusory realm, but they acted there only when necessary; otherwise, they remained as silent sentinels.

Once a victim's strength had been fully drained, his fate was sealed, and in the outer world his body became a corpse. Within the realm of illusion, Agashi consumed the victim's body as a spider consumes its prey— liquefying it with venom and drawing it in— while in the outer world, her six attendants tore apart and devoured the dead body, just as I had seen birds and animals feeding upon Hirvi. This was the common spectacle on a new-moon night— a victim offered to Agashi, and yet another of her victories sealed.

There was also a belief that she could be defeated— but then how was such an outcome possible? If a practitioner were to step into her realm of illusion with a vow to overcome her, he would have to know in advance that everything around him was an illusion, and that he must not attach his sensations to it in any way, but remain entirely detached. That Agashi would seek union with him was certain— this was her method, and the very key to victory or defeat. The practitioner would have to unite with her, but with complete mastery over his senses. He would have to know that only by surrendering fully within the act could he bring Agashi to her peak, while at the same time ensuring that he himself did not release.

In such a state, if the practitioner succeeded in granting her climax, then in those moments all of Agashi's powers would be wrung out of her and pass into the practitioner's body, making him a sharer in her strength. He would then acquire not only extraordinary powers in the outer world, but also immortality— becoming, like Agashi herself, beyond death. Such is the belief. Yet this has never truly occurred, and in any case it is almost impossible— because while a practitioner might display such control in a waking state, in the outer world, maintaining that level of mastery while asleep or in meditation, within her realm of illusion, is exceedingly difficult, for there Agashi has already gained access to the mind itself.

So what, then, had happened in my case, that I was left suspended between outcomes? Asimanand explained that because the powers bestowed upon me by Sainvani were still with me, I had become different from an ordinary practitioner— and that was why, while moving within her realm, I had been able to retain control over my mind. As for why Agashi had not changed form after her first failure, as Hirvi had— this was because, unlike Hirvi, she was immensely powerful and capable of maintaining control over herself even in utterly adverse circumstances, whereas others, by natural reflex, lose composure and revert to their true forms.

A single failure meant little to Agashi, because as long as the night endured, her game could continue. She persisted, and in the final watch of the night she succeeded in drawing me once more into the stage of union. Now, at the moment when she was nearing her climax and I was on the verge of release, when I tore myself away from her— at that instant the onset of her climax had already begun, and a portion of her power had passed into me.

Because my release had taken place entirely outside her, she was not given even the slightest opportunity to drain my strength. And since she had reached her climax wholly on her own, although I could not fully receive her power because of its dissociation, she nonetheless lost it— and that loss rendered her drastically weakened, a fact I sensed in the struggle that followed. Now, because she had been unable both to restrain herself from reaching climax and to draw my release into herself to siphon my strength, the failure at both stages provoked her to such an extent that she lost control over herself altogether. It was then that the realm of illusion — shaped according to my will— gave way to her true dark world, and we were cast down into the netherworld that was her real abode.

From that point onward, only two outcomes were possible. One was that she could kill me before sunrise, and in doing so— although she would gain no strength from me, which was ordinarily her primary aim— she could still preserve the rule of the new-moon sacrifice by taking my life. The other possibility, from my perspective, was that I could contend with her precisely because a portion of her essence had already entered me, granting me greater strength; because having lost her power she had become markedly weak; and because only a little time remained before sunrise. If I could somehow keep myself alive until dawn, then for the time being death would cease to be an option for me— because I had now become, in part, Agashi herself.

This was why my weight had become too great for her, and why neither she nor her forces were able to kill me despite every effort— though against their demonic strength my worth should have been no more than that of an ant. All of those soldiers were bound to Agashi; when she weakened, they weakened as well. And by human measure I had grown strong enough that neither their blows could break my bones, nor the lava burn me. In the end, when Agashi gathered all her remaining strength and came to the very brink of success, morning arrived at that exact moment, and the first ray of sunrise touched the temple. The opportunity slipped from her grasp— and I, too, was released from death.

I will remain beyond death until Agashi herself is destroyed or her powers are completely extinguished. In other words, until some practitioner defeats Agashi and chooses to free her servants, my death is impossible.

And how, after all, had they reached the illusory realm created by Agashi? I learned that they, too, were practitioners of Agashi— though of a different order, the nature of which they did not disclose to me. They told me only this: that they could not merely read my mind, but also intrude into my imagination and enter that very realm of illusion where I was. They had arrived at the temple that night when I was alone, cut off from the outer world, wandering in meditation through a mind-realm with Tashi. They remained gathered around me, continuously reading my mental currents, and in the final watch of the night— when they sensed I was in danger— they themselves entered meditation and reached the same place. Their task there was simply this: to protect me until sunrise. They knew that Agashi and her forces had been weakened— for in their normal state, restraining them would have been beyond their capacity. One difference between them and me was this: though we had all entered that realm by our own will, they could return whenever they chose, whereas I could not.

And by the time I lost all awareness, I had already become wholly a part of Agashi, unable to leave without her consent. I lay in a dormant state for months, because my body required stillness for healing and transformation. Now that I have awakened, I am no longer human; like Hirvi and that monk, I have been transformed into a vampire— into the vampiric state. My mind and my powers are bound entirely to Agashi, and I can feel her at every moment. By the laws of the ordinary world, I am already dead— the outer world holds only my body. My soul is imprisoned within Agashi's body in that dark world. I cannot separate myself from her, even if I wish to— she may use me whenever and however she chooses.

After telling me all this upon my awakening, that group of Aghoris moved on, leaving me to my fate. I am now condemned to wander these forests forever as a vampire. Agashi dwells within my mind; whenever she requires something of me, she issues her command directly there. All of us— including the monk and Hirvi— are bound together as if by telepathy, able to reach one another when the need arises. When I was still human, Hirvi had taken an interest in me, but now neither does she feel any interest in me, nor do I in her. Scattered through these forests are countless refuges — abandoned settlements, ruins, ancient temples, and subterranean caves— where we reside. Most of the time we lie dormant in these darknesses, and each month only one or two among us go out to hunt. Any young man found wandering the surrounding forests becomes our target— someone to be coaxed gently, deceived, or forcibly taken captive and delivered to that temple on the night of the new moon, to be presented before Agashi.

In the meantime, my body has changed completely. I can feel immense strength within myself. When hunger strikes, only raw flesh brings satisfaction— flesh taken from a bird or an animal. One of the greatest changes has been this: now, when I focus my mind and will myself into another form, my body assumes that form— just as Hirvi's does. This helps me hunt for flesh. As yet, I do not find within myself the capacity to consume a human being, and so I keep myself apart from the collective feast on new-moon nights. Even when I come across a lone woman wandering in the forest, I sometimes let her go unharmed, whereas the others rarely do— more often than not, they consume her.

Could I step beyond Agashi's sphere of influence and enter a settled, civilised world— or return to Calcutta? This question tormented me after I awoke as a vampire, until I finally attempted it. The attempt revealed that the moment such an intention formed within me, Agashi became aware of it. She summoned me at once into her realm of illusion and subjected me, for an entire month, to such torments that the very courage to think of it again was stripped from me. Since I could not die, she would mercilessly kill me to the brink of death and then abandon me there. As I endured the agony, my body would recover within a few hours— only for her to inflict another punishment of the same kind. This cycle continued for a full month.

In the outer world, my body had been lying tangled in a thicket. When I awoke, a young boy was present there. He lived somewhere nearby and came to me every day to witness what he believed was a miracle. When he came in the morning, animals would have eaten more than half of my body; when he returned in the evening, my body would be whole again. He believed me to be an accomplished saint, and for the past ten days he had been watching this cycle unfold. Fortunately, he had not yet spoken of it to anyone else.

I told him that I was a yogi, engaged in such a discipline. I said that I would now carry it out deeper in the forest, in a safer place, so that animals could not devour me and human beings could not disturb my penance. Saying this, I freed myself from his presence and swore never again to venture out of those forests.

Today, after many days, I am back in Agashi's temple, and after many months I have opened this dust-covered diary and begun to write again. I have tried, as best as I can, to set down everything that has been in my mind and everything that has happened to me. Tonight, once again, it is the new moon. By custom, one of our companions, Nimbuja, is bringing a victim who is to be handed over to Agashi before nightfall. At first, this cycle had felt abhorrent to me, because of my human nature— but gradually my sensitivities began to die, even though I had been in this state for only a few months. As for the others, who have been carrying on like machines for who knows how long, what sensitivities could possibly remain in them?

I can sense Nimbuja drawing near— so I am stopping my writing here. The victim she brings with her, I will meet in this temple in exactly the same manner in which, when Hirvi arrived, I once encountered the monk Namgyal.

ooo

It has been more than two years, perhaps, since I last put my hands on this diary… Today my mind is unusually restless, so I sat down with it. I do not know why this unease has come over me— but something feels wrong. Sometimes it happens suddenly and then I withdraw into some dark corner and remain inert.

Today, for the first time, I found myself walking toward Agashi's temple and opening this book.

In these two years nothing has changed… everything goes on as before and Agashi's hunt continues, uninterrupted and smooth. My sensibilities have completely died; in the meantime, I myself have brought two preys to this temple. I no longer shrink even from human flesh, and I attended the last seven feasts. After each such banquet I feel my power increase.

In all this I have not committed any open disobedience that would have brought punishment from Agashi. As I accepted their ways, becoming fully part of their society, a bond of trust formed between us and now we speak freely among ourselves.

Within Agashi's army, besides me, there were two men— the Bhutanese Buddhist monk Namgyal, and an Assamese yogi named Baro. The three of us had knowingly taken that deadly step aimed at defeating Agashi; because our attempt had been half-successful, we now existed neither truly alive nor quite dead.

Namgyal was the ascetic whose tale is known among the tribals; Tashi had told me about him. Our ages differed… Baro was said to be a hundred years old, while Namgyal was one hundred and eighty. The other four were women, some a hundred years old, some three hundred. I became close to Namgyal; he told me that the older we become, the more our powers grow.

The three of us men had become part of Agashi's force as a consequence of that half-successful sadhana aimed at mastering her, but how had those women come under Agashi's sway?

Namgyal explained: some surrendered themselves to Agashi in exchange for relief from torment, exploitation, or social ostracism; some, tired of life, came here and ended themselves; others had been trapped and devoured by cruel men and, calling to Agashi for help, had had their humanity and their souls taken as payment.

It is not that anyone can routinely do this— such a concordance of events happens perhaps once in fifty or five hundred years.

What will be the future of this cycle? Namgyal feared that as amavasya after amavasya Agashi continued to feed, she would grow enormously powerful over centuries and her sphere of influence would steadily expand… and one day she might rule the entire earth. Then she would have uprooted every other god and goddess, and only Agashi would remain — so powerful that nothing would lie beyond her might. The thought itself chills the blood.

Namgyal knew more about Agashi than the rest. He told me a legend of Agashi's past— unverifiable, but I had no reason to doubt it. In some vanished age an ancient city of yakshas and gandharvas once stood in these Himalayan reaches.

I no longer think those words need be taken literally as gods appearing as humans— they could have been tribal totems, common folk of a certain clan. Agashi was once that city's princess: beautiful like an apsara but full to breaking with arrogance; she considered no mortal her equal. For her, sex carried no moral bind— and in that era such notions lay beyond the framework of morality anyway.

Each month she offered a chance to any willing youth: take her to the peak of pleasure. Whoever succeeded would become her master; if one failed, his fate was at her whim. Almost always she remained undefeated: the youths who came, enticed by the promise of her beauty and the chance to consummate, returned in failure and were mercilessly slain.

Drawn by the praise of her charms, people came from far and wide; unable to succeed, they were killed. Over the years many such young men met their end at her hands.

Once, a party of ten yogis passed this way and heard of Agashi's fame. The idea of a woman hunting men thus offended them, and they challenged her: they would beat her at her own game— but their condition was that she grant them the chance to take her all at once.

Overcome by anger and pique, Agashi accepted. The crucial point was that these yogis had mastered absolute control of their senses; any one of them could have defeated her. Yet in their arrogance, they desired not a duel but a united humiliation: together, in a single night, they intended to conquer and shame her.

And so it came to pass. No matter how much control Agashi had over herself, she could not win against those who had attained mastery of the body. One by one she was overcome; when sunrise came, it was the most humiliating day of her existence— her pride was shattered.

The ten yogis became her masters. They stipulated that she must now live as their shared consort, wandering the forests with them. Agashi would not abandon her kingdom and luxuries to live with them in the wild; enraged, the yogis in public shamed and reprimanded her.

That humiliation ignited a terrible fury. She had them crushed under the feet of elephants. As they died, the ten united to curse her: that her entire empire and glory be destroyed, and that she be condemned to half-death— to become a pishachini and endure that curse until the world's end, neither truly dead nor truly alive.

They said it came to pass: soon storms broke, earthquakes and landslides swallowed the city, and the place was destroyed, returning to nature. The people perished or fled; their descendants now live higher up. Agashi herself perished in worldly terms, but because death would no longer take her, she was transformed into a pishachini and has remained so ever since.

For many centuries she was merely a common pishachini, but gradually she learned to cultivate power and systematize herself.

She constructed her own maya-lok where she would live out her curse with some dark gain: she learned to draw strength from men and to make a craft of devouring their power. To this day she uses the same game she once played in human guise. But if the ten yogis could not truly subdue her, what guarantee exists that some modern aspirant can defeat her by that same method?

Namgyal contended that though she lost at first, much of her authority remained, which she used to crush the yogis by elephants.

Now, he said, she does not possess the same sweeping force… We who serve her are in truth fragments of her. For her, bringing someone to the peak means transferring some of her power to the aspirant; then the aspirant may choose whether to enjoy those powers and the promise of immortality, or to renounce everything and bury her and her realm forever in the nether— after which she would have no contact with the outer world and neither would we.

The outer bodies we inhabit would decay in accordance with natural age.

This temple was built by certain aghoris who have been here for more than four centuries. Namgyal said they, too, used to worship her and practiced a form of sadhana— only of another kind.

That reminded me of the aghoris who had aided me; they had spoken in similar terms. Could they be connected to those who built this temple? We had no answer. Namgyal had been linked to this place for about one hundred and fifty years and had seen many aghoris come and go without knowing who they were or what they sought. Who they were and what they desired remained a mystery.

Namgyal also explained that when we enter a meditative state and move into Agashi's maya-lok, our being seems to divide: our conscious part travels within that inner world while the inert body remains in the outer realm.

That is unlike Agashi: she exists solely in the inner world; she has no dormant physical body in the outer sphere that must be rendered inactive or placed into meditation in order to enter the inner plane. She is only in that interior dimension, and whoever wishes to reach her must go from the external to that inner world— there is no other path to meet Agashi.

In any case, my spirit has been filled with a constant despair; no ray of hope appears on the horizon.

I do not know how long I must continue thus… the most painful awareness is that this life has no end. That thought makes me profoundly restless at times. My feelings have atrophied and the heart within my chest is turning to stone. If only I had not clung to that stubbornness.

Today I opened this diary after two full years, perhaps for the last time… from now on it will not remain in my possession. An unexpected thing has occurred that I must record— this will be my final admission. Four days ago, a happening stirred my deadened feelings back to life and it has left me anxious in a way that may not easily pass.

Yet it has given me a hope. Hope that I may be freed from this accursed existence. Hope that my unfinished mission might be completed by my fragment— my son.

Four days ago, I was wandering toward the plains when I saw a small child, terrified, trying to fend off some jackals. They were attempting to tear him apart… nearby was a hamlet of huts that looked vaguely familiar. Perhaps the child had wandered there out of play or curiosity and, misfortune, the jackals were present.

He had a little stick with which he beat at them, crying out, but his defense would soon fail. No person was in sight that way; maybe some women were inside the huts.

For reasons I cannot explain, pity stirred in my deadened heart and I lunged at the jackals, driving them away. The drowned child relaxed as the danger passed. My plan was to chase them off and move on— the child would run to his hut — but when I looked at him, I was stunned. Though he was wrapped in a scrap of cloth, he did not look like a tribal child by face or skin.

Most strikingly, he was exactly like me… the boy in the old photographs of my youth would have resembled him. He bore my features; the color of his eye pupils was the same as mine.

I turned toward the hamlet and a memory stirred: this was the settlement of Tashi and Boyal where I had once spent a recovery period; it was there that Tashi and I had become intimate. Could this child be the fruit of that union? The thought set my mind in tumult.

I did not wish to meet Tashi— so much time had passed that she must have rebuilt her life. My reappearance would disturb her world, and besides, I was no longer human. Yet I wanted to be certain that the child was mine. I spoke to him in his tongue to tell him to go to his home; he nodded and ran toward a hut.

The hut was indeed Boyal and Tashi's. My doubt vanished. Still, I hid to watch if Tashi lived there.

I waited, hours crouched hidden, and then she appeared… though distant, I could not fail to recognize her. She had come from the rear to throw something away, and the child followed, explaining in gestures what had happened in the afternoon.

Tashi glanced their way but could not see me. Once I confirmed beyond doubt that he was my son, I withdrew.

I returned, carrying the ache of my privations. I wanted to weep; I found a dark corner and I did weep. But as night fell I scraped the image of that child and Tashi clean from my mind— afraid that any trace of them in my head might be read by Agashi.

Who knows how she would take it… or whether, seeing my lapse into human attachments, she might turn against that mother and son. So, I steeled my heart to stone and sank into my nocturnal instincts: hunting, roaming through the night, keeping my mind so full of motion it had no chance to ring their bell and alert Agashi.

But at dawn the emotions returned with a vengeance— I was torn between the human I once was and the pishach I had become.

The whole day passed in that conflicted fog: what could I do, what ought I do? The others in Agashi's army were of another age; their ties to the world lay far behind them and their emotional attachments were gone. I, however, belonged to the present.

The people and relationships I had once known still existed. Those who were far away— those I had left back in Calcutta— I could forget; there was no bond with Tashi that should make me pine for her, so I could have kept away. But a son… how does one stop thinking of one's own flesh? He was a part of me.

The day slipped by in that inner struggle, and when night came, I had to brutally flense their faces from my mind again so Agashi would not learn of them.

I wandered through the dark all night, my thoughts snagged here and there. Two more days and nights passed without an instant's sleep. Though what does sleep mean to we who are children of the night? It mattered when I was human.

When the next day grew unbearable, I finally poured my anguish into Namgyal. Though he, like me, is a loyal soldier of Agashi, the residue of his human self still carries some sympathy; I hoped he might show me a way. He told me that since the child is my fragment, he must carry the powers I received from Sainvani.

Even if immature now, unable to recognize or harmonize with them, in time he will arrange himself around them— and not only see futures in visions as I do, but stand against demonic, pishachic, and illusory powers, perhaps as I do or even more powerfully.

That may happen. But if the boy stays here, I will not be able to keep away from him for long… and if that happens, Agashi will learn of him. She sees futures better than we do; for two reasons she will not let that child live if she perceives his potential.

First, the child would become a threat to her in the future; second, my falling into the human trap of attachment would be a deviation from the rules Agashi set— something she will never tolerate.

Therefore, the child must be taken away from here and sent far. Even if Agashi discovers his existence through me, he will be beyond her reach.

Namgyal offered another solution: if those powers indeed reside in the boy, he might be the instrument of my liberation. What I could not do— he could do for me. I failed, or at best achieved only half-success, because I did not fully understand how to face Agashi or what the encounter truly required; but through this diary I can prepare my son for everything ahead of time.

Knowledge is the supreme safeguard; I can hand him answers without forcing him to grope in the dark.

If he chooses, he could master the game and defeat Agashi — and after victory, he could bury her world in the nether, freeing me and the others who have borne this curse for centuries.

Thus, my son is not only my hope but a hope for the six others who have endured this damnation. Namgyal reckoned that it would be best for the boy to be trained to face Agashi after his twentieth year.

By then his body and mind will be mature enough. Agashi herself prefers to hunt young men of that age; a favored youth brought to union may not hold as much control as she expects, and in that moment my son's chances would be stronger. The future is never fixed— he may be defeated or meet only a partial success and gain my strength— but I do not want to dwell on those possibilities.

Maybe I am selfish, but what father would not cling to hope for his child?

Yesterday I persisted in that inner debate: what should I do? And whether Tashi would consent to let the child go— she had given herself entirely to me before. Would she, now, give him up? It seemed unlikely; still, I could not be certain. The child's safety was crucial.

If he stayed here, he would be killed. Would she accept seeing her son slain? I had to erase her from my mind again at dusk— at least for that night, at least until I arranged something to keep them safe.

At dawn I set out toward the place where my fragment lived. I took with me what I had: my belongings, the remaining money, and this book— I would send the child away with this diary. For an ordinary man the journey to the plains would have taken at least two days, even more if the route were straight.

I had needed ten days the first time I'd traveled from Tashi's hamlet to Agashi's temple. But I am no longer an ordinary man. I can leap down from heights, swing from tree to tree like a monkey. Thus, the long journey that once would have taken days I made in half a day.

At noon I reached them. The siblings were astonished. When Tashi saw me, she wept for joy. She brought the little boy to meet his father; I held him in my arms.

He was so young and innocent that, though he recognised me, he could not tell his mother that it was I who had saved him from the jackals three days earlier. There was no time to lose. I told them everything: the ordeals I had suffered, my truth. They were stunned, but what could be done?

I explained that because of me the child was in danger; as soon as Agashi learned of him, she would have him ended.

I wanted to keep him safe, but I did not want to place that burden on the two of them. They were not fit to live in civilized society as protectors; they could neither ensure his safety nor give him the upbringing he needed. I did not want to send the boy to my family for two reasons.

First, my orthodox, tradition-bound family would never accept an illegitimate child born to an adivasi woman; no one knows how they would treat him. Second, there was the threat of Agashi. Today she might not know, but tomorrow she might discover him and seek him out.

My family in Calcutta was prominent; finding him would be easy for her. If he were raised elsewhere, tracking him would be far harder.

My friend William seemed the better option. I wrote two letters— one for William, one for Deepdas babu— laying out the situation and asking them to follow my instructions. I told Boyal the address of Deepdas babu in Calcutta and asked him to safeguard this diary, to ensure that it reaches my son when he turns twenty.

For the boy's identity and the diary's safety, let them take whatever measures they deem fit. I also told Boyal not to reveal William's address directly; instead, he should arrange a meeting somehow so William will receive the message.

I asked William to consider transferring away from Calcutta for a few years for the child's safety; even if the boy eventually returns to Calcutta, a temporary relocation would make him harder to find. I do not know whether William still lives in Calcutta after all these years, or what post he holds, but given his father's standing in the British government, I hope he can be of help.

I did what I could to place the boy in his hands; from the little I see of the future, my hope is starting to take shape. Tashi remembered the lunar date of the child's birth; from that I converted to the English date so I would know when the child turns twenty.

I told William that he was free to choose any name he liked for my son, but that the child must carry his surname.

That will hide him further… I do not want any path that leads Agashi to him to remain open. In my letter I strictly ordered William not to tell anyone— neither of my past nor of me— before the boy's twentieth year. Let this matter stay between him and those I designate; let no one else know until the proper time. Now I am sending Boyal off with this diary.

A few final lines for my son…

My son, when you turn twenty, and if all goes well, one of my messengers— who may very well be your maternal uncle, Boyal— will reach you. He will place this diary in your hands and, if you wish, help guide you toward the path ahead. If you are reading this diary, then you already know what became of your father. Now, as I live this accursed existence, I cling to a single hope— that you will understand my suffering… that you will understand the suffering of a life that has neither an end nor any hope within it.

You can grant me release— if you feel even the slightest sense of responsibility toward me. Yet since you have never known me, never seen me, never lived with me, and since I fulfilled none of a father's duties, it is possible that you feel no bond with me at all, and that you may refuse to attempt anything of this sort. That choice rests entirely with you. If you do not wish to become the instrument of my liberation, I will respect your will, and I will hold no grievance against your decision."

••

CHAPTER 5

A rustle broke the thread of their conversation. Debu turned his head toward the noise as Bhagatram entered.

"Food is ready, sahib— shall I serve? Eat first, then talk at your leisure," he said with folded hands and great politeness.

"Hmm... do that, Bhagatram, bring it here. I have no desire to get up today. And Debashish babu might not prefer a formal lunch in my present state. Why, Debashish?" Saumitra babu looked at Debu as he spoke; Debu merely returned a formal smile.

Bhagatram nodded and left.

"Right, so there were a few instructions— what I must do, what I must not, and certain points to take special care of, along with ceremonial things that a father full of hope might get tangled in. Think of it as an attempt at emotional blackmail through words, which, given my mental condition at the time, proved an effective ploy.

I don't claim the diary quoted him verbatim, but broadly those were the points. Besides that, there were many small items that were unnecessary, and a host of sketches describing things they had seen, which helped me picture the powers and phenomena they mentioned."

"And after reading the diary what did you do? I mean, once you knew so much, surely you wanted to meet your father's family or close friends?" Debu asked, stretching.

"Of course... I spoke to my father and found he'd been transferred to the Madras Presidency for a few years, then returned and settled in Calcutta— in this very house. I went to see Deepdas babu; he told me more details about my father. He said Professor Frederick had died in some accident during an experiment a few days after my father had gone to Assam. Frederick himself had mentioned that he put the locket around my neck at my father's behest, so there'd be no trickery when the diary was handed over."

"And your grandfather or other family?"

"I met them too, and I told Dadaji everything… that was enough for him— the notion that I was his son's offspring. But he felt the rest of the family might not be comfortable adopting me, which my father had already written in the diary. I did not want any share of their property, nor would I leave my current parents, so it made no difference to me. I left the decision of whether to tell anyone else to Dadaji. I asked him what I should do next; he said I should try to free my father. Of course, he said that— his filial love would not let him say otherwise."

"And Saavri… did she not come to see you at Deepdas babu's house?"

"No… but she had told Deepdas babu that should I need her help she would appear of her own accord. How she would 'appear' he did not tell me, nor did she hint to him. The truth is, Saavri was the main reason I decided to go— I don't know why I felt so drawn to her; I wanted to understand her. She clung to my senses so that I even began to see her in waking dreams. Still… I could not tell my parents the full truth and expect them to let me go."

Bhagatram returned with two plates of food and stood silent. After half an hour, when Bhagatram had cleared the dishes, their conversation resumed.

"So— what were you asking?" Saumitra babu reclined against the tall bedhead and looked at Debu.

"Just this: after reading the diary, what did you do? You must have planned to go— how did you contact that girl?" Debu, switching his voice recorder back on, asked with interest.

"I didn't decide to go lightly… I didn't feel any special attachment to that father that would make me willingly risk my life— something I had only glimpsed once, when I might've been three and a half. It took time to prepare myself, but in the end, I recognized I was being driven. Think of this: the visions kept appearing in my mind— a father wandering a cursed life in forests and wastelands, looking at me with pleading hope.

Seeing those visions filled me with fatherly tenderness; I felt drawn to them. Finally, I decided I had to go— if not as a son, at least as a human who could not refuse the plea of another suffering being. I still could not grasp how, even with powers, I could help against Agashi, whose strength overwhelmed me. Besides, her encounter is fought in a world separated from our bodies and faculties, one created by imagination; how would I keep control of my mind there? It was hard to understand.

Another complication was that the diary said Boyal, my uncle, would come with my father's message and show the way— but no such man arrived. Instead Saavri came, who in no way looked like an adivasi. And truth be told, Saavri was the primary spur to my going… I cannot say why I became so fascinated with her; I wanted to know her. She had become a constant presence in my thoughts— even while awake, I dreamt of her. Nevertheless, I couldn't tell my current parents everything."

"Did Saavri meet you then?" Debu pressed.

"Yes. It wasn't false; she had promised to appear if I needed help. When I reached the railway station to depart for Assam with my belongings, she was there, waiting with two reserved first-class tickets. Seeing that removed my irritation completely— she knew what was coming."

●●

CHAPTER 6

The evening had fallen and the train clicked and rattled toward Bardhaman. Fields and trees blurred past both sides; the sun, a red disc, slid behind a distant tree and sank. Our coupe held just two berths— ours. She, careless, stared out the window; I kept stealing glances at her. Her face held an arresting charm.

A maroon gown enhanced her beauty. Compared to that earlier meeting where she had come empty-handed, now a bag hung from her shoulder. If she had not brought a bag even on such a long journey, it would have increased my puzzlement.

"The diary said Boyal would come with a message— but you don't look like Boyal, Saavri," I said at last, aiming to break the silence.

"No— I am Boyal, only in disguise," she replied, with a teasing air, and I smiled.

"Well then, uncle— how did you know I'd decide to go to Assam? Maybe I wouldn't have paid attention at all. I do not know the father the diary speaks of."

"What does not knowing matter? Blood ties are like that. If they are in pain, you cannot stop yourself from helping."

"Okay— but how did you know the exact day I'd leave?"

"A bird circles me and tells me— it tells me what I need to know." She fixed me with her first serious look.

"If you are Boyal in another guise, how will you guide me? I mean, I know I must help my father, but where? He was said to be somewhere near Manas Park among the heights— it's a huge area. How would I find him?"

"Who said you must search him out?" she asked, slightly surprised.

"Then how will I help?" I was at sea.

"Don't overstrain your mind. Just keep moving. What has reached you now will be revealed further in time. Knowing everything at once sometimes puts a person into such confusion that he cannot act. Things will emerge at the right time and you'll understand them better." She turned back to the window; her manner showed she had no desire for talk.

I breathed out and lay down on the berth, closing my eyes. She was a mysterious girl— so beautiful and attractive that despite myself my gaze kept returning to her. Oh, my romantic nature— I could not stop thinking about her.

The country had gained independence, but Bengal had been left with deep and grievous wounds— ones that would take a long time to heal. First came the chaos of the World War and the Japanese attacks, then the famine that, driven by misguided policies, swallowed millions of lives. After that followed the riots of Calcutta and Noakhali, and finally the violence of Partition. I belonged to that unfortunate generation which witnessed all this with its own eyes and endured it.

Because my father served in the British government, the protection that came with his position kept me personally safe from the famine and the riots— but all of it unfolded around me in terrifying proximity. The most dreadful phase was the famine, when people poured into the cities from the villages in the hope of finding something to eat, and Dhaka and Calcutta were flooded with the starving. During that time I saw countless living skeletons around me. Driven beyond endurance by hunger, people were eating grass— even snakes. The government had become utterly merciless.

Before we had fully recovered from this, the frenzy of Partition led to the call for Direct Action Day, and riots erupted. Hindus and Muslims, who had lived together for centuries, were torn into opposing camps. In Calcutta, bodies lay everywhere, and the images carved themselves so deeply into the mind that they were not easily erased. When the fires of Partition finally subsided, innumerable people had been left homeless. East Bengal became the new country of East

Pakistan, and a flood of refugees poured in from there— its impact felt most acutely across Bengal and Assam.

Gradually, conditions were beginning to settle, but economic ruin remained. And the effect of those times was such that trains carried people only in name. In any case, in those days who travelled from Calcutta toward Assam? Only those compelled by work.

Night came and with it the hunger to eat; I ate, she refused, claiming a troubled stomach. After the meal I tried once more to speak with her, but she persisted in aloofness. I bade her good night and turned off the light.

I don't know when I slept. Even sleeping did not quiet my mischievous mind. The face I could not shake in waking haunted my dreams. There, in sleep, I had dominion. In an instant I found myself wandering a lovely place, and she slipped willingly into my arms. The touch was intoxicating. Our faces came close; breaths tangled; lips grew urgent. Once lips were breached, hands advanced without restraint. Clothes were torn.

When the two naked bodies rubbed against each other, my mind took a sudden jolt. It felt as though the instant an obstruction arose, the mind split into two— one part desperate to rush headlong along that slippery path, the other struggling to restrain it, warning that something was wrong, that this should not be happening. The conflict seemed to seize the entire body and leave it paralysed. My eyes were open, yet I was unable even to move my eyelids. It felt as though someone had me firmly pinned down.

Even in that state, I could see that the compartment light was on, and Saavri was sitting very close to me. Her large eyes were fixed on me with a mysterious intent, and the same smile played upon her lips— the kind that appears on a hunter's face when the prey has been caught.

Then her hands began to move toward my neck, and even in that rigid state my heartbeat started to sink— but those hands stopped at my shoulders and began to shake me. Her shaking broke the paralysis that had overwhelmed me, and it was as though I were suddenly released. The breath trapped in my chest burst out, and I sat up, gasping violently.

"What happened— are you all right?" she asked, staring at me.

"Y–you're Hirvi?" I managed in a strangled voice.

"Who Hirvi… my name is Saavri. I told you that before." Her tone held a hint of annoyance.

"Y–you came into my dr–my dream and all that—" I could not get the words out.

"If you think of me a lot you'll see me in dreams as well. What's the big deal in that— and what is all that?" she peered into my eyes.

I couldn't speak. I couldn't very well accuse her of barging into my dream and playing with my honour.

"Why were you smiling when you saw me in that state?" That was the only accusation left to hurl.

"Are you mad? When was I smiling… on the contrary, seeing your state I thought something was wrong and tried to wake you. Your eyes were closed— when were you even seeing me smile?" she said, a little irritated, and I was thrown into confusion: were my eyes really open, or was my mind simply imagining her?

When nothing further came to mind, I lay back silently and stared up at the coupe ceiling. She sat beside me a while watching, then went back to her berth and lay down.

Was all this the mind's play, stirred by what I had read in my father's diary, or had it really happened? True, I had always been somewhat rakish in temperament— dreaming of dalliances was not new, and in youth I had often suffered nocturnal emissions because of such dreams.

Perhaps my unconscious was repeating that old pattern, and after reading the diary some new element lodged in my mind, which the subconscious treated as a threat and intervened— and in that struggle I, like my father, fell victim to sleep paralysis. Perhaps I wasn't really seeing a smiling Saavri with open eyes at all; perhaps my doubting subconscious had merely shown me her image.

I remained deeply perplexed.

After watching me for a while she had turned away and lay with her back to me; looking at that back I tried to sleep. But sleep did not carry me through the night. During the waning hours I heard some sounds and opened my eyes.

The coupe lamp burned; though blinking I could see that Saavri was gone from her berth.

I felt sure the train had stopped. Voices drifted by outside — perhaps that had woken me. Half-asleep, I thought she might have gone to the toilet.

Why had the train stopped? Surely there was a signal ahead. I glanced at my wristwatch: it read three. We must have passed Rampurhat and should be somewhere between Farrakka and Malda. I had closed the window before sleep, so the landscape was unknown, but I guessed we were either halted in the open or at some small halt; no sign suggested a large station.

Hoping the train would move once the signal cleared, I tried to sleep again; but my mind kept returning to Saavri—why hadn't she returned? How long does one spend in a toilet?

I had awoken while she was already gone, and ten minutes had passed with neither the train moving nor Saavri returning. Worry stole what remained of my sleep. Ten more minutes passed, and still neither expectation was fulfilled. The train had not moved; she had not come back.

I sat up and pulled the window sash aside to look out.

The view showed nothing but desolation. There was just enough moonlight to prevent total blackness. No artificial lights marked any settlement; only trees and scrub were visible, and a vague flat expanse that might be fields. The compartments showed faint light seeping from doors and windows, but no one could be seen to ask. The oil-lamp on the halt's little hut burned, but its circle of light did not reach far; the sky bore a half-moon leaning toward the horizon, and a few wandering cloud fragments periodically dimmed that pale light.

A thin mist hugged the ground, not smoke but spreading as if cold, heavy air pressed it low and carried it out.

Puzzled where Saavri had gone, I put on my shoes and stepped out to search. The toilets of our coach were empty; the other compartments were also vacant. We seemed to be the only passengers. One door on the carriage stood ajar— perhaps she had stepped down.

I peered out— no one was visible. A little further on, a small halt glowed under a single lantern— perhaps the train had been stopped there by the halt-keeper.

I made my way to that hut. The ground was uneven; sleepers and ballast strewn along the line made walking difficult. Under the lantern's light an old man sat dozing; when he noticed me, he woke and peered through the barred window.

"What's happened, uncle? Why is the train standing so long? Has something happened?" I leaned on the window ledge and asked.

"A tree has fallen across the track ahead, son. What can we do in the night? Workers have been called; they'll clear it in the morning and the train can go on then," he said, groggy and hoarse.

"Is this Farrakka?" I asked.

"You've crossed the Ganga, boy… Farrakka's behind you."

"I'm with a memsahib who went somewhere and hasn't come back— did you see any beautiful memsahib passing by?" I asked.

"No, I didn't see any memsahib. Some people did come and ask why the train was stopped. She might be in a toilet somewhere. At this hour where would she go?" the old man shrugged.

I had searched every toilet and found none there. Could she have slipped into another carriage? No; first-class toilets rarely fail. Shrugging, I walked back and sat on a crude bench by the halt, resting my back against it, and closed my eyes to try a concentration.

Concentration meant emptying the mind to a single point so completely that contact with the outside world and its sensations was cut, and one's consciousness traveled elsewhere. It is not easy.

Before reading the diary, scattered times in my life I had fallen into such states involuntarily and seen visions; now I had been practising deliberately, but had rarely reached the level required to disconnect. Tonight, for some reason, I did.

My body remained at that bench while my mind slipped away. What appeared was not clear enough to be grasped at once: shadowy shapes wrapped in a thick haze moved and tangled. It was the train, like a corpse in the dark; my berth's coupe appeared— Saavri lay sleeping there.

Shadows boarded the train, leaping about in ways that offered no solid forms; they felt like gusts of air or transparent figures whose presence could be sensed only by their motions, not by sight.

Those same shapes drifted toward the coupe where Saavri slept… and then, abruptly, her eyes snapped open as if by a jolt, and at that instant the vision shattered. I came back with a start to the external world— the same silent stalled train; no wind seemed to have hit me, yet I felt as if a gust had broken my concentration. The trees behind were still and ominous as if frozen by a curse.

What had that been?

Merely seeing a vision was not enough; understanding it was far more difficult. Was Saavri truly in the compartment, or was this some other train, some other night? My mind refused to accept it as an event belonging to another place or time, because whatever had appeared in the vision— however veiled in haze or smoke— belonged to this very location. Then another thought surfaced: why was she alone in the compartment… and why was I not there?

At that moment, I sensed a change in the surrounding atmosphere.

The place where the train stood was semi-wild and uninhabited. There was a halt, but no settlement nearby. With no habitation, there were no sources of artificial light— only near-total darkness. In the twelve-coach train, a faint glow came from a few compartments, filtering out through doors and windows. A lantern burned on a pole near the halt's cabin, but its light was so limited that it did not reach beyond the coach standing directly in front of it. In the sky, a half-moon hung low toward the horizon, its pale glow just enough to keep blindness at bay, yet even that light was being repeatedly interrupted as fragments of cloud began to drift across it. Near the ground, a mist was spreading— not quite smoke, yet expanding in the same manner, as though the cold, heavy air above was pressing it downward and forcing it to spread far and wide.

Watching that uncontrolled mist expand, a sudden flash struck my mind: the vision had been of these very moments. Saavri was sleeping alone in the compartment because I was here. The instant this understanding dawned on me, I sprang to my feet.

At that very moment, a gust of wind struck my body with such force that it wrenched my planted feet loose, leaving me staggering. I looked in the direction the gust had gone— only a swirl of air could be seen passing through, though there was no wind anywhere. In the same instant, sounds reached my ears, as if people had jumped onto the roofs of the train coaches… yet there was no one there. For a brief moment there was the illusion of movement, as though something had stirred— but then nothing at all could be discerned.

Then— as if from inside my head— I heard Saavri's voice: "Come back."

A shiver ran through me and I began to look around in alarm, but there was no one anywhere. The mist had spread and enveloped the lower part of the train, and now, around the coaches, I could see the same kind of movement I had witnessed in the vision.

My feet quickened, carrying me back the way I had come.

As I trampled over the uneven ground along the tracks, strewn with loose stones, moving toward my coach at the rear, the mist kept rising, swallowing the train upward. When I looked carefully toward the lower sections, it seemed as though that part was growing old and decayed. The mist had the effect of rust— or of compressed time— so that whatever portion of the train fell within its reach appeared to age by decades and crumble away. It was a sight that was as astonishing as it was deeply unsettling.

All at once, my attention turned to another thought: was this mist of compressed time also draining the people inside the train, just as it was consuming the train itself? I checked myself— though I, too, was within the mist, it was not consuming me. That meant its effect was limited to inanimate things. Now those airy, shadow-like forms could be felt moving over the coaches, along the windows and doors, as though they were trying to imprint themselves upon them. When the moon peeped out even briefly, they fell within sight because of their movement; the moment the moon hid its face again, they vanished.

As I drew closer to my coach, frightened voices and muffled screams from inside began to reach my ears. I quickened my pace still further. I did not know why concern for Saavri had seized me. When circumstances were changing so rapidly and growing so dangerous, why was it necessary for me to go toward my coach— when by all reason I should have been moving away from the train altogether? Saavri could take care of herself— as she had said. And even if she could not, how could I possibly help her? In such circumstances, what was there that I could do at all? It was beyond my understanding— yet still I rushed toward my coach like a madman.

At the very moment I reached it, a man came running out of the coach behind mine, screaming in a hoarse, terror-stricken voice. Behind him, I saw a disturbance in the air, which condensed into a dark shadow and clung to him. He collapsed onto the ground, and the shadow mounted his chest, pressing its mouth against his. When it drew in a long breath, I could hear it even where I stood— and the man writhing beneath it began to shrivel, as though he were an air-filled balloon being slowly emptied. Within moments, he appeared as a desiccated corpse, as if he had been dead for years.

Then the shadow lifted its face and looked toward me.

It had no clear form— nothing but a mass of black shadow, from which certain limbs seemed to emerge, though even those were shadow-like. Only the two eyes in its face were distinct, gleaming with a feline sharpness. At the sight of them, my entire body began to tremble, and with unsteady steps I climbed into my compartment.

I was by no means a weak-nerved man, yet it was also true that I had never before encountered a situation that truly tested my courage. Now it felt as though I was not as strong as I had believed— and that I would surely fail my father's expectations. Overwhelmed by the circumstances, my limbs refused to function as they should; and if this was my state now, how could I possibly face those phantoms?

I had just started toward my coupe when a gust of wind struck with such force that the door of the compartment ahead flew open and I was hurled inside.

Turning quickly and scrambling to my feet, I saw a black shadow at the doorway— its eyes alone clearly visible. Though the light inside the compartment was off, the corridor outside was lit, and from within I could see it plainly. For the first time in my life, I felt such fear that my body seemed to freeze in place— my heart pounding up into my throat. My calves shook violently, and the fate I had just witnessed below now began to replay before my eyes as my own.

The shadow lunged and seized my arms. It did not feel like air at all; the grip was that of flesh and bone— so strong that I was unable to wrench myself free.

It tried to bring its face close to mine, and I tried desperately to turn away— because I knew what would happen next. Then it seemed to exhale a startled breath and began dragging me out into the corridor. I steadied myself as I struck the window opposite, and then I saw Saavri behind it— she had grabbed the thing from behind and pulled it back. The moment it was torn away from my body, as Saavri shoved it aside, it dispersed into air with a sharp whap, vanishing as dense black smoke scattered backward.

Turning toward me, Saavri seized both my arms and shoved me back between two windows. Bringing her face level with mine, she stared straight into my eyes and began to growl—

"What did you really learn from your father's diary? What did you think— where you were going, and what kind of forces you were going to face? Look at me. Look into my eyes. On the journey you have set out upon, you may have to confront situations like this at every step. You cannot get past them by being afraid— you must gain control over your fear. Human fear is their strength. The more fearless you are before them, the weaker they become before you. Yes, they can kill you— but just as much as they are allowed to kill you, you are allowed to survive. You can fight them without fear — your fearlessness itself is your weapon. And the boon of the goddess Sainvani, inherited from your father, is with you: these powers can dominate you only as long as you surrender before them… otherwise, you stand on equal ground. You are one, and they may be hundreds— but still, you are equal."

I drew a deep breath. These were words my father had written in the diary, addressing me directly, urging me to absorb them— words I had forgotten at the very moment I needed them most.

"And you?" I asked, turning to her.

"I am not afraid of them, so they cannot harm me. Now come." She said, gripping my hand and pulling me along.

"Where?" I asked, startled.

"Toward the engine— the driver will be dead by now. We will have to run this train and get out of here. We cannot stay here… they will drain the entire train before morning." She said, stepping down.

"But there's a fallen tree across the track ahead." I said, climbing down after her.

"That will have been their doing— there will be nothing there now. The tree was only an illusion… its purpose has already been served.

The moment I stepped down, a powerful gust of wind slammed into my body and sent me staggering back against the coach. In the same instant, that gust condensed into a black shadow and clung to me. I steadied myself, brought my mind under control— convinced myself that I could fight it — and engaged it. As I grappled with it, I saw several such gusts turning into black shadows and lunging at Saavri as well, but she moved swiftly, striking out with hands and feet and flinging them away. As they were thrown back, they dissolved into the air and vanished.

"Not like this, Saumitra Babu— stir your anger and think of them as nothing more than unruly children. Drive them off the way you would them, and keep moving forward." Saavri said sharply.

And treating it as an equal opponent, I fought on. I closed my eyes for a brief moment and gathered all my strength, summoned anger within myself, and with one hand lifted it and smashed it against the train coach. Until then it had felt stronger than me, but the instant my mental state shifted, it suddenly felt light— as though I could lift it easily and hurl it away. Though it dispersed into air the moment it struck the coach, it left me with the unmistakable sensation of having become a lion. A fierce confidence surged through me.

"Well done!" Saavri said, watching me with approval. "Now come."

The mist kept climbing upward, and the lower portion of the train was growing increasingly decayed. I began to doubt whether it would even be able to move. The screams were growing louder now— mostly from the general compartments. Through the mist, above and below the train, around it on all sides, those airy shadows were visible— at one moment forming a black presence, at the next dissolving back into wind. People attempting to flee by jumping down from the coaches could also be seen— and they were falling prey to those shadows.

We began to run swiftly in the direction of the engine.

I was astonished at how effortlessly she was running despite wearing a gown, almost as if she were gliding— while

I, even in trousers, was struggling for breath as I ran across that uneven, stone-strewn ground. Nor was it as though she were lifting the gown with both hands. Every moment she left me filled with wonder; I could not make sense of what it was that set her apart.

As we ran, the attention of the shadows began to turn toward us as well. They kept trying to block us, seize us, drain us— but neither of us was yielding to them. As for Saavri, they made no impression at all. And now, striking them away, hurling them aside, I too felt such confidence surge within me that fear vanished entirely from my mind, and I became even more aggressive against them than Saavri herself. Running toward the engine, I remembered my father's past as etched into the diary. He had never been able to attain such confidence until the very end of his human life, but by learning from his mistakes he had shown me the path. I had faltered because this was my first confrontation— but Saavri had set me back on the right course. Only now did I fully understand what it meant that my father's messenger would guide me.

By the time we reached the halt's cabin, still battling the shadows, one of them had already drained the old man inside and hurled his empty, desiccated shell out of the cabin. When we arrived, the shadow confronted us as well— but it had no power over us.

Somehow we made it to the engine. By then, the lower half of the train had already been drained, and two shadows inside the engine were about to consume the drivers. We reached there at that precise moment, and they abandoned their task, drawn toward us instead. As we climbed up, they tried to wrench our bodies apart as gusts of wind— but we were prepared for the impact. We steadied ourselves, and the instant they transformed into black shadows, we seized them and hurled them down.

"Drive the train— now!" Saavri shouted at the drivers.

"B-but there's a fallen tree on the track ahead," one of them stammered.

"There's nothing there… that was all their doing. Get the train moving— quickly."

Sensing the gravity of the moment, both men understood. One began fumbling rapidly with the controls while the other opened the furnace mouth and shoveled coal inside. Meanwhile, more shadows rushed in to aid the two that had been flung out, and both of us positioned ourselves in the narrow space outside the driver's cabin, trying to hold them back. It was true that, given our state of mind and strength, they could do us no real harm— but it was equally true that we could only drive them away. We could not damage them further, because the moment they were flung aside, they dissolved back into air.

Then the train surged forward with all its might, as though wheels rusted and jammed for years were finally grinding free, shrieking and groaning as they began to move. For a moment it seemed as though the shadows stirring in the mist spread far around the train had faltered, drawn toward the engine… and then they began advancing toward it.

"You watch that side— I'll handle this one," Saavri said, looking at me.

She was right. Otherwise, we might have remained occupied on one front while they slipped in from the other and drained both drivers. Neither of us knew how to run a train— at least I did not; whether Saavri did, I could not say. Protecting the drivers was essential. Without hesitation, I moved to the other side of the engine. Shadows were already converging there, and I began to engage them.

The train started crawling forward with a harsh, creaking clatter. As it did, the shadows began racing along the ground, then clinging to the train's windows, doors, and roofs. From the rooftops they made their way toward the engine, trying by any means to wrench us from our positions. But by now I had hardened myself mentally to such a degree that I faced their assaults with complete fearlessness and resolve, repeatedly flinging them away.

Above us, the moon and drifting clouds played their restless game— and between darkness and moonlight, our struggle went on.

A short while later, the tree lying across the track— the very one because of which the train had been halted— came into view in the engine's headlight. The train's speed was certainly increasing, but now a stark question rose before us: if the tree was still there, then the train's charge was pointless. It would collide with the tree and derail. The surroundings were dense with trees and shrubs, and on either side of the track the ground sloped down four to ten steps into water-filled pits and pools.

In other words, there was no hope of escape. Still fighting the shadows, I began bracing myself for the impending collision.

And just as the train reached the tree, at that precise instant, a gigantic bat-like shadow shot toward it from the direction of the train itself at an inconceivable speed— and before the impact could occur, it lifted the tree and flung it far away. Since I was on the opposite side, I could see little more than the train crossing past that enormous shadow as it vanished somewhere beyond.

What was it?

My mind refused to supply an answer. But then I noticed that the shadows fighting me had begun to ignore me and move toward the roof. When even the last of them released me, I turned back and climbed atop the coal car behind the engine— and there I saw it: that same colossal bat-like shadow was striking down the black shadows on the roof of a coach. One moment it was visible, the next it had dropped away to the other side. The train was now running at a fair speed. When I went inside and looked, both drivers were staring at me, shaken and pale. This was far beyond their comprehension— none of them could understand what was happening.

I looked to the other side, where Saavri had been fighting — but she, too, was gone. The mist that had been spreading beneath the train did follow us for some distance, but then it fell behind. Before my eyes, the moon slipped away behind clouds, and complete darkness descended— darkness that the headlight on the engine's brow could pierce only faintly. Everywhere else, the darkness spread as though some monstrous entity of night had risen there, swallowing everything in its path. The train was now racing through the dark exactly as though it were hurtling through a pitch-black tunnel.

How all this was changing, I had no answer— nor did the two of them. We could only stare at one another's ashen faces in stunned silence… while Saavri remained nowhere to be seen.

I turned to look back, toward the side where she had vanished while fighting… and despite the pitch darkness, on the first coach adjoining the coal tender there was the distinct sense of a colossal shadow. Then, sensing light behind me, I twisted my neck forward— and it felt as though a wall of lava stood before us.

Only a few seconds later, a violent jolt tore through my body and I was flung out of the engine. Outward— into the air. And it was not as though I had been hurled toward the ground nearby; rather, both the train and I were now plunging into a vast abyss.

It felt exactly as if the train had passed through a tunnel and emerged directly into a great, bowl-shaped chasm, where the track simply ended— causing the train to sway in midair and plunge downward. And this place was anything but ordinary. It was like a colossal cup, ringed on all sides by towering mountains, from between which streams of lava poured down like waterfalls, collecting at the bottom of the chasm into a massive lake— a boiling lake of lava, into which the dead train, the two living drivers, and I were all about to be consumed.

Because I had been flung free of the train, I lagged behind its momentum. The engine struck the lava before me, plunging into it— and the screams of the two drivers rang through my ears. I was moments away from meeting the same fate, about to come into contact with the lava myself— when someone seized me, and the lava passed beneath me and receded into the distance.

Whoever had grabbed me could fly. Clutching me tight, it carried me upward.

Behind us lay darkness, making it hard to see— but here, with lava spread wildly in all directions, there was abundant light. I turned my head and saw that it was the same colossal bat-like creature that had torn the tree from the track earlier. I was clenched in its talons, my head pressed against its chest. The instant I felt that chest, my mind jolted again— and the shape became clear: it was the body of a woman, whose arms had transformed into enormous wings, and whose legs had taken the form of a bird's talons. From where my head rested, pinned by those talons, I could see only the lower edge of her chin; her face lay beyond my line of sight.

Yet for reasons I could not explain, my heart told me that it was Saavri.

"Saavri," I cried out, calling to her— but she did not respond.

We rose so high into the air that the mountains encircling the lava valley began to pass beneath us. Though I came from an elite family, I had never travelled by aeroplane before, and this was the first time I was experiencing any kind of flight. To see the earth spread out below in this way was exhilarating — and had my mind not been overwhelmed by the awareness of danger, the thrill of the ride might have been something else entirely.

In any case, once we had crossed beyond that place, we began to descend over a wild stretch of land. And when the distance to the ground had reduced enough for impact to be survivable, the bat-like shadow released me.

With the involuntary scream that escaped me as I was dropped, I crashed through bushes and reached the ground, rolling on and on. Sharp branches scraped my body, sending stabs of pain through me— but by the time I managed to come to a halt, the angel that had brought me this far had already flown so far away in the opposite direction that, in the moonlight which had begun to reappear, I could see it only as a distant shadow. Try as I might, I had not seen its face, and I was in no position to claim with certainty that it had been Saavri.

All around me was desolation. The silent trees and plants stood as though they were staring at me. In that moment, it felt as if the entire world had ended and I was the only human being left. Now even Saavri— who had been protecting me and guiding my way— was no longer there. If that bat-like creature was not Saavri, then where was she? And if she had remained trapped on the train, had she gone down into the lava along with it? My heart grew restless with concern for her.

"Saavri… Saavri!" I began calling out to her like a madman.

After a few moments the sound of her voice did come, calling my name. I turned toward it— and everything violently unstitched. Sky and moon fragmented and tumbled down; the darkness folded in upon itself and collapsed.

From the belly of that fallen dark Saavri's face emerged, bent close to mine; her voice called from a distance that drew near with each syllable.

Then a sharp shock hit my mind and I snapped awake. I was not in that chasm but in my berth on the train; we were racing through a forest. The light beyond the window told me dawn had come. Saavri sat beside me, watching me with anxious eyes.

I cradled my head in both hands and filled my lungs with ragged breaths. The first thought that seized me was: was that a dream— or had it really happened? My father's words came back at me then: if you set out for this journey, plant this in your mind— all the fights will be fought inside your head; you must not only keep your wits about you in waking hours but must hold yourself even in sleep.

In other words, the trials my father had faced in Agashi's mayalok were being replayed— could I now be within her sphere of influence?

"Where are we?" I asked, blinking and looking out.

"I don't know— we haven't reached Malda yet." She replied, keeping her eyes fixed on me. "Were you having a bad dream? You were calling out to me."

"You didn't know?" I asked, incredulous.

"How would I know what's in your head?" she shot back.

"If you truly are my father's messenger, and the one meant to guide me onto the right path, then you should know everything about this snare— that here, dreams are not merely dreams. They are used to draw the prey into a kind of virtual reality, where everything that occurs in that world happens as real events, and their impact is felt on the outer body in exactly the same way. If I had died there, my death here would have been inevitable as well."

"And how did you survive?" she asked, sardonic.

"Because you saved me. You were there; you taught me how to fight those powers. Twice you prevented me from being swallowed."

"So you should be pleased— grateful to me— and instead you're glaring at me," she said, twisting her mouth in irritation and turning her gaze away.

"Because I want to understand the whole truth… I want to know who you really are."

"You claim that I entered your dream and helped you, saved you from death. Can you yourself do such a thing to someone? Who is even capable of that?"

"Agashi's soldiers," I replied. "Just as Father wrote in the diary."

"So according to you, I must be one of Agashi's soldiers. Then why would I help you at all? Why would Agashi want you kept alive? She would want you dead— so that your father's hopes are crushed."

"But you could also be my father's friend— like Namgyal." At this point, I felt thoroughly entangled.

"Even so— do you really believe that during the night, any soldier of Agashi— even if he were your own father— would defy Agashi's will to show you sympathy or come to your aid?" She stepped closer and looked straight into my eyes.

All at once, I remembered what Father had written on the final pages— that during the periods when he was locked in mental struggle over me, the moment the sun set he would cast me out of his mind, so that Agashi would not discover my existence. He had written clearly that they were all fragments of Agashi herself, and that while during the day she might be indifferent to them, at night she remained mentally connected to all of them. Which meant that if, in apparent reality, Saavri was saving me as one of her soldiers, then in essence it was Agashi herself who was saving me… but why would she do that?

"Perhaps I'm being protected because this new moon's sacrifice is meant to be me," I said after thinking for a while. "And at the very least, keeping me alive until the new moon is your responsibility."

"Then from whom were you in danger?" she asked, her voice now edged with sarcasm. "Who possesses the power to enter your dreams, or drag you into some illusory realm, and attempt to kill you there?"

At this point, my capacity to think failed me once again— because where I stood, two mutually opposing forces were present. One was trying to kill me, the other to save me. They could not be one and the same.

Now, entering someone's dream or dragging them into a virtual reality in order to kill them was something only Agashi and her army were capable of— or, as a counterforce, the Aghoris my father had written about, those who had helped him against Agashi. But he had also said that they could do so only when Agashi's prey was physically present before them— as my father himself had been. Here, on this train, even if such an Aghori existed, he was certainly not in this compartment. Then who?

And if one were to assume that those black shadows were the Aghoris themselves, then what motive would they have to kill me? If they could go against Agashi to help my father, why would they attempt to kill me instead? I bore them no enmity, nor were they an obstacle on the path to my father's liberation. In that case, only one possibility remained: that the black shadows were acting on Agashi's behalf— and that Saavri was not Agashi's soldier at all, but rather an ally of those Aghoris, capable— just like them— of entering the virtual realm through the mind of Agashi's prey.

"Who are you— are you not my father's companion?" I asked after a while, looking at her as I lay back.

"How can you say that?" she asked, with interest.

"Because the state my father has reached— no human can truly be his companion anymore. Those who once were, were Agashi's soldiers— and at night, none of them can act against her will. If my uncle Boyal had reached me instead, that would have been different. As it stands, only one possibility remains: that you are allied with those Aghoris."

"Which Aghoris?" she asked, narrowing her eyes.

"Don't pretend. The way you know everything about me, the way you intruded into my dream— you cannot be an ordinary human being. And to my knowledge, only two forces are capable of doing such a thing, and of having an interest in me."

"So you think I belong to some group of Aghoris," she said, with a faintly mocking air.

"Appearance itself is the greatest illusion of this snare," I replied. "Here, what seems to be is rarely what truly is. Look at it this way: to the eye, you appear like a woman of the modern age, shaped by Western civilisation— yet someone entangled in these horrors should have no connection with such a world at all. And whether you are my father's messenger as one of Agashi's soldiers, an ally of those Aghoris, or someone tied to my mother and my uncle in some other way— none of these possibilities fit this attire, this manner, this way of being. That is why, before setting out on this journey, I convinced myself of one thing above all else: that I must trust my eyes the least. Because it is through them that deception comes most easily."

Something shifted, and she suddenly burst into laughter. It was the first time she had laughed like this in front of me. As enchanting as her smile was, her laughter was just as lovely. For a moment, I forgot everything and was lost in it

— it felt as though a string of pearls had snapped, and the beads were scattering far and wide, bouncing across a glass surface.

"Yes, my outward form is a disguise," she said at last, "but not to the extent you imagine. One has to do this for one's own safety— otherwise, forget dark powers, even ordinary men would tear apart a woman they find alone."

"Then tell me who you are… at least trust me enough to know that I would never harm you." Seeing her soften, a flicker of hope rose in me. I turned onto my side, propped myself on my elbow, rested my cheek against my palm, and looked at her.

"You will regret knowing this," she said. "I am the daughter of your mother's brother, Boyal."

Her words struck me like a blow. It felt as though an arrow had been driven into my chest, and a fit of coughing seized me.

"What do you mean?" I sat up abruptly, my voice weak with shock.

"Baba had no one except your mother… and she had already given herself to your father. They lived far above, away from his settlement, at such a height that travelling back and forth was extremely difficult. One day she went away with him, and after that your father never came down again. No one knows in what condition they are— whether they are even alive. Baba was left alone, and so he abandoned that place and moved to Cooch Behar. There he married a widowed Bengali woman— my mother— who already had a daughter. That daughter was me.

He fell prey to an illness for which there was no cure. Knowing his death was certain, he told me everything and asked me to fulfil the task your father had made him promise to carry out. He knew the task was dangerous, so from my childhood he taught me many things himself. Later, he placed me in the tutelage of a Buddhist yogi, with whom I stayed until I grew up, learning a great deal. After that yogi left for Tibet, I returned to live with my mother.

I was not his biological daughter, but he never allowed me to feel that distinction— not even for a moment. He did not even father a child of his own. He passed away before the riots and chaos of Partition, sparing himself that catastrophe — but my mother and I endured it alone, without his support. For two women living on their own, that time was anything but easy. Everyone saw us as easy prey, ready to tear us apart— but I had learned enough since childhood to somehow protect ourselves.

It was during those days that I understood how necessary this disguise was. A girl who is well dressed and appears to belong to a wealthy household— people, even with ill intent, restrain themselves, thinking she is beyond their reach. Any wrong move could drag their entire family into the streets. But if they see a poor, helpless girl, it takes no time for ill intent to surface and for a human being to turn into a beast.

That is the only reason I look the way I do. In truth, I am neither a modern woman, nor highly educated, nor truly of the manner I appear to be. I am just an ordinary village girl, living like this to protect myself from two-legged wolves— so that when they look at me, they do not give themselves permission to become animals."

It felt good to see that she had finally opened herself up— and there was a deep sense of relief in knowing that she was not my mother's brother's biological daughter. Even if she had been, I would not have been able to stop myself from thinking about her. In that case, I would only have had to take refuge in the argument that she was, on my father's side, a Naga maiden, while I was a Shaandilya Brahmin through my father— so there would have been no binding prohibition preventing me from thinking of her.

"So you're admitting that you know tantric practice as well, and that— like the Aghoris and Agashi's soldiers— you can enter someone's mind… and that you were the one who entered that virtual reality and saved my life?"

"No," she replied firmly.

"No?" I stared at her, my mouth hanging open in disbelief.

"No. I can do no such thing, nor did I do anything like that. You were calling out to me in your sleep, and that woke me. I thought you were slipping back into that same paralysed dream-state again, so I tried to wake you. Yes, I know many things because of what Father told me— but I did not intrude into your dreams." She said this with a faintly annoyed expression.

And now I was truly bewildered— if it was not her, then who?

What had happened was far too real for me to accept it as nothing more than a dream. If she had not entered my mind, then who was it that had been playing with it in this way?

"If it wasn't you, then who was there in your form— who not only instilled confidence in me, but saved my life twice in such a way that without you my death would have been certain? And the second time, you weren't even in that form at all— you were something else entirely." I said, my voice knotted with confusion.

"Tell me everything— perhaps then I can explain. But before that, tell me what your father wrote specifically for you in the diary. I know the rest, but not what he wrote for you alone."

This time, without any hesitation, I told her everything— what was written there, and even what I had seen in the dream before that, when I had fallen into sleep paralysis.

"This is clearly the combined effect of both those things," she said. "Everything that happened to your father, and everything he learned as preparation to face those forces. Your mind is now not only recreating those situations for you on its own, but also preparing you, in its own way, to confront them. First, it showed you a predator in my form, trying to stop you— because of which you fell into sleep paralysis. The second time, it showed you another form of mine, one that guided you and helped you. That happened because, from the words written in your father's diary, you must have formed this image of me as his messenger— so your mind created events accordingly and showed them to you."**

"Do you mean all of that was my imagination? I was not trapped in some mayalok?" I could hardly believe it.

"No— all of it was the product of your own mind."

That was a hard thing to swallow. She could say it sitting opposite me, but I had suffered it. Dreams do not usually follow such continuity; they break into fragments, springing from one place to another. What I had endured had come in perfect order and unbroken continuity. A dream it could not be. On the other hand, perhaps she had not really been there but something else had taken her shape.

My thoughts spun in a hundred directions while the train ran on, indifferent to my confusion.

••

CHAPTER 7

Getting to Assam hadn't been so painful before, but after Partition Assam's links to the rest of the country were disrupted and the railways now had to make new efforts. It took us three days to reach Bongaigaon.

At Malda we had to change trains and then pick up buses, trucks and other means: Barsoi, Katihar, Kishanganj, Naxalbari, Bagarkot, Jalpaiguri, Madarihat, Hasimara, Fakiragram, Kokrajhar— by the third day's end we reached Bongaigaon and then the question was where to spend the night.

In the meantime, on two nights I had again been pulled into that virtual reality… and, strangely, both times Saavri had tried to make love to me in that state and both times I had thwarted the attempt. It wasn't that I suffered sleep paralysis those times as I had earlier; I had been able to steady myself.

The first time the hesitation had been the cause; in the later two there was no hesitation— I had resolved that if these things happened to me, I must keep absolute control of my senses so that they could not make me yield. Yes, I could have surrendered by my own will, but before that I wanted to understand why this was happening.

She insisted she had not entered my dreams. The key puzzle remained: if not her, then who else?

Clearly, the beings who tried to overwhelm me had different shapes and effects on both occasions, yet on both occasions Saavri's help was necessary for my survival. That made one thing clear: this was not merely the product of my imagination or the diary's influence preparing me; these events were really happening— when I sank into deep sleep I was being drawn elsewhere, and in that virtual reality life-and-death games were being played with me.

Who was behind it remained a complete mystery. Even after I had said everything, Saavri remained an enigma.

From Bongaigaon we were to move on early in the morning, and lacking shelter within the town we camped at the eastern edge of the settlement where a survey team had pitched their camp.

We joined them for the night… the team were reluctant at first because of our Bengali origin, but when the chief engineer ascertained our identity, he graciously accepted us. We completed the camp preparations and I set out wondering how many more nights we would have to spend like this. For safety, like my father, I carried two weapons; you can never trust the animals in the forest, and you might need to hunt for food.

The chief engineer, Manik Roy, accepted my story that my maternal relatives lived in Barpeta and that I was going to visit them; to avoid complications, I introduced Saavri as my wife.

Manik and his crew were a little surprised at our sudden marriage. He said that after independence the country had to be rebuilt from scratch— new structures, projects across north to south, east to west. They were surveying on behalf of the railways; they would be staying longer, while we planned to move on at dawn.

Food had been served and several of them sat around a fire. Manik's team numbered thirteen; seven sat by the flame, the rest in their tents.

Saavri was with our camp while I lingered among them, in a light mood. One of them had a violin and was playing an Assamese tune that suited the atmosphere; we snapped fingers and clapped along. The dark spread wide; a few lights from Bongaigaon glimmered in the west, otherwise there was the night. A soft breeze moved the trees like black monsters slowly to a rhythm. Crickets chirped at a distance, logs popped in the fire, and the violin's delicate strings wove with the claps. When the song finished, we applauded.

"Do you have any hobbies, Saumitra babu?" Manik looked at me.

"Why not— a sensitive temperament, certainly. We Bengalis lean to literature. From Ghalib to Mir and Faiz, we're fond of such things. Ask, and I'll offer a ghazal." I said cheerfully.

"By all means," said a bearded fellow who loved poetry.

So I began, letting the phrases flow, and the violinist caught my rhythm with a light harmony. The mood became rich and sweet; after each matla the team cheered.

Just as the ghazal ended, a man's sudden shout struck our nerves like a whip and we stared at one another, startled.

The moment that scream tore through the air, we all rushed in that direction.

The tent we ran toward belonged to Manik's team— two men slept there, one of whom had been with us at the campfire while the other had stayed back, unwell. He wasn't inside the tent when we entered; instead, we found him behind it— collapsed on the ground, trembling like life itself was ebbing away. We tried to hold him up.

His entire body was shaking, his eyes wide, his lips quivering, as though his mind had not yet returned from whatever horror it had seen.

"What happened, Bijoy? Wake up— what's wrong?" Manik shook him by the shoulders.

"Th-there… over there…" he stammered, pointing toward a heap of thorny bushes cloaked in darkness.

"What's there? I don't see anything." I placed a hand on his shoulder, trying to steady him.

"S-something was there… something strange… a monstrous creature. I don't know what it was. I must have fallen asleep in the tent, and then I felt myself being dragged out. When I opened my eyes, it had already pulled me all the way here. I screamed… and then it left me and ran that way." His voice trembled, breaking between words as his hand went to his chest.

"What was it like?" Manik crouched beside him.

"I don't know… its body was like a giant lizard's… its face like a wolf's… and it had enormous wings on its back." He shuddered as he spoke.

The others seemed confused, but my senses sharpened instantly. Such a creature could belong only to Agashi's world. My father had described something similar— the forms of Hirvi, of Agashi herself— and I had seen that same shape once, the one that had pulled me from the edge of the lava. But why here? Why now? And why Bijoy?

"Come on, man," Manik said gently, trying to soothe him — "It must've been a wolf. You woke up suddenly and imagined the rest." But Bijoy's face didn't suggest belief.

We brought him near the bonfire and made him sit close to the warmth. Meanwhile, the others who had gone to sleep in their own tents were now awake, alerted by the noise. Saavri hadn't come out yet, and I deliberately didn't go looking for her. I didn't want to face the possibility of her absence— that thought alone was enough to unsettle me. I trusted she could handle herself. If she needed help, she'd call for me.

Those who'd stepped out to check returned to their tents soon after, while Manik and I stayed with Bijoy near the fire. Someone handed him a bit of brandy to calm his nerves.

"Are there wolves around this region?" I asked Manik quietly.

"They're in the deeper forests," he replied. "Not near inhabited areas. Maybe one wandered too close." He bent down to examine Bijoy's leg. "Let me see— any bite marks? Could be infected."

Under the flickering firelight, we saw scratches but no clear bite. Still, the tear in his trousers looked like it had been ripped by teeth. His story wasn't just a fevered dream— something had happened. Perhaps he hadn't seen it clearly in the dark.

"Lucky you," one of the others said, patting his shoulder. "Could've mauled you, if not killed."

Then I asked, almost casually, "Tell me something— have any of you ever heard the name Agashi?"

They all looked at each other, puzzled. No one responded.

"Who's that?" Manik asked, brow furrowing.

"The Goddess of Darkness," I said softly. "A center of all dark power. Think of her as a supreme spirit of shadow. There's no organized cult around her, but among certain tribal groups, she's believed in— worshipped even. Some offer sacrifices to please her… others to keep her away from their lands, or to protect their kin from her wrath."

Manik's men exchanged uncertain glances. Then one of them spoke. "I think… yes. I heard something like that once, when I was in Panbang. Met a few monks— they mentioned a spirit with a name like that. I'd forgotten it until you said it now."

His words gave me a strange reassurance— that someone else, too, had heard her name whispered in this world.

"Do you know anything more?" I asked. "My mother once told me about her, and that curiosity never left me. I've tried to study all the dark goddesses across mythologies, but Agashi… she's a void. There's almost nothing written about her— just fragments passed down by tribal shamans."

He shook his head. "No, nothing more than what you've already said."

Manik leaned in. "You mentioned dark goddesses— who else are you talking about? Never heard of any."

"Oh, there are many," I replied. "Across the world, polytheistic cultures have always had their own dark mothers. The Greeks had Nyx— the primal goddess of night— and Hecate, the keeper of witchcraft and shadow. The Aztecs worshipped Itzpapalotl, Tzitzimimeh, and Yohaulthicetl— spirits of darkness and death.

The Canaanites had Araphel, the Egyptians Nut, the Greeks again Artemis— who, though known as a huntress, was also tied to the moon. The Lithuanians had Ausrine and Breksta; the Polynesians had Hine-nui-te-Po, Ira, Tao'nul, Mao'hi… and we, in India, have Kali— worshipped both for destruction and for protection. Agashi's nature reminds me of Hecate, though Hecate belongs to mythology, while Agashi… perhaps does not."

"Why?" someone asked. "You mean she still exists?"

"Why not?" I smiled faintly— "She was here just now, wasn't she? Came for Bijoy and missed her chance."

That made the group burst into uneasy laughter. Bijoy scowled and looked away.

"You said yourself something strange attacked you," I reminded him— "There are no such creatures known to science— but my mother told me Agashi could become such things. She isn't bound to one form. She takes the shape she needs."

No one replied after that. Silence spread like mist among us. Then, to drive away the tension, someone plucked at the violin again. A few men began singing softly, and laughter returned— false, forced, but enough to make Bijoy breathe a little easier.

We sang and talked until midnight, when sleep began to take hold. The fire crackled low. One man was assigned to keep watch with a rifle, and the rest dispersed to their tents.

I trudged back to ours, my legs heavy with exhaustion. Saavri was asleep, her face calm in the dim light. The sight filled me with a quiet peace. The tent was small— no space to keep distance— so I lay down beside her. The warmth of her body, the soft rhythm of her breath, all of it was oddly reassuring. I'd grown used to it now.

Despite that closeness, I always kept a certain line untrespassed— a silent promise not to wound her dignity. If ever anything more were to happen, it would only be by her will, not mine.

For now, I was simply content to be near her, like a child clutching a piece of the moon. In the realm of dreams, she often came closer— offering what I had learned to refuse. I'd begun to wonder: if the Saavri who shared my nights was not truly her, then who was she? Because whatever it was, I knew — it wasn't merely my mind's creation, as she kept insisting.

Perhaps I'd slept only a few minutes before sleep took me whole. The mind, too tired to resist, simply gave in. No strange visions, no voices this time— just ordinary dreams, so unremarkable that by morning I remembered nothing. For the first time in four nights, I had slept in peace.

When the body was rested, the fog of sleep began to lift. Sounds reached my ears— voices outside, hurried, anxious. Light pressed against my eyelids. I opened my eyes. Morning. Saavri lay beside me, still in deep sleep, her face soft, almost childlike.

I stretched, sat up, and listened again. The tone of those voices wasn't normal— they carried fear. The haze of sleep vanished at once. I slipped on my shoes and stepped out of the tent.

Everyone was awake, but not everyone was there. Those who were, looked pale and shaken. They were running toward the northern edge of the camp— the same direction from which Bijoy had been dragged the previous night.

The sun had not yet risen, though the sky was silver with dawn. This was the hour when men usually went out for their morning needs. In a place like this, there were no washrooms — just the wild beyond the tents. Perhaps something had happened to one of them out there. My first thought went to Bijoy. Had something happened again?

"Hey! What's wrong?" I called to a man rushing past me.

"H-hemanta…" he stammered in broken Assamese— "Something's happened to Hemanta. Over there."

And he ran on.

So, one of their men— Hemanta— was hurt. But how? At this hour? My curiosity got the better of me, and I followed.

The path curved through low bushes and uneven earth. The camp sat on a small clearing at the base of a hill, with thick forest on every side. Under one of the trees, a group had gathered, speaking in terrified whispers. I saw Manik among them, his face pale, his lips pressed tight. I didn't approach him immediately. Instead, I moved closer to where most of the men were standing— peering at something on the ground.

When I reached the spot and looked down, my breath froze.

It was a body.

One of their own. Dead. But death alone wasn't the horror. The horror was what had been done to him. He hadn't merely been killed— he had been eaten. His clothes were torn to shreds, his chest ripped open. One arm, a leg, half his face— gone. Devoured. The sight was so ghastly that I could look for only a few seconds before turning away, nausea rising in my throat.

It was Hemanta— the same man who had been assigned night watch duty.

I stepped back slowly, the realization sinking like ice. Bijoy's story had not been a delusion. Something truly existed out there— something that hunted. It had failed last night, but it had come back for another.

Who could it be? What creature could do this? Bijoy's description fit nothing known. My thoughts circled back to one name— one fear— Agashi. Or one of her soldiers.

But if so… why here?

Was it just a random hunt… or had it come for me?

••

CHAPTER 8

Given what had happened, we couldn't leave the place at once. The police were called from Bongaigaon, and by the time they finished their formalities it was already eleven.

In front of the policemen there was little I could say about our journey or about Saavri— half-truths and evasions felt safer than the full story— and they accepted our account without pressing. Perhaps the fact that I was connected, however distantly, to two respectable families in Calcutta spared us extra questioning.

At eleven we finally moved, and by noon, after catching a lift on a truck bound for Barpeta Road, we were back on the road.

The driver and his helper were both Bengali; they warmed quickly when they learned something of our background. Both had their own Partition tales to tell— losses and wanderings that had become common conversation among those who had survived that terrible stretch of history.

We listened as the long hours went by, stopping three times: twice to load or unload cargo, once to eat. Saavri spoke very little, mostly dozing with her head on my shoulder.

One small oddity remained— since she had been travelling with me, she had very rarely eaten a full meal. She would pick at food and claim stomach troubles— not that she refused entirely, but she ate only a little. At times that made me suspicious. I voiced the suspicion even at the roadside dhaba: did she perhaps hide something— was she some kind of pishachini?

If she were one of Agashi's, why then had she twice saved my life in those dream-worlds? If she truly belonged to Agashi's hunting nights, who, then, had been attacking me? Saavri denied, flatly, that she had any such nature; when I pressed her about the contradictions, she only told me that if

I wondered whether she could be a pishachini, I should first answer the two questions above— and that was where our conversation ended, with no more clarity offered.

Fifty to sixty kilometres of road should have taken a couple of hours, but the driver's unhurried pace and the stops stretched it into five hours.

By the time we reached the turning toward Narayangudi it was five in the evening and dusk was edging in. The truck couldn't go all the way to Barpeta, so we left it at Simlagudi and began looking for transport toward Narayangudi.

Here a practical problem surfaced— where exactly were we to go? Father had spoken of delivering a message, of liberation, but he had not given a clear place— only hints and the promise that a messenger would guide me.

Saavri refused to accept that she had any special map of the route; she said her father had only ensured she delivered the diary to me and would accompany me like any attendant. I wanted to follow the route father had once taken; if they expected me at a particular place after I turned twenty, it made sense to stick to the same track.

Within ten minutes we found a small vehicle— a mini-truck— headed toward Khelgaon with four labourers on board. Apart from the driver and his helper, there were four Bengali workers seated in the rear where goods were usually carried. Considering our apparent status, the driver sent his assistant to the back as well and asked us to sit in front.

Once we were seated, the vehicle sped off.

Before long, habitation fell behind us and the landscape opened into fields, lush meadows, and stretches of wild vegetation, through which a narrow road ran on and on. One concern lingered at the back of my mind: the sun was close to setting. Within half an hour darkness would spread, and it was uncertain whether we would even reach Narayanguri by then.

"Why are you heading that way— do you have relatives there?" the driver suddenly asked. He introduced himself as Basanta.

"Yes— my maternal family lives there," I replied, repeating what I had been telling people all along. In a way, it was not entirely untrue. A flicker of surprise crossed his face.

"People like that don't live there— people who could be related to someone like you," he said after a pause, shaking his head.

"And how can you be so sure?" I countered. "Can't a poor tribal girl from there become the daughter-in-law of a respectable household?"

"She can," he conceded, "but I'm from that very area, and I've never heard of such a family. It's a small settlement— everyone knows everyone else. Whose house are you going to?"

The question caught me off guard. I had no answer.

"We're going beyond Narayanguri, to Bodhanbari— Bibhās Boyal's place. He's his uncle," Saavri said, turning toward him. Basanta fell silent at once.

I found it slightly strange. By her own account, this was her first journey in that direction, and yet she seemed to know the surrounding places well. Then it occurred to me that she must have learned these details from Uncle Boyal himself.

"There isn't really a proper road beyond that," Basanta said after a while. "You'll have to go through forest tracks. There are animals there— so apart from that gun, have you made any other preparations?" he asked, glancing at the rifle propped in a corner. The question struck me as odd— why should my preparations concern him?

"Yes, there are other preparations," I replied curtly, fixing him with a stare. "When someone sets out on a dangerous journey, they do so fully prepared. Why do you need to know?"

"Oh, nothing, sir… I was just asking," he muttered, flustered, and said no more.

Half an hour passed like this, and we had left Barpeta Road far behind. Where we were now, there was no habitation in sight— only scattered trees and shrubs along sloping ground. To our left, far off, flowed the Beki River, sometimes visible, sometimes disappearing from view. In the distance, a structure could be seen— something like a building— but the fading light made its outline indistinct. As we drew closer, it looked like an old hunting lodge or rest house, perhaps once used as a stopover by those heading toward Manas for hunting expeditions. It appeared quite old, possibly crumbling from neglect, and clearly no longer in use.

Just as the vehicle neared that structure, Basanta abruptly turned the truck toward it, steering off the road and driving straight into its dilapidated courtyard.

"What's going on— why are you stopping here?" I snapped at once, instinctively alert.

"I'll tell you," he said curtly.

The moment the wheels came to a halt, his left hand shot back and locked around my neck. At the same time his right hand came up to my throat, a long fruit knife clenched in his grip, its blade pressed directly against my skin. A feral, violent glint surfaced in his yellowed eyes.

"Make even the slightest move and I won't hesitate to slit your throat. I've done it before— plenty of times," he growled.

"W-what do you want?" The words stuck in my throat. Animals and spirits had already been looming threats in my mind— but the idea that human beings could turn predators too was something I had completely ignored.

"What we want, we'll take ourselves. And madam— no cleverness. Sit quietly. Come on, you lot," he barked, thumping toward the rear.

The sound of people climbing down followed, and within moments all five of them stood around us, a vicious gleam etched across their faces.

Basanta yanked me down from his side, while one of his accomplices wrenched my arms behind my back. On the other side, two men dragged Saavri down and restrained her, while the remaining two seized my rifle and our bags.

I looked frantically toward both ends of the road, hoping — absurdly— for help. But the road lay deserted in every direction. This was a near-uninhabited stretch; only a handful of people ever passed through here. There was no realistic hope that someone would appear out of nowhere to save us.

My heartbeat spiraled into chaos. It felt as though, in trying to free my father, I had brought myself to the brink of destruction. Physically, I was no weakling— but against one or two men, perhaps I could have fought back. Against six, there was nothing I could do.

They began shoving us toward the interior of the crumbling structure.

Had anyone seen my face at that moment, it would probably have appeared drained white by the terror of death itself. There was no reason— none at all— for me to expect mercy from them.

In contrast, Saavri's face did not reflect the same raw panic. Instead, her expression carried a strange mix of helplessness and irritation.

Inside, it was almost completely dark. Outside, there was still daylight, but it no longer had the strength to penetrate the darkness of an enclosed space. They shoved us into a room with a broken-shuttered window; once it was pushed open, light spilled in, dispersing much of the gloom. They forced me into a corner. Two of them then opened our bags and began rummaging through the contents. The pistol lay in the smaller bag— one of them picked it up and aimed it straight at me.

"We're bandits, babu," Basanta said, fixing his gaze on me. "Before Partition, Rangpur was our territory. Then this cursed division put our lives at risk, so we fled here. We're nomads— no fixed base. From Siliguri to Tinsukia, we roam like this, hunting wherever we find prey, taking whatever we can from whoever we get hold of. If we don't get cash straightaway, we sell whatever goods we manage to loot. This vehicle was stolen the same way— we'll use it till it lasts, then sell it off too."

"And the driver?" I asked, moistening my parched throat with saliva.

"Killed him, of course. What else?" he replied casually. "We never leave prey or witnesses alive— nothing that might trouble us later. Now remember— since you're going to die anyway, don't try anything clever. Killing is routine for us. But anyone who tries to fight back— we make them suffer. Slowly. Brutally. Otherwise, we just slice this vein—" he traced the blade along my neck as he spoke— "less pain, quicker death."

A violent shudder ran through me. I felt cold waves ripple through my body, and the very image of that death made me tremble.

"And the women?" I asked, licking my dry lips as I glanced toward Saavri.

"We're men— needs come with the body," he said without hesitation. "Marriage isn't part of our lives. So wherever and however we get a woman, we satisfy ourselves. If she's for sale and we're in the mood, we pay something. If she falls into our hands for free, we use her and let her go. But if she's taken as prey— then killing her afterward becomes necessary. People of your status and standing can't be left alive. Once the police get wind of it, they'll hunt us down."

He finished speaking with unflinching cruelty.

I looked again at Saavri, half-dead inside— but her expression remained unchanged.

"Guru… there's a thousand rupees here, the pistol, about two-and-a-half dozen rounds for both guns, and the rest is clothes and essentials," one of the men searching the bags reported.

"There's camping gear too— looks like they set out to make *mangal* in the jungle," the second man said with a mocking laugh.

"Yes, their *mangal* has indeed been celebrated," another added. "Now their souls will roam the jungle, celebrating forever."

They all burst into laughter— laughter steeped in cruelty. It seeped into my ears like poison, making my body writhe. They pocketed the money and the pistol, shoved the bags aside, pulled out a thin blanket from among them, and spread it over the crumbling floor. Basanta took the lead, dragging Saavri onto it.

What followed was exactly what one would expect in such a situation. We were in no position to resist, and Saavri seemed to have laid down her arms entirely. For me, even turning my eyes in that direction felt like a slap across my dignity. I curled in on myself, buried my face into my knees so I would not see anything, pressed both palms hard over my ears so I would not hear— but palms can only do so much.

The sounds tortured me. They pressed against my nerves, tightening, tightening— until the pressure grew unbearable. My senses failed me, and with a mind slipping into darkness, I collapsed right there.

Then the sharp prick at my throat dragged me out of that darkness. I forced my mind to focus; Basanta's words about slitting my throat came rushing back, and I jerked my eyes open. A blast of air struck my body— enough to jolt me. How could there be wind inside that closed room?

Ever since the first night of the journey, it had become a habit: after waking, I needed a few moments to understand whether I had risen in the real world or opened my eyes inside some other realm. Today, too, the sensation of wind triggered the same doubt, and I stared around, trying to grasp where I was.

That, more than anything, confirmed whether I was dreaming or inhabiting another reality. In dreams— no one can think this clearly, or remember what preceded sleep with such precision. When my mind functioned this way, I knew it was not a dream but a form of reality. Which reality— outer or inner— was revealed by what lay before my eyes.

The wind told me I was in the open— yet moments ago I had been inside a sealed room of a ruined building. That could only mean one thing: I was inside a virtual reality. My physical body outside was under immediate threat; at any moment those killers could slit my throat. Why I had been dragged into this world made no sense— but since I had not come here by choice, I could not return by will either.

What pricked my neck was not the tip of a knife, but talons.

I was trapped in the claws of a gigantic garuda, flying over a forest of shifting black shadows that writhed in an uncanny way. One talon pressed into my back; the other clamped my neck, its nails digging in with painful sharpness. Half a moon hung low in the sky, descending, yet its light was enough. Bathed in that cool moonlight, I could see the living forest below— and the road winding through it like a snake, where a mini-truck swayed along like a drunk.

In the open rear of the truck were large, wolf-like humanoid figures— looking up at us.

This was the same vehicle in which Basanta had given us a lift, and the wolf-shaped humanoid figures riding in the back could only be his companions. I forgot the pain blooming in my neck and kept staring at them. Was Saavri among them? I searched desperately, but I could not glimpse her anywhere.

This was the first time I had been dragged into this mayalok where Saavri's presence seemed unlikely. As I kept watching those wolves, my gaze shifted forward and a dark silhouette of a structure emerged ahead. We— meaning I and the garuda carrying me— were flying directly above that very mini-truck, and as the structure drew closer, I recognized it at once: the same ruins where Basanta had brought us.

For a fleeting moment, a thought crossed my mind— could Saavri herself be this garuda? But this form was entirely different from the bat-like shape I had seen earlier, so it was difficult to believe she could be Saavri in this guise. Even her bat form had never been fully confirmed. And during the two nights in between, she had helped me directly, like a warrior, without changing form at all. That made it even harder to accept that she could do this at will. Besides, it was still unresolved whether she was truly the one appearing in my visions— or whether someone else merely took her shape. She herself had clearly denied it.

The moment the truck reached the ruins, the garuda released me and veered away at an angle, disappearing to the other side. I slammed almost screaming into the rear of the truck and scraped along with it. In that instant, it felt as though my weight had multiplied a hundredfold— like the impact of an elephant. The truck lurched violently, smashed through the half-collapsed outer wall of the ruins, crossed the courtyard, brought down another section of the structure, and finally came to a halt inside. I, along with all the riders, was flung in different directions.

Though the place had been engulfed in darkness earlier, much of it had now collapsed, allowing moonlight to spill inside. Everything was clearly visible. Two figures lay scattered near me, and one— who had been thrown out after the driver's side door burst open— was unmistakable. They were Basanta and his companions. Their bodies had transformed into eight-foot-tall wolves, yet even after the transformation, their faces remained recognizable. Razor-sharp fangs protruded past their lips, and their hands bore the claws of beasts— enough to terrify anyone at a glance. Seeing me, they began to snarl in a horrific manner, sending shivers through my body.

The creatures I had faced over the past three nights had been more like airborne formations— entities that could dominate both body and mind. They felt solid to the touch, yet dispersed into air the moment they were flung away. This was the first time I was facing beings that were entirely solid — and they appeared far stronger than me.

Until now, Saavri had always been by my side, teaching me how to fight, filling me with such confidence that I had been able to face everything successfully. But today, Saavri was gone.

Today was the true test.

I had forgotten that the battle I needed to fight for my father's liberation was one I would ultimately have to fight alone. If I wished to win, I could not depend on anyone— I had to be capable of fighting my own battles. Yes, I could be killed facing them, but there was no option of retreat anyway.

Pushing aside a slab of wall that had fallen over me, I stood up. For a moment, I convinced myself that the protective shield inherited from my father— the boon of Goddess Sainvani— was with me, keeping me on equal footing against such powers. After all, it was my impact that had driven this truck into the ruins; that alone meant I was no ordinary human in this reality.

In that instant, I remembered something Saavri had once told me in a similar moment: You can defeat anyone— if only you can convince yourself that you can. I had seen this proven again and again, and that belief now formed on its own.

In the outer world, I would have been nothing before six well-built killers. But here, the fight was equal.

I convinced myself that I was not weaker than them.

I could defeat them.

By then, one of them had slammed into me with full force, knocking my feet out from under me. It felt as though a body of steel had collided with mine, and we both crashed backward, bringing down a section of the wall as we sprawled apart. For a fleeting moment, a wave of fear and doubt passed through my mind— was I truly capable of facing them?

At once, Saavri's words returned to me: If you ever find yourself in such a moment, summon anger within yourself— only that will help you. I began telling myself they were nothing more than unruly children. I could control them. I could teach them a lesson. To ignite that anger, the thought alone was enough— that they had defiled Saavri, that they had meant to slit my throat. There, in the outer world, I had been helpless. Here, I was not.

When another grabbed me by the collar and hauled me up, it felt as though lifting me demanded real effort from him. And then I remembered something else Saavri had said: The more you give in to fear, the weaker you become and the stronger they grow. The more you rise above fear, the more their strength flows into you. Doubt your ability even for a moment, and you lose. Believe in yourself— and fight.

The one who had lifted me was broader and taller than me, his muscles seeming forged of iron. At a glance, anyone would assume him far stronger. But when I drove my head into his chest, he staggered back with a groan. In the next instant, gripping his arm, I hurled him sideways with all my strength, and he collapsed along with the wall behind him.

At that exact moment, Basanta lunged at me, and in the momentum we both crashed to the ground. Without hesitation, I rolled over, seized his throat, mounted his chest, and began choking him with both hands. He clawed at me savagely with his nails, but the pain was no worse than what an ordinary man could inflict. Seeing this, two of his companions threw themselves at me, trying to tear me away from him— but in those moments, I felt an extraordinary power surge through me. Basanta's eyes bulged, flooding red, as he writhed beneath me. Seeing him convulse, the others joined in, piling onto me— but even while enduring their blows and brute force, I did not loosen my grip. He was released from my hold only when his breathing had ceased.

The remaining five descended upon me at once, and walls, ceiling, windows, and doors began to fall like casualties of war.

Having killed one, my confidence multiplied many times over. Despite their monstrous forms, fear had drained from my mind. I knew that fighting all of them together would be foolish, so I tried to scatter them, hunting them one by one. In this process, I managed to bring the next down and smash a large chunk of broken wall onto his head— splitting it open. With a heart-rending scream, he went still.

By then, two of them had broken away toward the truck and returned carrying an iron rod and an iron chain.

I realized what they intended only when the iron rod struck my back— by sheer luck, my head was spared. I staggered forward, and at once the other tried to loop the chain around my neck. I thrust my arms out in time; his attempt failed, and as the chain came into my grasp, I shoved him toward the man with the rod. The three of us tangled together and went down in a heap.

By then, the remaining two had recovered. Each seized one of my legs and began to drag me. As I flailed to resist, the iron rod of the man who had fallen entangled with me came into my grip. The force with which they were pulling me worked in my favor— the rod stayed in my hands. Even as I was being dragged, I swung it at the head of the chain-wielder who was trying to regain his footing nearby. His skull split open, and he reeled back with a groan.

Pooling their strength, the two dragging me hurled me aside. I crashed into a half-collapsed wall, bringing it down, and sprawled across its bricks.

The rod remained in my hands— that was a blessing. As one of them came close to lift me, I grabbed a loose brick and smashed it into his leg. When he hissed and bent down, I swung the rod with both hands and brought it down on his head with all my force. His skull burst open, and with a guttural growl he collapsed beside me.

Of the remaining two, one tried to hurl a large chunk of wall at me, just as I had done earlier. At the last instant, lying on my back, I kicked upward and deflected the piece to the left. It crashed onto the chest of the man who had already fallen to my rod. The blow struck him higher, near the legs, where it was less lethal— but the impact was still brutal, and it jolted my own body as well, tearing a muffled cry from my throat.

Even so, I gathered myself. I surged up, wrapped my arms around the legs of the man who was rising, and lifted him with me. Lifting him was not the goal— slamming him into the others was. I did exactly that. All three went down together, tangled and sprawled.

I had a few seconds to recover. Holding the rod in my left hand, I snatched a brick smeared with grit and mortar and hurled it with all my strength at the face of the man who was just lifting his head. His face collapsed under the blow, and with a scream he began thrashing, clutching his ruined features. As soon as the brick left my hand, I gripped the rod with both hands and smashed it down on the head of the man with the chain— the same one whose skull I had already cracked. He tried to shield himself with his arms, but against the force I wielded in that moment, it was useless. The rod shattered his forearms and still reached his head.

At that same instant, the third man had partly recovered. He kicked my legs out from under me, and as I staggered back, he sprang at me from a crouch. We collided and crashed against a wall, locked together.

This was my one advantage— he was alone now. The rod slipped from my grasp as he reached for it, and in that brief distraction I seized my chance. Sliding my arm around from behind, I clamped both hands around his throat. He got hold of the rod, but it no longer mattered. Gathering every ounce of strength in my body, I tightened my grip on his neck, and he began to writhe helplessly in my hold.

Just as his body went limp and I was about to release him, someone struck my head— perhaps with a brick. A sharp explosion of pain followed, and for a few moments darkness flooded my mind. I lost consciousness— but even as I slipped, I knew that losing consciousness here meant certain death. Fighting the pull of that deepening blackness with everything I had left, I struggled against it— and won.

I came back to myself at the precise moment when the one who had struck me had dragged me onto a flatter patch of ground and was about to bring that same iron rod crashing down onto my skull. A second before the blow, my awareness snapped fully back. I jerked my head out of its arc, and the rod struck the floor beside my face with a sharp, ringing clang, cutting nothing but air. The missed strike must have sent a brutal jolt through his arms.

Seizing the rod, I drove my boot into the face that had dipped forward to strike. It was the same man whose face I had smashed with a brick earlier— and taking another blow to that ruined face sent him screaming backward.

I was on my feet in an instant, the rod clenched in my hands. Before he could recover, I went at him, raining blow after blow. He tried desperately to regain his balance, to defend himself— but the frenzy driving me overwhelmed him. When he finally collapsed, I finished it with a single strike that split his skull open.

My own head had split as well— blood ran down over my neck. Letting the rod fall, I bent forward, bracing both hands on my knees, gasping for breath.

Only a few seconds passed before I sensed movement behind me. Before I could turn— before I could even tense — something looped tight around my neck.

The chain.

I had forgotten the man with the chain. He was badly wounded, yes— but neither dead nor incapacitated. Now he was behind me, the chain cinched around my throat.

There was nothing left for me to do— nothing but thrash.

He hauled back with all his strength. The chain tightened. My breath collapsed inward. My vision dimmed. Darkness poured into my mind once more.

Then the darkness cleared. For a moment, it felt as if I had died and arrived in heaven— or hell. Light brushed against my eyelids, and when I opened my eyes, a beautiful face hovering close to mine drew back. I did not recognize it at once. But a few seconds later, realization struck. It was Saavri.

The same beauty, the same gentleness, the same quiet allure that had always pulled me toward her was there, unchanged. Only then did another question take hold. Where was I? I looked around and found myself in a beautiful garden. A river flowed through its heart with calm serenity, and on the river was a shikara-like boat, inside whose solitary cabin we seemed to be. The cabin was adorned with fragrant flowers on all sides, and on three sides there were transparent glass windows through which the view to the right, left, and behind was clearly visible. Outside, sunlight was spilling generously, everything sharp and distinct. No— if I had died, this could not be hell… and if it was heaven, then what was Saavri doing here? She hadn't died— and why would I have died? As I tried to think, everything that had happened came rushing back, and I sat up almost with a start.

"What happened?" Saavri said softly, running her hand over my head.

The touch on my head made me realize there was a bandage wrapped around it. The moment my attention went to the bandage, a dull ache surfaced in my head— and as soon as the pain registered there, the injuries all over my body began announcing their presence. I couldn't tell whether I was dead or alive— asleep or awake… whether I was in the real world or still trapped in the realm of illusion. Wherever this place truly was, it felt unlikely to be anywhere around this part of Assam. Which meant I was still inside that virtual reality. Then why was the pain so real— if I had already crossed that threshold? If I wasn't dead, then how had I survived?

"I-I had died— so how did I end up here? What place is this?" I asked, confused.

"You are exactly where you want to be— on your journey, and at one of the places that lie along it. And who told you that you had died?" she asked, in the same gentle tone.

"What do you mean who told me— I felt death myself, and there was no chance of survival there." I said, clutching my head with both hands.

"No— you came very close to dying, but you didn't die. You lost consciousness, and now you've regained it."

"And the one who brought me that close to death?" I stared at her.

"He was badly injured himself. In trying to kill you, he exerted so much force that he ended up knocking himself unconscious. The others were already dead— so I took you and left. I had to drive the vehicle myself— got your wounds dressed by a vaidyaji in Narayangudi, brought you as far as I could by road, and then found this boat to carry us further." She tried to settle my questions.

"How did you get the boat— and who's rowing it?" I asked anxiously, trying to look ahead, but the wooden-shuttered window there was closed.

"A boatman, who else— it's his boat. I paid him ten rupees. He'll take us as far as he can. We're on a tributary of the Beki, which will get us to Bodhanbari a little faster."

"Where were you when I was fighting them?" The thought struck me suddenly— she had been completely absent through that entire fight.

"Right there— where else would I be? You weren't even looking at me. You were charging at them like a madman, tearing into them and killing them one by one. When the man with the chain grabbed you, I tried to help— but he collapsed on his own. He'd already lost so much blood that he later died while unconscious."

"You mean I wasn't fighting them in some other realm— but in the real world?" My eyes widened, disbelief flooding my voice.

"Yes— you fought them in reality, and you killed them in reality. The injuries you took were real too, which is why their presence and their impact are still with you." She gestured toward my head.

"And I'm not in any illusion now either— I'm in the real world?" I still couldn't believe it.

"Yes— you're not in any other realm. You're in the real world, and we're continuing our journey." She said it with absolute firmness.

I clutched my head again and shut my eyes. It was a strange, maddening mess— what I took to be real later turned out to be unreal, and what I dismissed as unreal was proving to be real. How was one supposed to make sense of anything? She pressed a hand to my chest and eased me back down.

"Go to sleep— your mind isn't stable right now. You need rest." She said, kissing my forehead.

There were countless knots to untangle— but the pain in my head was genuinely intensifying. It felt right to shove everything out of my mind and try to sleep. That's what I did, and slowly, sleep finally took me.

When I woke, I felt cold— and found myself lying on bare, broken flooring, shivering. The cold hadn't just broken my sleep; it had snapped my senses fully awake. Blinking hard, I pushed myself up.

I was startled again to see that I was not somewhere else, but in the very same room of the same ruin where we had been brought. Outside, the pale light of dawn was beginning to spread, and the chirping of birds was dissolving into the air. Almost every part of my body ached with injury, and my head, in particular, throbbed like an inflamed wound— blood that had flowed from it had reached my neck and soaked into my clothes, and the sting and abrasions from the chain around my throat were still painfully fresh. I looked around in disbelief… Saavri was there too, still lying on the same blanket, completely naked. Her clothes lay scattered nearby, and like me, she was badly curled up from the cold.

Of all the others who had been there, five corpses lay scattered around the room, but one man was missing— the one with the chain, the very reason I had lost consciousness.

The first thing I did was rush to cover Saavri with her clothes and then drape the remaining part of the blanket over her, so she might get some relief from the cold. After that, I examined the bodies. I had been certain that I had confronted them in a dream-world and not in reality— but the astonishing thing was that they were dead exactly the way I had killed them. Every wound I had inflicted was visible on their bodies, and I could still feel those blows and sensations on my own body— the ones they had inflicted on me. Which meant that whatever dimension it had happened in, it had been a hundred percent real… yet by that logic, this place too should have been utterly wrecked, just as it had been during the fight— but it wasn't. The place looked exactly as it had the previous evening, not a trace of change anywhere.

So where had the sixth man gone— the one who had tried to kill me? If he had passed out while trying to choke me and then died during that unconsciousness, his body should have been here as well. Searching for him, I examined the ground carefully and noticed streaks of blood— marks made by something being dragged. Following those marks led me behind the crumbling structure, where the corpse of that sixth man lay… but the body was in such a condition that it looked as though it had been brutally mauled and half eaten. It reminded me disturbingly of Hemanta's body, found some distance away.

The sight made my head buzz and nausea surged so sharply that I had to clutch my chest and turn back at once. He seemed to have fallen prey to some flesh-eating animal— but what was strange was that it hadn't touched anyone else, and if it wanted to feed, why drag him all the way here instead of eating him on the spot? Or was this too the work of one of Agashi's soldiers— or that other faction, the one that had turned into my enemy inside that virtual reality?

When I returned to the room, Saavri's sleep— or unconsciousness— had broken as well, and she was quietly putting on her clothes. She did glance at me briefly, but didn't feel the need to say anything.

Leaning against the wall, I began to think: if I had left this place and gone ahead toward Bodhanbari by river and boat, then how had I come back here? If I had lost consciousness here and woken up there, and then fallen asleep there only to wake up here again— what, among all these layers, was the true reality? Was I in the illusionary realm then, or am I in it now? The confusion was so overwhelming that I felt like smashing my head against the wall and splitting it open again.

"Who killed them?" I finally asked Saavri, gesturing toward the corpses.

"I don't know— if you were awake, if you were conscious, then you should know," she said, irritation edging her voice.

"You mean none of this happened in front of you?" I stared at her in disbelief.

"No— I lost consciousness the moment he forced himself on me." She gestured toward Basanta. "I thought that after I passed out, you killed them."

"No— I've only just come to. I blacked out too, right when that bastard was forcing himself on you. The strain and rage hit me so hard that I think my consciousness slipped away… and then I was dragged to that place where I'm tested.

They were there in the form of wolf-men— but you weren't."

"Why would I be there? I've already told you— it's someone else who appears with you in my form. So tell me — if I wasn't there yesterday, then what did these men do to you, or what did you do to them?"

"I killed them. For the first time, I faced those dark forces alone in that realm— and still, I overpowered them and finished all five. And what's astonishing is that the way I killed them there, they're lying dead here the same way— and the injuries I took there are present on my body here as well."

"Then why were you asking me who killed them?" She went completely still and stared at me.

"Because I killed them not in the real world, but in the world of dreams," I protested.

"It makes no difference— you should know that if you die there, you die in the outer world too. The same applies to them. Yes— but there was one more, wasn't there— the tall one with the cut on his cheek."

"He nearly killed me there, and I lost consciousness in that realm. But he himself was so badly injured that, in trying to kill me, he passed out— and died from loss of blood. You told me that yourself— in that very dream."

"What? Just now you were saying I wasn't there at all, and now you're saying I told you."

"After I lost consciousness, I came to on a boat somewhere on the way to Bodhanbari— you were there, and you told me that I hadn't killed those men in a dream but in reality. I just wasn't fully in my senses, so even seeing you in front of me, I wasn't really seeing you."

"I had passed out, and I have no idea what happened after that… or where the sixth man went. I can only see five bodies here." She looked around with a searching gaze.

"His body is lying behind the building— some animal must have dragged him there and eaten him halfway. No idea whether it was an animal or some vampire or vampiress… here, guessing anything feels impossible."

"Whatever it was— let's get out of here. If someone turns up, we'll be in trouble." She said, folding the blanket.

I gathered whatever belongings of ours were lying near the bodies, secured our bags, and we stepped outside. In the direction of the road, the same silence lay scattered as the previous evening, and it could safely be said that no one saw us leave from there. We took over their vehicle and drove away.

••

CHAPTER 9

Leaving six corpses behind, we reached Narayanguri— a small hamlet of barely four houses.

By some stroke of fortune, we met an old vaidya there who dressed my wounds and gave me some herbal medicines that, he assured, would help heal the injuries faster. I still had a small stock of allopathic medicines with me for emergencies, but I decided to keep those safe for whatever lay ahead. For a few rupees, the vaidya also let us use his house to bathe, relieve ourselves, and have a proper breakfast.

The mini-truck we had seized from the bandits was left there. On Saavri's suggestion, we hired a boatman who agreed to ferry us as far as Mathanguri for a small payment.

His boat was shaped like a shikara— the kind he once used to take Englishmen and their staff through the Manas forest when they came for hunting or sightseeing. But after independence and the chaos of partition, his business had nearly collapsed. These days he collected flowers from further upstream and sold them at Barpeta Road.

He had planned such a trip today, and since our request meant he would lose eight rupees' worth of flowers, we paid him ten instead. That settled, he rowed us onward.

In the middle of the boat was a small cabin where two people could sit or lie down. Its right, left, and rear sides had glass windows that offered a clear view of the surroundings. The front side had a similar window, but since the boatman sat there, it had wooden shutters for privacy— which Saavri had drawn. The entire cabin was filled with fragrant flowers he had gathered early that morning.

How strange— it was exactly the same scene I had seen in my vision. The same clothes on my body, the same fragrance of flowers, the same transparent windows, and Saavri sitting just as she had in my dream.

Only one thing was missing: the river didn't flow through any garden-like landscape as I had seen before. Still, I decided not to tell her that I had already lived this moment somewhere inside my mind.

"Where are we going, finally?" I asked, trying to probe her.

"I think we should first go to the place where your mother and my father once lived. From there, we can understand what must be done next. Perhaps when we reach there, your mind will establish contact with your father— and he will show you the way himself," she said quietly.

"And that place… is Bodhanbari?" I asked, recognizing the name I had once heard from her.

She nodded simply.

"I can't understand you," I said, my frustration slipping through— "At first, you behaved as if you knew everything — that you would guide me to my father. Then, suddenly, you acted ignorant, claiming to know nothing, insisting that I make every decision while you merely follow as a servant. And now again, you're suggesting where we should go— as if you've known the path all along. What are you, really?"

She only smiled— that same mysterious smile that revealed nothing.

"And you once said you learned many things from that Buddhist monk and your father— that you knew how to protect yourself. You were confident enough to roam Calcutta alone at night. Then where did that confidence and skill vanish? Yesterday you were assaulted, and yet you did nothing. How am I to believe you're capable of anything? What good can it do me to drag you along on such a dangerous journey if you can't even defend yourself?" My tone was edged with irritation.

"Then assume I lied," she said softly, almost with innocence— "I never learned anything that could help me fight such men. I just pretend— to keep up the illusion."

Perhaps that was indeed what I had suspected, but hearing it so bluntly from her lips made me doubt it even more. No woman who wandered alone at night through the streets of

Calcutta could be entirely helpless. Her calmness had never betrayed the slightest fear. So why had she allowed last night's events to unfold? Why hadn't she stopped Basanta before it was too late?

"Then why stay with me at all? Should I fight my battles or keep protecting you?" I asked, narrowing my eyes.

"Do what you must— and leave me to myself. It's for me to decide how much use I can be to you," she replied, utterly composed.

What a strange woman— never revealing, never letting me walk away either. I leaned back and closed my eyes. She sat silently beside me, watching. After a while she rose and stepped out of the cabin, leaving me to rest.

My body still ached; the heaviness in my head from the wound throbbed steadily. Lying down felt easier than moving. I let my mind drift through the chaos— this journey, this search for my father's salvation, everything built upon uncertainty.

At times I wondered if I was still in the real world or trapped again in that virtual plane. Thinking so, I must have drifted into sleep.

When I opened my eyes again, Saavri's face hovered above mine, drawing back the moment my lids fluttered. I turned my head and looked outside— the boat was gliding through a place that looked exactly like the garden I had seen before. I sat up in shock. It was happening again— the very same sequence, repeating itself before my eyes.

"What happened?" she asked, puzzled by my reaction.

What could I tell her? I tried instead to determine whether I had awakened in the real world or if this, too, was the same virtual repetition. Every time I woke— from sleep, from fainting— my first struggle now was to figure out where I truly was. Asking her made no sense; even in the dream-world, she would swear it was reality.

"We were here before," I murmured. "I've seen you like this, in this same place, in this same light. It's all happened inside my head already. Where are we now?"

"In one of the tributaries that joins the Beki," she said. "He can't take us any farther. From here, we'll walk northeast to reach Bodhanbari. Don't ask how I know this— the boatman told me himself."

"Why can't we go further by river?"

"Because it isn't a river," she said, standing up. "Several hill streams meet behind us to form this shallow flow, and farther ahead it merges into a larger one. Beyond this point there's no depth left for rowing. Now get up and gather your things."

The boat slowed and touched the muddy bank. We stepped out. The water grew shallower ahead, and beyond it the land sloped upward. It was noon; the sunlight was fierce but the breeze was cool enough to soothe the skin. The forest thickened around us, alive with birdsong.

We bid farewell to the boatman and began following the narrow stream upward. I carried two bags— the larger one on my back with the camping gear and provisions, and a smaller backpack with clothes and essentials slung across my chest.

The rifle hung from my shoulder. Saavri had a single large bag of her own, heavy enough to strain her small frame, though she never complained.

After walking for some distance, we rested under a tree's shade. We ate some food that the vaidya's wife had packed for us; as usual, Saavri barely ate a morsel, claiming her stomach could never handle more. I often wondered how she survived on so little.

After a brief rest, we walked on again. Soon we reached a dirt track that led toward Mathanguri— where the Indian border ended— but we didn't take that road. Instead, we turned onto a narrow footpath veering northeast.

Coming from the cities, it was hard for me to grasp why people would live in such remote corners, so far from civilization. Saavri smiled and said, "Man began here— in forests like these. These are his real homes. What we call civilization is only a retreat from nature, a gathering of artificial lives. These people are happy with little; it's the so-called civilized world that suffers endless conflicts despite its abundance. We think of them as backward, but they think of us as beasts— machines killing themselves in cities."

Talking thus, we kept walking, resting when tired.

By the time evening fell, the forest opened up to reveal a small village— mostly mud huts roofed with straw and wood. A few patches of cultivation surrounded it, and behind, a line of fruit trees. By then the villagers were returning home from their day's work, yet a few still lingered outside and stopped as soon as they saw us.

They weren't bare-bodied like tribal hunters— they wore clothes of hide and rough fabric.

A strange feeling swept over me. This was the place— where my mother had lived, and where I had spent the first three and a half years of my life. I tried to recall something, anything from those early days, or that moment when my father had saved me from the jackals— but nothing came.

"Father wrote that it was a cluster of eight or ten huts," I said to Saavri— "This looks like a proper village."

"Seventeen years is a long time," she replied— "Children grow up and build more homes. In a place without family planning, a settlement can easily double in size."

"Hmm." I nodded and fell silent.

"Do not mention my father or your uncle here. In their society, leaving one's people behind like this is not looked upon kindly— it is considered a kind of social exile. There is no need to tell anyone that I am his daughter. If anyone asks about me, just say that I am your wife. That will be enough. Besides, you won't understand their language properly anyway— I will have to do the talking. You just stay alert." She said this in a tone of warning.

I nodded in agreement like an obedient child.

When we entered the village, the people stood watching us with a mix of surprise and uncertainty— there was no trace of the kind of warmth with which strangers are usually welcomed. This reaction felt strange, because although they lived cut off from mainstream civilization, they were not completely disconnected— the clothes they wore were proof of that. Even so, such coldness and suspicion made little sense. Among those who had gathered around us were men as well as a few women, but their eyes too held the same odd scrutiny and unspoken distance.

I folded my hands in greeting, but it drew no response.

Saavri began to speak to them. The language wasn't foreign— it was Assamese, but an older, rustic form. I could make sense of it if I listened closely, though I could not have spoken it myself. The villagers were astonished that a city-bred woman could speak their tongue so fluently.

Gradually their stance softened— until she mentioned that I was Tashi's son.

At once they stiffened, eyes filling with unease. Even though I was one of them by birth, there was no warmth in their gaze. When she explained that I had come only to see my mother's village and would leave by morning, their tension eased a little. Still, their fear puzzled me.

Then Saavri asked about my mother's house, and a few villagers pointed to a hut standing at the far edge of the settlement. We thanked them and started that way.

"Why are they so afraid of me?" I asked quietly.

"Well," she said dryly, "you're the son of a pishach— what else do you expect? They don't see you as Tashi's boy alone but as the offspring of Saumik Banerjee, the man who became a vampire and still roams these forests preying on the living. Be glad I told them we'd stay only one night, or they'd have driven us out at once."

"Look at their doors," I said suddenly— "They've written something in red— looks like dried blood."

"Totka," she muttered, "to ward off evil spirits."

"Do such charms really work?"

"Maybe they do," she said with a small shrug. "How would I know?"

When we reached the hut that must have once been my birthplace, the light had already thinned and dusk was spreading its net.

The little dwelling looked long unused from the outside— its walls sagging, the thatch roof and the door badly weathered— yet stepping inside gave the impression that someone had come in now and then to put things right. Cobwebs were few; the interior was not entirely abandoned.

There was no heavy lock on the door; only a stub of a wooden peg, which we removed, and the door opened easily.

It was dark by then, so we lit a thick candle and drove back the gloom. I wiped a patch of floor with a handkerchief and spread the thin blanket I'd brought for just such a purpose. We inflated two pillows the way a tired traveller makes do, propped them beneath our heads, and lay down.

We had been walking for half a day; our bodies were bone-weary and demanded rest.

"Perhaps I was born here," I said, staring at the roof.

"Yes. You lived here for almost three and a half years. Is there nothing at all you remember?" she asked, turning on her side to look at me.

"No— only blurred, scattered images: the circle of jackals or hyenas, father pulling me out. Faces won't come. Nothing clearer than that. Tell me something— does it not bother you, being called my wife in front of people?"

"No. Why should it? My life is what it is because of the father who took responsibility for my mother and me when we stood at death's doorway. If he asked me to pledge my life in service to you, then nothing else matters to me."

"And if I were to ask for intimacy?"

"Then I would take off my clothes— I would consider it an honour that you thought me worthy." She said it without fluster.

"My mother's dialogues... I truly don't understand you. In Calcutta you were trying to act like my mistress, and now you present yourself like a handmaiden. I've heard about it, read about it, and perhaps even seen a couple of cases where a woman who has been violated remains in a traumatic state for some time— shocked, unsettled, needing time to return to normal. But you seem untouched by what happened last night, as though Basanta's assault on your dignity made no difference at all."

"That was not my dignity," she said, twisting her mouth in distaste. "My dignity does not reside there."

"Even so… something should have affected you."

"Why should it have?" bitterness crept into her voice. "They committed an outrage, and they received the highest punishment for it. Why should I continue to suffer for their crime? Does a man only feel satisfied when a woman is seen crying, breaking down, and carrying such incidents in her heart forever?"

"No— no, that's not what I meant. Forget it. Tell me this — have you ever been in love?"

"Life never allowed such opportunities," she said curtly, and lay down straight.

"Is love something contemptible to you, that you respond like this?" I protested.

"Think of it that way if you wish. For me, my duty is paramount, and love can only be a part of that duty. My role is to serve you and stand by you like a handmaiden. If you expect love from me, I can offer it as another form of service — but beyond that, it holds no meaning for me."

Hunh. Who would ever want love performed like an obligation? Love is instinctive— it cannot be done on command. It is something that happens on its own. Perhaps she did not truly understand what love meant at all. I fell silent, left her to herself, and began thinking about my own situation— I had come this far, but what lay ahead now?

An hour or more passed in that hush when there came a knock at the door. Saavri rose and went to the threshold. She returned with two plates of cooked rice and two glasses of water.

"A neighbour— your mother's friend. At least someone remembered to feed us." She set the plates before me.

"You'll eat so little?"

"Just a little. You need energy." She smiled simply.

There were some condiments— a pickle, a chutney— and a bland vegetable the neighbour had brought. With those accompaniments the rice became bearable and I ate my fill. Afterwards we spoke idly— mainly about how she survived on such meagre food and about her stomach trouble, which she said had worsened of late and kept her from eating much. She insisted this malady had lasted only a week and would be borne for as long as necessary.

Night drew down; silence settled across the village.

Before sleeping I went outside and looked: every hut was dark and still— not a light, not a person in sight. It felt like a town of the dead, not a living hamlet.

I wandered a little and then returned to sleep beside her, alert to the unwelcome possibility that some new night-vision might snatch me away. Sleep came late, but it came.

A bird's sudden cry woke me. I opened my eyes to find a brown heron perched in the small ventilation opening on the right wall, facing me and calling as if to rouse me. The morning light had spilled into the hut.

For a while I lay lazily, then sat up and found Saavri absent — perhaps gone to relieve herself. I waited, then rose and went outside. Oddly, the village seemed empty. The sun was peeking over the trees to the east; birds flitted, but no livestock, no human figures answered the sound of my footsteps.

I moved toward the neighbour's house— she wasn't there. I checked every hut— no one.

I returned to my own threshold perplexed. Until now, it had never truly occurred to me whether I had awakened in the real world or in some virtual one. But now, sitting on the threshold of my hut, that very question gnawed at me— had I genuinely woken after proper sleep, or had I been drawn into this virtual reality while still asleep? I had no way of knowing, not until something happened here that simply could not occur in the primary world. Until then, there was nothing I could do except wait.

If I had indeed been pulled into that other realm, there had to be a purpose behind it— one that had yet to reveal itself.

Suddenly, a pelican's call made me lift my head and look in its direction. At a distance, near a tree, I caught a glimpse of Saavri, gesturing for me to come closer. My heart thudded sharply— what did this mean? For a moment, I hesitated, unsure whether I should go. But if this too was a Maya-realm, then sitting still would lead nowhere. I would have to move, to act— only then would those who had brought me here reveal themselves.

With that thought, I rose and began walking toward her in long strides. Seeing me approach, she slipped behind the tree and vanished from sight. I continued forward, guided only by where I believed she had been. When I reached the spot, she appeared again, just as far ahead as she had been before— as if she had never stopped at all, but kept moving onward while logic dictated that she should have waited. She did not stop even now; she merely glanced back to confirm that I was following, then disappeared once more behind a thicket.

Her behavior struck me as strange— whether this was the real world or a virtual one. Then it occurred to me that she had always been enigmatic, inwardly and outwardly alike. When had I ever truly understood her?

She continued this way, offering fleeting glimpses of herself, leading me on— until suddenly she vanished altogether. Only then did I realize that I had wandered deep into the forest. The part I stood in was dense; even sunlight struggled to penetrate it. There was no path, not even a faint trail, to guide me. It felt like a trap, laid deliberately to ensnare me— but why would Saavri do this? For the first time, I felt convinced that the Saavri who appeared in my dreams was not her at all, but someone else entirely.

And now, what was to become of me? I was lost in the forest, searching blindly for a way out. After everything I had witnessed, one thing became clear— I was not in the real world. Otherwise the village would not have felt so dead, and Saavri would not have been nowhere to be found. In such a place, the greatest difficulty was this: I could never leave it of my own accord.

I remembered that on the first night aboard the train, when I had endured those incidents, I had tried to meditate and had seen fleeting glimpses of scenes yet to unfold. That meant I had been capable of receiving visions even while existing within that Maya-realm, whereas my father had written in his diary that the moment one entered Agashi's sphere of influence, the ability to see visions diminished to almost nothing. Now, if I had been within Agashi's domain even then, I should not have been seeing any visions at all— or else that Maya-realm had been created by some other force altogether. But could I repeat that experiment here? I decided to test it.

A little ahead, I found a place suitable for sitting, and there I settled into a meditative posture, attempting to draw my mind toward the highest point of concentration.

After about ten minutes, it felt as though I had entered a vast cavern in the form of a camera— without a body, existing only as an eye that could observe what lay before it. At the far end of the cave stood what appeared to be a tree that had pierced the ceiling and vanished somewhere above, while its roots spread below like a tangled web. Those roots were contained within a circular boundary, at the center of which stood a raised platform. Upon it sat an elderly ascetic with Bhutanese features, eyes closed in deep stillness. On the ground before him sat seven others, bearing faces and builds similar to his own.

Among those eight faces, not one was familiar to me— they were all complete strangers. Then, as if the elder seated on the platform sensed my presence, he opened his eyes and slowly turned his face toward me. I felt distinctly that he was not merely looking in my direction, but was looking directly at me— as if he were aware of my existence and could see me clearly.

The moment our gazes met, the vision rippled, dissolved into smoke, and I jolted out of my meditative state with a shiver running through me.

What this vision meant, I could not understand.

Just then, a faint sound drew my attention toward itself. I turned my neck in the direction of the noise and saw a leopard emerge from the bushes— and my limbs began to tremble. Only then did it strike me that I had wandered into the forest without any weapon or protection. Even if I was not in the physical world, my life was still at risk in this Maya-lok, and if

I were to die here, death in the outer world would be inevitable as well. I had seen that happen with Basanta and his companions with my own eyes.

With my throat drying up, I looked around desperately, but no solution came to mind— one cannot escape a leopard even by climbing a tree. In that moment, the only option that occurred to me was to run, and I did exactly that.

As I ran, I did sense that the leopard may not have come with the intent to attack, but my sudden flight startled it, and it began chasing me. Running through a forest with no clear path is no simple task— I kept sprinting blindly, leaping and stumbling, earning scratches from thorns, colliding with tree trunks, getting entangled in bushes, driven by a single thought: escape the leopard somehow. I had no idea where I was headed. Then it dawned on me that it was not just one leopard, but several, emerging from different directions and joining the chase behind me.

After about five minutes of this frantic run, I reached a comparatively clearer patch— still part of the forest— where trees were being felled. Seven laborers were cutting trees there, and among them stood a temporary open hut, inside which an elderly man sat with his eyes closed. What filled me with sheer terror was that these were the same faces I had seen moments ago in my vision. As I arrived, the woodcutters stopped their work and turned to look at me, while I came to a halt near the hut, bending forward and gasping for breath.

I turned once to look behind me and saw that the leopards had also arrived from different directions and now stood still. Their attention shifted away from me toward the seven woodcutters— there were seven leopards as well.

At that moment, the old man suddenly opened his eyes and looked at me in a way that made it feel as though he could see my exact position even with his eyes closed.

And at that very instant, it was as if an eagle or a vulture let out a piercing cry. Then it felt as though the beat of a distant drum resounded— like a wave forming and spreading outward. With that sound, countless egrets perched on the surrounding trees burst into flight, and in the very next moment, everything began to change.

The entire scene seemed to transform in an instant, as if driven by some spell. One moment it was morning— and the next it was night, with the moon blazing at full strength, flooding everything with light. The green, living trees standing on the ground turned into leafless autumn stumps, and in the same moment the egrets that had flown up from them changed into crows, circling in place and tearing through the silence with their harsh cawing. The hut ahead itself became a stump, before which the old man, who had been sitting cross-legged, rose to his feet without a single movement of his body.

Eyes wide with stunned disbelief, I looked around. The woodcutters were now advancing toward me with their axes, and their expressions made it clear that I was their prey— one that had wandered straight into their grasp. Panicking, I turned to look at the leopards that had chased me there. Before my eyes, they began changing form, turning into human figures. Even though the distance kept me from seeing everyone clearly, one among them I recognized at once — it was Saavri. Of those seven leopards, three had become men and four had become women. In that moment, it was impossible to tell who was ally and who was enemy.

I had barely turned my head to look behind me when a violent blow struck my body, tearing my feet from the ground, and I went flying backward into the dry bushes behind me.

The crows' harsh cawing grew louder.

As I fell, the seven woodcutters charged toward me screaming, as if they were about to tear me apart. But before they could reach me, the seven who had turned from leopards into humans leapt at them and attacked. They all became entangled with one another, bringing down dry shrubs and stump-trees in their struggle, while the frantic flapping of the crows intensified.

I guessed that this team of humans who had been leopards might, in reality, be Agashi's vampire legion— seven in number, including my father. If that was so, it also meant that Saavri was, in truth, a vampiric being herself, allied with me, and that one among them had to be my father. What baffled me was why they were helping me at all— and who these others were, the ones now trying to destroy me, and what enmity they held against me.

I had no time to think further. The old man sprang toward me in a single bound and drove a powerful kick into my ribs. I skidded across the ground, scraping along the earth. Irritated and shaken, I lifted my head to look at him. He gestured with one hand while beckoning me with the other, daring me to rise and face him. My blood boiled. He looked well past seventy, and his body hardly seemed robust. True, he had shown astonishing agility and strength in those two strikes— but still, the idea of an old man challenging me like this felt humiliating enough to make me want the ground to swallow me whole.

All right— I was not alone. The people helping me could handle the others; the old man was mine alone. That meant I could focus entirely on him, and he did not look capable of truly facing me. Filled with rage, I lunged at him and fell upon him in my own estimation— but immediately realized that he was deflecting every single strike with remarkable ease. Not only that, each deflection was accompanied by a punch or a kick that landed on me. My irritation and anger kept rising, and I began attacking wildly— but not a single blow found its mark. Instead, he beat me down using nothing more than defense. Had he gone on the offensive, I did not know where I would have stood against him.

During one failed attempt to strike him, a powerful kick to my lower back sent me crashing to the ground against a dry stump. Right there, two others were locked in combat, and in that very moment a vampire lifted his opposing woodcutter high in his arms and hurled him forward. Seeing me fall, he reached out his hand toward me. As I took it, a shiver ran through my body. Rising, I looked at his face in the moonlight— it was my father. For a brief instant our eyes met, and his face trembled. Then, as if shaking off his emotions, he turned his gaze back to where his opponent had fallen.

I wanted to speak— to call out to him, to embrace him— but before I could do anything, the old man's body came whistling like an arrow and slammed into my father. He was knocked from his place and sent rolling far back. The old man, meanwhile, was back on his feet the very next second, beckoning me again in challenge.

I looked toward my father; he too was rising. As he fixed his gaze on the old man, his eyes seemed to ignite, and with a terrifying growl his face and body began to change. He transformed into a massive wolf, eight or nine feet tall, staring at the old man with the intent to tear him apart. He had barely stepped toward us when his opposing woodcutter suddenly leapt at him, crashing into him and dragging him rolling far away.

Everywhere I looked, Agashi's legion was transforming. The men shifted into towering, ferocious wolves, while the women took the form of gigantic bats. Saavri was now in the very shape in which I had first seen her on the night of the lava valley. Then, I had been denied a clear view of her— but now I could see her from the front. Against the fearsome woodcutters, they appeared even more terrifying.

I was still looking toward Saavri when another kick struck my lower back, and I was flung through the air once more, getting tangled in a bush before crashing down. Turning, I saw the same old man calling me toward him in challenge.

My mind burned with fury as I got back on my feet— but then I thought it through. In all this time I had not managed to touch him even once, while he had beaten me relentlessly. Why? Because I was attacking blindly in anger, while he was observing every move with a cool, controlled mind— evading each strike, and then injuring me the moment my balance broke. Anger was useful for mastering fear, but not for fighting. Where it helped me in one place, its darker side was turning me into a plaything here.

Taking a deep breath, I changed my state of mind.

I sprang toward the old man as if my intention was to take him down with me. I knew he would give way, and my eyes were fixed on that very movement. The moment he began to shift aside, I adjusted my own line and stopped directly in front of him. The hand that should have struck the back of my neck instead came within my reach— I caught it with my reverse hand, dipped low, drove my left shoulder into his abdomen, and lifted him off the ground. Before he could recover, I hurled him away. He went face-first toward the ground, and naturally could not turn back at once. As he tried to rise after the fall, I leapt through the air and struck his waist from behind with a kick. He lost his balance completely, crashed into a dry stump ahead, and went down again with it.

From that point on, just as the other vampires and vampirines were beginning to overpower their opponents, I too gained the upper hand, and that small clearing descended into utter chaos. Above us, the crows still wheeled in the sky, screaming as before.

He may have been old, but within that seemingly frail body lay astonishing agility and strength. More than that, he was a seasoned fighter, which made me a natural target in his eyes — one he kept treating like a child, repeatedly giving me openings. But the moment I succeeded in throwing him off balance, I did not allow him a single chance. Keeping my mind completely cool, anticipating his every possible move, thinking through its counter in advance, I stayed on the attack — and I repaid him with a beating slightly worse than what he had dealt me in the first phase.

And yet... at one point, I misjudged. One of his companions— when we had drifted close to him during the fight— lost balance after taking a kick from his own opponent and collided into me. We both went down. Because all my attention was fixed on the old man, I never saw him coming, and in that instant my advantage slipped away. When I shoved him aside and stood up, the old man had already regained his footing. Now, when we clashed again, neither of us was weak— neither willing to grant the other any opening.

We both took heavy blows, and then the fight reached the turn where my game was nearly over.

During the struggle, his hand found an axe lying nearby— one that must have belonged to one of his own men. From that moment on, survival replaced combat, and he landed several injuries on me. Finally, after taking a kick, I fell— and as I went down, he leapt toward me. Not only did he close the distance, he swung the axe as well, and before I could steady myself or even fully grasp what was happening, the sharp blade had reached my neck. Yet, astonishingly, at that very instant he arrested the motion of his arm so precisely that the edge did not sink in, merely grazing my skin.

I looked at him in stunned disbelief. His face appeared utterly expressionless— but even so, there was something there that pierced me deeply.

At that very moment, another sharp sound rang out, like the piercing cry of an eagle— at the same time a ripple passed through the air. The scene before me shuddered for a split second and then vanished with a sudden snap.

In its place, the same hut returned— the one where I had been sleeping, my mother's house. The door stood open, and a crowd had gathered inside and out. Several men were already inside, and some of them had seized Saavri. At the exact instant I seemed to snap fully awake in this real world and sit up, they dragged her out of the hut by her legs. She cried out, wailing and calling my name, but her voice was swallowed by the uproar around us.

The light made it clear that the night had passed and morning had spread its arms— but why had the entire village gathered outside my hut, and why were they hauling Saavri away like this?

"Saavri— Saavri." I shouted, lunging after her.

I was seized as well, several strong men locking their grips around my body. Waking like this, my senses were already unsettled— then the scene unfolding before me seemed to paralyze my mind even further. I had weapons, and I had to help Saavri, I should have used them— but in my blind rush toward her they grabbed me too, and the chance to reach my weapons was gone.

Again and again I tried, in their own language and in broken words, to ask what Saavri or we had done, but it was as if they could not hear me at all. They were violently enraged, filled with fury, raising a din that sounded like a call for Saavri's death— or for the killing of us both. Once outside the hut, it became clear that almost the entire village had gathered there. Men and women, children and elders alike— all were consumed by rage against us, hands raised as if urging our execution.

At least I was being hauled along on my feet, but Saavri— they dragged her with merciless cruelty by both legs. In that state the lower part of her gown had ridden up toward her stomach, leaving her legs exposed. Being dragged along the ground must have scraped her back raw; her hair had come loose and spread behind her. As if that were not enough, people walking alongside kicked her, drawing broken, agonized cries from her. The savagery burned into me so fiercely that I wanted to break free, run back, fetch my pistol, and shoot those bastards one by one.

They were in no mood to listen or understand— only to drag Saavri away while pushing me along behind. Those nearest us were already overflowing with hatred; from the rest of the crowd trailing behind, there was no hope of mercy either.

In this way they dragged and shoved us far from the village, toward uneven, grassy ground where the forest began. There stood the stump of a dried, dead tree— and there they tied Saavri. Her clothes were torn and disheveled, her hair scattered, her face distorted, blood flowing from her lips down her neck.

"Tell me at least something… why are you doing this to her? What crime has she committed?" I pleaded again, struggling.

They had no answer for me. Instead, they picked up stones and chunks of rock lying nearby and began to hurl them at Saavri. With every blow she cried out. That was more than I could bear. Summoning all my strength, I tore myself free from their grasp and, stumbling and falling, ran to Saavri. I pulled her into my arms so the stones would strike my body instead of hers— and they did. The hands throwing stones did not stop, and now my body began to take the blows.

"Go away— leave this place. They won't kill you. Save yourself. Don't worry about me... nothing will happen to me," she said, writhing, her voice choked.

"No... no. To watch this fate befall you before my eyes is something my honor cannot accept," I replied, anguished.

"You'll die for nothing because of me... you should save yourself... go," she tried to push me away even while bound.

"If death is written for me like this, then so be it," I said, refusing to move or let go of her.

"You have to free your father," she snapped.

"If I can't save you from ordinary people like these, then even imagining that I'll save my father from demonic powers is pointless... I'm not going anywhere."

Those may have been my last words— because at that very moment a large piece of stone struck my head. My head had already been injured since the night before last; now another brutal blow landed on the same spot. My mind reeled, consciousness slipped away in the next instant, and after that I remember nothing of what happened.

●●

CHAPTER 10

During that blackout I sank into such a deep faint that no vision reached me and there was no pulling into any other world. When I came to, I was in a hut, lying on a bed of straw; dusk was descending outside. If I had dreamt between passing out and waking, nothing remained upon opening my eyes.

The memory of what had just occurred returned sharp as pain: the blows I had taken to save Saavri. My head hurt violently at the wound— touch made it feel like my life would leak out— yet I saw with surprise that a plain cloth bandage was bound there, placed after the new wound had been tended.

Who, in that village of such brutality, had shown mercy enough to bring me back and dress my wound? The straw mattress suggested someone lived in the hut.

I pricked together the scattered memories and a few things came back which the earlier chaos had not allowed me to notice. That old man came to mind— the one who had the chance to finish me and did not. Why had he not taken that chance? I remembered a look pass over his face as if with relief… but at what? If it was those same people and his own companions who had been pulling me into that virtual reality to kill me, why had he refused at the crucial moment?

Why had they tried so many times before then, only to stop?

For the first time I had faced my father— not in a meeting, but in the thick of it— and he had acted as if the matter was of no consequence.

How could they expect me to liberate him? If those who made up Agashi's army included Saavri… then had she lied to me? Or had someone been appearing in her shape all along? There remained two facts in Saavri's favour: first, if she truly were a pishachini, how had she let herself be robbed by Basanta and his men?

Second, if she truly were one, how had she been so helpless before the villagers that they were able to beat and kill her like a powerless woman?

I thought of all this and my head started to spin; then someone's presence made itself known outside and I tensed, looking toward the door.

"Who is there?" I sat up and called.

At my voice the person at the door seemed drawn like a magnet; he came in. A man of perhaps forty-five or fifty, an adivasi wrapped in a heavy cloth, entered and sat on a small low bench opposite me.

"You're awake, son." He spoke with a gentle voice and sat down.

"Where am I?" That was the first thing I needed to know.

"Not far from Bodhanbari— the place I brought you from. You were unconscious and your head had a bad wound; I brought you here so I could dress you." He said this with a fatherly tone.

"And Saavri— what happened to her?" I asked, anxious.

"That girl who was with you? She was beaten to death with stones and the village set her on fire with the dry tree they tied her to. Even if she hadn't died from the stone blows, she would have burned. They had probably meant to kill you too, but your father's name frightened them; so they left you there instead. I reached them after they left— she was already burned and you lay there unconscious." He told me with sorrow.

"What?" The pain in my head flared and darkness flashed before my eyes. A girl treated that way— the thought stabbed me with grief and fury both. I felt my fists clench and my eyes burn red.

"Why— why did they kill her? What crime did she commit?" I demanded, near tears.

"Was that girl your companion? Did you know her?" he asked, peering into my eyes.

"What do you mean?" I asked, baffled.

"I don't know, son— I only heard it from them. They said she was a witch. Two of them claimed they had seen her wandering the night and taking a goat to eat. At night they feared her and kept quiet, but in the morning, they told the whole village and their anger exploded." He spoke hesitantly.

"What!" My head filled with a cold numbness. Could this be true? She had been with me, acted like a woman who refused full meals yet never looked hungry. In my visions she had stood among my father's companions in Agashi's ranks — the things did point in that direction, but the idea that Basanta or the village could conquer such a being didn't fit. Had Saavri lied? I gripped my head.

"Are you alright, son?" The man laid a hand on my head.

"Who are you? Why show me kindness when I have become an enemy to these people?" I asked, raising my head.

"I am different from them— that's why I live here in exile rather than stay in Bodhanbari with others." He said in a heavy voice.

"Why?" I asked.

"Because my sister, unwittingly, became a slave to a pishach— and one day she left with him. While she stayed in the village, Saumik Babu— your father— would come to see her and people feared it. When Tashi left and they no longer saw him they stopped fearing, and they cast me out. They don't want Tashi or your father to come near the village anymore." The man told his story and my eyes widened.

"Boyal Maama… but Saavri said you died of illness." It seemed she had lied about everything.

"Who is Saavri? That girl who was with you— what does she know about me?" Surprise showed in his face.

"She said she was your daughter— not by blood, but because she was still a child when you married her widowed mother. She said your health failed and you died." I told him.

"How can that be? I never married. After being thrown out by the village I never went elsewhere; I stayed here. Who would give me a girl? I left only once to take you to those people in Calcutta, the ones your father had named." He seemed troubled.

So Saavri had told lies. I grabbed my head again.

"But Father's diary itself said that when I turned twenty, you would come to Calcutta to take me with you and tell me everything. Then why didn't you go?"

"Yes, he did tell me to do that," he replied. "But I'm not an educated man— someone who keeps track of dates and years. I thought that when the time came, he himself would come and give me the word. But he never came to me again."

And Saavri knew the exact date— but how? If she was among my father's companions, wouldn't Agashi know all of this as well? Then how could Saavri move beyond Agashi's reach? And in that case, why would my father side with them at all— if Agashi's true purpose was to see me as a threat and eliminate me, or to make me her prey on this very new moon? An urgent need seized me to see Saavri.

"Maama… where is Saavri?" I asked, gripping both his shoulders. "I mean, where is the place where she was burned?"

"The path that goes out in that direction leads to Bodhanbari— through there," he said, looking at me with concern. "But the sun has already set. Going out now is not without danger."

I gave no reply. I rose and began putting on my shoes. Seeing my manner, he thought it best not to say anything more. Once I had my shoes on, I stepped outside.

The sun had already set— or was just about to— but there was still enough light to walk by. A red glow lingered along the western edge of the blue horizon, and flocks of returning birds were scattered across the sky. I moved fast, almost running, toward the road that led to Bodhanbari. On the way I encountered a small herd of wild pigs, but they posed no threat, and I passed through the forest without obstruction.

By the time I emerged from the trees, darkness had begun to spread. In the distance, the huts of Bodhanbari were growing quiet. Their inhabitants were retreating into shelter, and the faint, hazy silhouettes I glimpsed from afar vanished into one hut or another as I drew closer.

When I came to where Saavri had been tied, I stopped. She was still there— except there was no longer a woman, only a charred heap. The dry tree she had been bound to had burned and she seemed melted into the coal-black stump. Nothing of a body remained— only a blackened shape that suggested a human had once been there. Night had thickened; I could not see clearly.

Seeing her like that, I sank to my knees before her. My mind roiled with the images of what we had passed through; tears came unbidden and my face fell into my hands.

Then a touch startled me— fingers under my chin lifting my face. I looked up. The fingers were the bones of Saavri's skeleton; for a moment she seemed to stir and movement came back into her.

Then, to my astonishment, flesh began to return to her body before my eyes, and within moments she stood before me in her former shape.

The only difference was that, since her clothes had burned, she was completely naked. She gave a loud stretch, and the charred stump that clung to her back collapsed with a crack and scattered into a heap— watching this, my mind began to function again and one by one all my doubts began to resolve.

"I told you nothing would happen to me— save yourself." She said this with a trace of reproach.

"Then I didn't know what you were… I took you for a human because you asked me to. Are you still hiding something?" My voice carried the sting of complaint.

She said nothing. She paced, watching the direction of Bodhanbari, and slowly a flame kindled in her eyes.

"I never intended to harm these people— I ate a single goat. Don't their cattle get preyed on by animals? For that, they punished me with such cruelty… what do they think they have done? They do not know what trouble they have courted. What was not intended until now— is intended now, and I will not step back until I put it into action." She spoke each word as if chewing it, lips drawn tight with hate.

"What fault of theirs… this is human nature— who would not feel threatened seeing a witch-pishachini in their village? If you were human, you'd have done the same." I said, rising to my feet.

"You… you side with those who burned me alive— who rained stones on you." She grew visibly furious.

"No— it's not about taking sides; it's about understanding the circumstances. Any human who faces an unknown power threatening their people will choose such means to protect themselves." I tried to reason with her, but her anger only swelled.

"Now I will teach them a lesson." she snarled.

"No, Saavri— you will not do anything like that." I stepped forward and gripped her arm.

She turned to me and hissed like a cobra; the force of it made me stagger back. Then she gathered herself, coiled inward as if drawing power, and in a single convulsion her body expanded fourfold— her arms became immense wings, her legs reshaped into talons like a bird's. She beat those wings and recoiled; the pressure of the air threw me off balance and I stumbled backwards.

"No— they must pay for what they did. They think their charms will protect them from me… today they will learn whom they have made an enemy of." She was completely out of control.

As she launched toward the settlement on huge wings, I snatched up a half-burned plank that lay nearby.

"Stop, Saavri, or I will kill myself." I shouted at her, and she turned, stopped; seeing that the words had an effect, I pressed on, "I know my life or death doesn't matter to you, but it matters to Agashi— and Agashi will not like me being killed prematurely, nor will my father."

"If you die, how will you free your father?" she snarled.

"I don't expect success anyway— think about your own loss. Will Agashi like that?" Seeing the doubt cross her face bolstered my courage.

"You can't do this— you're making empty threats." This time her voice wavered, revealing an inner turmoil.

Instead of answering, I raised both hands as if I would plunge the plank into my belly, and then I dropped my hands so that her "stop" rang true. I knew she'd peered into my mind in that moment, so I left no ambiguity in my resolve; I intended to stab myself with that wood. For some reason I felt certain she would stop me.

And in the end, she did— the plank had pierced my stomach before her command finished, but by fortune it had not gone in.

She landed, wings folding; her talons turned back into feminine feet and her wings shrank into arms— her body contracted back into the familiar shape I'd grown used to. She stepped forward, took the plank from my hands and flung it away.

"Coward!" she ground through her teeth.

"No— human," I answered— "Perhaps human life means little to you, but it means a lot to me. I'm not opposed to killing the wicked— I killed Basanta and his cronies in those ruins— but killing ordinary people isn't right. The crowd that beat you included women, elders, children— in truth they were frightened people who saw you as a witch. If you view them through human eyes, you might not find them entirely blameworthy. You refuse to look at yourself while you accuse them— are you a friend to humans? Aren't humans your prey?" I gripped her shoulders and spoke, but she shrugged my hands off and turned away.

"I don't want to see the face of this cursed village… if I stay here, I will lose myself. Come, let's go. If I stay, I will lose control. Why are you still here? Why offer yourself as Agashi's prey?" She said this last, turning back toward me, and her voice held deep entanglement.

"I'm in love with you," I said with a mischievous tone even in that atmosphere.

"Nonsense." She clicked her teeth.

"Not a joke— I mean it. I've been flirtatious and fond of many girls, but the feeling that has arisen for you I've never felt before. Even if that feeling formed when I was ignorant of your truth, I cannot change my heart now." I told her, looking into her eyes; she looked away. She was completely naked now, and my few words affected her so that she shrank inward as if suddenly aware of her nudity.

"Let's go— I need clothes. You walk ahead— I'll follow. Maybe they haven't rifled our things yet." She said, hesitating, and pushed me forward.

"Your name is Saavri, right?"

"Yes— and don't talk now. I am trying to control myself… your idle words can again anger me and then I'll have no hold over myself. At night I'm less in control and more under Agashi— you understand that." She warned.

I grunted and stayed silent, sensing the delicacy of the moment. I reminded myself at every step that she was not a mere human— far from it at night.

We walked through the village in silence and headed toward our hut. Darkness had deepened; no light shone outside. A few huts showed faint glows at windows, but it was not enough to cut the dark. The stillness lay heavy, as if everyone were cowering in fear of some impending misfortune. Misfortune had indeed risen— and by some twist it had passed without striking— thank God, I had reached the right place at the right time. Had she truly unleashed herself in full fury, ordinary folk would never have stood against her. It was good I'd arrived when I did.

Our hut was as it had been: it looked as if no one had even peered inside. Everything lay where we'd left it. She donned clothes first; then we packed our gear and set off.

"Where to— any idea?" I asked as we left the village.

"I don't know— just move away from here. This place is suffocating me." she said, irritated.

"Then let's go to Boyal Maama's— we'll spend the night there and leave in the morning."

"What— whose place?" she stopped, startled.

"Boyal Maama's— the man the village exiled who lives alone in the forest." I explained how I'd learned the truth after coming to.

Once the truth was out— that she was no mere human and not Boyal Maama's adopted girl— there was nothing left to object to. She followed silently. When we reached Boyal Maama's hut, he was outside; upon seeing me safe, relief softened his face, but he stiffened at Saavri's presence— which was only to be expected, for he knew her true nature.

We decided to spend the night there. After our arrival Boyal Maama cooked rice for us, and my hunger was stilled, but Saavri could not eat— she slipped out without a word to forage. We slept; she returned during the night and in the morning lay sleeping among us.

The night passed peacefully.

••

Chapter 11

Daylight came and we continued our journey. Even though Boyal Maama tried to stop me and send me back, I no longer cared. I wanted to see this mission through— even if it meant death. My inheritance from my father was not only the blessing of Devi Saivani but a stubbornness that made me finish what I began.

We were cutting up a steep path through dense woods. Tall trees barred out the sun; the air inside the thicket moved little though leaves trembled in the breeze.

"Think again." she said as we walked; when I looked at her quizzically, she went on— "Now you know why I brought you and what I intend by taking you to the Amavasya— why still go? Why not run away?"

"You tell me— you said you would present me to Agashi on Amavasya… why would you want me not to go or to return?" I asked, flashing her a look.

She did not answer. Once more she looked at me as though she wanted to say something, then mastered her feelings with a faint smile and walked on.

"You've fallen in love too, haven't you?"

"Don't be ridiculous— humans are nothing but prey to me. Remember, the shape you see now is only a disguise. I probably left this world three hundred years ago. By the measure of my age, many generations have passed while I remained in this form. Love and affection are worldly experiences we abandoned long ago."

"Hmm."

She was right— what common ground could there be between us? Not age, not body, not desire. Could such a bond grow between such dissimilar beings? Yet the heart is a strange thing; once it decides, who can command it? Dreams are harmless— if a dream breaks, the heart only aches— what worse can happen?

"Tell me the truth— why do you still want to go there? Do you really think you can defeat Agashi and free your father?" she asked again.

"I don't know, but there is a stubbornness inside me that, once set on a mission, it must be completed. It's been my nature since childhood, and perhaps that's why I want to see an end to this chain."

"Even if that end is your death?" she taunted.

"Yes— even if it's my death."

"You know that if Agashi swallows you, your corpse out there will be consumed by us— by me and perhaps even by your father." she said.

"I know— so let them eat me if they must. But my heart… you eat that. It's only for you." I murmured.

She said nothing— only looked at me and pain passed across her face.

"Alright— drop that thought, and answer some of my doubts. You could protect yourself alone, and that's why you could walk the streets of Calcutta at night— I understand that now. You broke into my dreams, saved me, and planted the courage to fight in me— yet publicly you kept a false story, playing the innocent who denied her virtual-reality performance. I can see why you didn't want your truth exposed to me before taking me to Agashi's temple. Still… a few questions remain."

"Ask. Now that you know everything, I don't think there's anything left for me to hide."

"When you handed me father's diary and I read it, I was not intending to begin this quest to free him… then those recurring dreams about him kept pulling me, and finally I decided to come and prepared myself. You already knew that —you'd reserved tickets. How did both things happen? Were those dreams also planted in my mind by intrusion, and did you already know when I would decide to leave?"

"Like your father could catch glimpses of the future through visions, which sometimes came to you as well— I can see a little of that too. Not everything, not always, but when I need to know something particular, I can glimpse that future in a vision. I had to know what decision you would make— I saw you were going to come, so I prepared."

"And who was it that invaded my mind again and made me ready to come?"

"That I don't know— that wasn't my job. Maybe it was Maling." She spoke, thinking.

"Maling? Who is that?" I looked at her in surprise.

"We'll come to him later… ask whatever else you want."

"When you attacked Bijoy at Bongaigaon and Hemanta was killed— that was you?"

"Yes. Your daal, rice, vegetables, pickles don't flavor or fill our stomachs— we need raw meat. When no other prey was available, we had to hunt them. The first one cried out and escaped, but I put the second to sleep so he wouldn't scream."

"I don't understand— if you can enter someone's mind, why not go in and finish them there? Why was an attack necessary?"

"We aren't spirits who can possess a conscious mind. Any of us can enter someone's dreams or mind only when they are unconscious, asleep, or otherwise in a zero-consciousness state. We could have killed the sleeping men in the camp by slipping into their minds, but then we'd have to go into the camp to eat them— doing so might wake someone else. So, we only hunt those who are already outside themselves."

"And the man at the rest-house, Basanta's companion: you ate him too, not some animal."

"Yes. When there's easy food in camp, why go searching outside?"

"What exactly happened that night? I need to know. How did you allow Basanta to force himself on you?"

"Bodily union means nothing to me— in my three-hundred-years-ago life I've lived through countless such moments. What mattered then was that it wasn't yet nightfall; I refused to create any danger I could not handle. I sensed that once the sun set the odds would swing back into my hands, and then I could teach them a lesson."

"So that's why your face showed no fear even then… but what happened next? I lost consciousness with the stress— who took us to that dream-world after that?"

"I don't think you actually lost consciousness. You were probably put into that semi-unconscious state and pulled there, as those others were. It wasn't only you who went inactive— they all did; all were drawn into that place."

"Who drew us there?"

"Maling. Think of him as the one who's been pulling you into that virtual world from the start, and whose people have been trying to take your life. Don't ask who he is yet— I'll tell you later."

"Does he pull only me there, or you too?"

"Only you or whoever the thieves decide to lure… he doesn't need to pull me, because he knows I can come on my own if you are around."

"Then why didn't you appear in that reality— the same place where the wolves appeared and the people fought? You weren't there."

"Because I wanted to see if you could face them without me. If help was necessary, I would reveal myself; if not, I would watch quietly. You took them all down— that proved your growing confidence— but when you got trapped in the chain-man's grip, I intervened from behind and split his skull. By then you had already gone limp, but luck held your breath."

"All of them were killed there, and by your reckoning they were all food— still, you alone ate the chain-man and, more than eating, you butchered him horribly afterward. Why so much hatred for him?"

She didn't answer that; I watched her retreating back and, when she said nothing, let the question go.

"Tell me this: you're so powerful that you could have razed all of Bodhanbari. Yet how did those people manage to humiliate you so helplessly— even burn you alive in public?"

"Because by day we are almost like ordinary people— our powers are nominal. After sunset our powers awaken and then no human can stand against us. Please don't make me remember. I've only just managed to swallow my rage."

"I won't force it. Now to the main point: the things father wrote in the diary— theoretically they should have been known only to him, to my mother and to Maama— that at twenty years I would meet him, and reading it I would come here… how did you know these things?"

"There's an English word— network. Do you know about it?" she asked me.

"I know the word— how did you? How do you keep such modern knowledge, so you could pose as a city-bred woman? I've wondered that before."

"I'll answer that another time. For now, think of it this way: Agashi's mental powers are boundless, and she not only sees the future but stays mentally connected to us so that, in a sense, we become part of her. It's a cerebral network through which we are linked, and she is the centre. By day she may be dormant, so our actions might not register with her; by night she roams the outer world through us.

Whatever your father did, he did by day and wiped it from his mind at night, but his repeated longing to meet your mother after you were sent to the city eventually betrayed him. Agashi didn't need to ask; she extracted the information from his mind and saw the vision of the future in which you would come— to her you were a threat.

She sent Baro and Sachi to search Calcutta, but by then your new guardians had already moved you, and the man with your father's diary had gone on. Agashi became furious; she tormented your father in many ways, and then, when her wrath cooled, she left him some relief. Most of us are gone from this time long ago and have no emotional ties; your father, though, exists in the present and carried attachments.

For another reason, Agashi finally allowed your mother to live— she figured that forty or fifty years would pass, the woman would age and die, and your father would be free of worldly ties. Also, when you learn the truth and come searching for your real parents, she can catch you."

"Wait— why did she need me then? She could have taken any man. I was living my life; why make me learn everything and pull me here?"

"Maybe she saw some future in which you were a threat."

"I'm glad to know I mattered to Agashi. Still— father must have known what would happen, no? Didn't he object?"

"No— perhaps he still hopes for you."

"Alright. What next?"

"Nothing immediate— when the right time came, I was equipped with all the information and sent to fetch you. The rest you know."

"Father wrote that as we age, our powers grow, and as Agashi consumes prey on new amavasya nights, her power and domain will expand— but when he wrote the diary her influence reached only as far as the Manas forest. How then did Calcutta or Farakka come under this reach and pull me into virtual reality there?"

"First, Agashi had never pulled you into her world before, so the idea of an influence zone is irrelevant. It was Maling who pulled you— and in his domain zones have no fixed rule. Two things are necessary: the prey must be in an unconscious state, and the one doing the pulling must be within the prey's vicinity.

If you ask when he was near you, the answer is this: the same mental network was at work. Maling's people not only saved your father from dying when he was to be transformed, they linked themselves to his mind and infiltrated our network. We may be scattered physically, but mentally we're connected.

So Maling could reach your father's mind, then reach mine through it, and from mine reach yours— using that network to pull you anywhere. He has done this repeatedly. I've done it too, at times— when I wanted to have sex with you. That was the kind of contact I made. But you were often too guarded and missed those moments."

"Help— what kind of help?" I blinked, but she fell silent; the question died there and I moved on— "When I was pulled into that reality and for the first time saw my father and your companions, why had I not seen them before?"

"Although we're mentally linked, distance matters, and everyone isn't always idle— by night most are occupied within themselves. Neither had Maling ever shown himself before. When, for the first time, all his people materialised, the rest had to be summoned too, and that's why you saw almost all the players in that battle. Dawn was approaching, so that reality collapsed."

"The leopard I saw first— was that you?"

"Yes. And I had come only to keep an eye on you, but you noticed me. Even then, I chose not to change my form, so you wouldn't panic. But you ran anyway, and from the visions dancing inside your mind, I could already sense what was about to unfold, so I called the others too. That fight was meant to keep you safe from our side, but when he had the chance to kill you and still didn't, that's when I realized I had been made a fool all along."

"What do you mean? Who was that old man?" I had to gasp again.

"That was Maling— he wasn't just playing with your mind, he was playing with mine as well. Anyway, at that moment I was still trapped in that same reality, when the villagers reached there and began dragging me away. When you came out of the dream, at that exact moment, I came out too."

"How do you even know that Maling pulled me into that reality— you were roaming the forest at night to hunt, weren't you?"

"In the middle of the night— when you were in deep sleep. I had moved away from you only for a short while, and even then someone spotted me while I was hunting. The rest of the time I stayed right beside you, keeping myself connected to your mind in such a way that the moment you were dragged somewhere else, I would know."

"You just said that last night you finally realized you were being fooled by Maling— how?"

"For that, I'll have to explain the entire web Maling has spun."

"Then explain it already— who exactly is this Maling, so deeply tied to everything, and yet not mentioned anywhere in Father's diary?"

"An ascetic from centuries ago— a yogi, a monk— who is still very much alive, still walking in a human body."

"You mean not just you creatures of the vampire realm live for centuries, but even humans can?" My eyes widened in disbelief.

"The world is full of mysteries— surely you haven't seen them all. Think of Maling as one such mystery. He's probably Tibetan— a devotee of Lord Shiva— but he and his disciples also worship Agashi. The temple where the monthly sacrifice takes place on the new moon… that temple was built by Maling himself."

"Wait— these are the same aghori monks who entered Agashi's shadow world to save my father, right? If they were against her, and yet have kept fighting me— even though I was being taken there as Agashi's prey— then what kind of devotion is that?"

"Why not? Doesn't every devotee, in some form, wish to conquer his god— to become one with what he worships? That's what Maling desires. He prays to Agashi so she may bless him with power, but secretly he longs to absorb her powers for himself. Over centuries of penance, he's cultivated extraordinary mental abilities that have kept him alive and capable of controlling any human mind. Inside the mind, he creates his own world— a world of illusion, where he plays whatever games, he wants… the same games he's been playing with you. Through this mental strength, he's enslaved many wandering ascetics who entered the forest over the ages, making them his pawns— just like now, he controls a band of aghori sadhus led by Asimanand. It's that same group which helped your father in Agashi's realm— the same you saw last night.

No one truly knows where Maling's physical body resides — but even if someone reached it, they couldn't use their mind against him. He takes over every mind that comes close. His desire is simple yet terrifying— he wants Agashi's full powers so he can reclaim his youthful form and grant immortality to his followers, just like Agashi's army. Right now, he can't do that… but with her powers, he can.

But why would Agashi grant her powers to anyone? However skilled Maling may be in mind games, Agashi reigns supreme in her own shadow world— no one enters it without her will. Even if he could somehow reach her through her permission, he might have the strength to challenge her. That's why she never summons anyone she can't defeat. She chooses only those young men whose defeat is certain. She doesn't exist outside her realm, and she'll never allow Maling to enter it. So the only way left to him is to use a human vessel — a pawn— who can draw Agashi to a vulnerable point, where her strength wanes and she can't stop Maling and his followers from invading through the prey's mind. That's what happened in your father's case.

Then Maling keeps searching for young men who could serve his purpose— who can be brave enough to face Agashi, right? That's why his disciples roam in monk disguises from Dhaka to Guwahati, from Calcutta to Thimphu, luring fearless, curious souls to come here?

The monk who revealed Agashi's secret to your father didn't meet him by chance— he was sent to find him. And your father, by his own curiosity and pride, fulfilled Maling's wish. Through him, Maling's followers got their first chance to infiltrate Agashi's domain. They saved him not out of kindness, but because he was their only link— through his mind they entered our mental network and could one day reach her realm again."

"But my father wasn't the only one who fought her. Namgyal and Baro also survived their battles. Didn't Agashi's powers weaken then? Why couldn't Maling's people enter her world afterward?"

"Because they fought until sunrise. We never had to enter, so we stayed guarding their human forms outside. Maling's people never got near them. But in your father's case, we all had to go in— and his unguarded body was left behind. That's how they reached him. And now that Maling is part of our own network, if we go to Agashi's realm again, he and his people will come too— unless we go at a time when Agashi is weakened. That hasn't happened since your father's time."

"So, according to you, it was Maling who showed me those dreams in Calcutta— my father's agony, his pleas for deliverance— to make me come here. But if he wanted me to come, why did he try to kill me repeatedly in those virtual realities?"

"Are you sure his purpose was to kill you?"

"Yes— though… last night, in that final illusion, it all got strange. If he meant to kill me, why did he stop? And if he meant to spare me, why chase me for so long?"

"Just as Agashi can see fragments of the future, Maling can too. He must have seen you as a possibility— a hope. And you had two qualities that made you unique. First, you carry the blessing of Devi Sainvani— inherited from your father— that if you truly overcome fear, no demonic force can harm you. Second, you are mentally far stronger than your father — it takes you less time to regain control over fear. That makes you a beacon of hope for all of us— and a threat to her. That's why she wants to consume you quickly, while you're still human enough to feel fear. Your father often drowned in his own dread, but you haven't— remember, your fear is our strength, and your fearlessness our weakness."

"And Maling's interest— this strange contradiction of saving me and threatening me?"

"He wants you to defeat Agashi, and at the last moment, when you succeed, he'll seize your mind and take over the game. His intent was never to kill you in those illusions— he was training you, shaping you to face danger, to stay balanced in chaos. He knew that because I was charged to protect you, I'd intervene— and in trying to help you, I'd end up strengthening your defences against my own kind. Because in the end, in Agashi's realm, the roles will reverse. We will be your enemies, and they— your protectors."

"Oh… so that's what it was. Now I see why, in all those fights, they could've killed me but didn't. So all this time, the battles inside those illusions were a rehearsal— a shadow game— both sides preparing me for the final confrontation." I gave a weary smile— "Alright then— tell me, when you tried to tempt me into sleeping with you, what kind of help was that supposed to be?"

"You tell me— if you were offered eternal youth and immortality like us, would you take it?"

"Never. I'd rather age and die like any ordinary man. Eternal youth may look beautiful from the outside, but I know it's a curse inside."

"That's what your father and the others never understood. Greed devoured them. But it's good that you don't carry that lust— it's your greatest weapon against Agashi. This life is no blessing; it's an endless curse. Somewhere deep inside, we all crave release. Even if we stand as your enemies, our hearts still long for your victory. That's why I tried to help you in my own way. Maling was training you for battle— I was preparing you for the trial beyond it. You don't have to fight Agashi with weapons— you have to… unite with her. That is the real test. Tell me, do you truly believe you could hold yourself back long enough for her to lose control first? Have you ever even tried?"

"Hmm… so through sex you wanted to prepare me for that final moment— where the battle is fought not with weapons but with will. Well, I grew up under the British, where sex isn't taboo. My first time was at sixteen, and since then… many times, many ways. I've even practiced holding myself back— but against Agashi? I don't know how long that trick will hold."

"There are no tricks. If you try to distract your mind, she'll feel it— she'll freeze herself into ice. No woman can be defeated that way. The only way to win is to give yourself completely— body, mind, and will— and yet stay in control. Your victory lies in making her reach her peak before you do. That's the only way you can defeat her in her own game."

"That sounds impossible," I said, swallowing hard.

"If it were easy, someone would have done it long ago— and we'd either be free, or have a new master by now."

"Alright, suppose I do win— what will Maling do then?"

"He'll take control of your mind instantly. You may want to banish him into eternal darkness, free us all— but he won't. He'll share Agashi's powers, make himself the ruler of her world and ours, restore his fragmented body— and then he'll kill you, because by then, he'll have absorbed everything he needs through your mind."

"Fragmented? What do you mean by that?"

"You wouldn't understand. When you see him… you will."

"So either way, I die— if I lose, Agashi kills me. If I win, Maling does."

"Exactly."

"Then this whole game makes sense from Maling's view, and from Agashi's too— but not from yours. Why would you or the others, including my father, still want to help me— still hope for release through me?"

"Because only now do I truly see Maling's plan. All this time, I thought he meant to kill you before you could reach her— that maybe he'd foreseen something in the future that could threaten him. I never realised he was preparing you. Now… the hope that you could free us feels almost foolish." Her voice fell, and her eyes dimmed.

After a long pause, I asked quietly, "Still… was there ever a real chance of defeating Agashi?"

"Maybe— but if someone is practiced at union, in those fragile moments they can hold back their excitement. A new body will fire you quickly, while a body that's been used many times gives you chances to steady yourself. It's true that Agashi is uniquely beautiful, but she will not meet you in her true form; she will come as someone you find easy to make love to. As she came to your father in the guise of your mother, she may come to you in my guise— and, almost imperceptibly, change from Saavri into Agashi before you realise it. If you have already shared many embraces with me, the novelty that would otherwise make you lose control won't hit you all at once; you will be able to steady yourself."

"Yes— there's a point to that… but what good is steadying yourself if afterwards you fall into Maling's hands?" I shook my head in frustration— "Is there no way to get rid of this Maling?"

"Not that I know of… we never had to think about it, so we never made plans. Maybe if we think— a way might appear."

"Where is my mother now?"

"At Agashi's temple. She lives there as a servant now. I don't think she'll be happy to see you… she has seen what happened to your father and she has seen every hunt carried out there on new-moon nights. Both things would be unbearable for a mother."

"When will we go there?"

"If I hadn't told you everything, I was planning to take you three nights from now— the new moon falls on the third night. But since everything's out in the open, there's no point in disguise. I can take you there in one night now. It's up to you when you want to go."

I fell silent, thinking. A greedy part of me wanted only to reach my mother quickly so I could spend a little time with her— but would she be at peace watching me walk into death? Or should I use whatever time remained to prepare? Any time near my mother would demand restraint; there would be no practising the bodily endurance I needed.

"Maybe I am capable, but before you I am nothing— I'll leave the choice to you. Tell me: what do you think I should do?" I said at last, defeated, looking at her.

"Today is Tuesday; you have Wednesday and Thursday before you— Thursday's night I can bring you to the temple. You'll have the day to be with your mother, and when evening comes the new moon will begin— then who knows what will happen. Use today and the next two days to prepare; you must ready yourself for Agashi, and also try to find some way to guard against Maling." She thought a little and then spoke.

"And how, exactly, do you expect me to prepare?" I asked, trying for a grin.

"Plainly— you must practise the union you will have to enact with Agashi, because she will first appear to you in my form here. Practise the game of physical union with me by day, and in the virtual world by night... perhaps Maling will be less inclined to meddle if he sees me acting in his one role." She sounded almost light when she said it.

"So, in plain language: a honeymoon in the jungle. Well... I won't complain. Is there a place nearby where we can stay safe from wild animals and other dangers for this time?"

"There are three earth caves nearby, but they're occupied by bears and wolves. About three hours from here lies a ruined temple from Agashi's age— most of it collapsed, but parts are intact and we can camp there. It's a beautiful spot: a clear stream forms a pond and the greenery is rich. The only problem is there are spirits there; they won't trouble me, but they might trouble you. It's the same place your father once spent a night with Hirvi and felt those spirits."

"Right... I remember. Never mind. When you're with me, I'm not frightened. Besides, I know any spirit or demonic force can only prey on me if I surrender to fear— so I won't." I smiled and reassured her.

We walked in silence toward that place.

••

CHAPTER 12

Night had fallen. Crickets and the small night sounds filled the air. I had lit a fire for warmth and to keep the dark at bay, and sat before it.

The place had once been a temple or monastery, now surrendered to ruin and time; nature had stitched the stones into the forest. Still, parts remained that offered shelter. We cleared a small area and made camp; there were no large predators about, only small animals that had fled human footprints. It had been twenty-one years since my father was here— the place would have changed in that span— but it was still good enough for two nights.

It struck me as strange: ten or twelve days ago I'd never pictured myself sitting on a ruined temple floor in a haunted forest, waiting for the ugly game of those spiteful spirits who had tormented my father to begin again and test me.

From the shelter of the half-collapsed roof above the fire I could glimpse stars; around them the forest lay like a dark smear.

We had reached the place by dusk, cleaned a little, and settled. I had cooked a little rice and eaten with achar; she had gone hunting for food and left me waiting by the fire to see whether the spirits would show themselves. She had gone into the trees; I stayed.

I tried to steady my thoughts. I was different from Agashi's ordinary victims in two ways: I wasn't ignorant, and I knew the rules now; and I wasn't the sort who could be frightened into helplessness. With those two facts in my favour, it wasn't inconceivable that I could reach the threshold of defeating Agashi— though it would certainly not be easy.

The last, lethal problem was Maling: even if I beat Agashi, Maling would claim me. The million-rupee question remained — how to avoid Maling, defeat Agashi, and free everyone.

As I sat brooding, a sudden gust of air struck me. The blaze at the centre of the circle guttered— not out, but it shrank; the logs still smouldered red, throwing an ember-light about.

I felt the pressure of breath around me. A string of low whistling noises rushed past my ears and ran away into the trees; before they could fade, a harsh laugh rang out— ugly and very close.

A sudden chill ran through every hair on my body— but I quickly pulled myself together. I reminded myself that the boon of Devi Sainvani was with me— if I did not give in to fear, no force, however many in number, could harm me. That thought strengthened me... for the first time in many days I was facing such a thing fully conscious and in the real world— until now every such encounter had been inside the virtual reality Maling had made.

I steeled my heart and told myself to let them do whatever they wished. I would sit like an unmoved spectator and watch their horror show as though it were a child's game.

Then I heard something behind me and, by instinct, turned my neck toward the sound.

My camp lay behind, but the dark recesses on either side still showed, and in one of those corners I saw movement; looking more closely, I realised something was crawling toward me.

My first thought was an animal— I readied myself accordingly, pistol in hand, and waited for the movement to come into the firelight.

When the creature slithered into the glow of the embers, I involuntarily let out a little gasp... for it was no animal that a pistol could stop. A human torso it was, but every bone seemed broken and painfully misjoined; it dragged itself forward on all fours like some distorted quadruped.

Its head, horribly twisted, faced the wrong way— more like a spine than a chest— and its white eyes shone even from a distance. The rest of its face was a torn, ghastly ruin; it growled, mouth agape, the wolfish teeth jutting out. Its body was wrapped in something that could have been cloth— or perhaps it was merely its own skin, flayed and ragged, hanging in places.

Such a sight in the ruins of a forest under the dead of night would stop any heart, but having faced similar creatures in Maling's virtual worlds before and having prepared myself mentally, the effect on me was blunted. Adrenaline did set my body trembling at first, but within seconds I had gathered myself and slid the pistol back into its belt.

I made sure my face betrayed no fear; I looked at it with deliberate indifference, as if it meant nothing to me.

A low, similar growl rose to my left. I straightened my neck and saw another one slithering that way. Before I could steady my gaze, the same sound came from the right— another creature.

Then, from the direction in front of the fire, yet another dragged itself in. They were all converging on me; I drew a cold breath.

"Come, friends— I never believed in spirits, ghosts, witches and the like. When I first encountered them, my curiosity only grew: why do they choose humans? What feeling compels them to frighten a man? How do they decide what to do, which guise to assume, or what force to use? Since you have come, let us converse— so that my understanding may increase." I said it calmly, watching them.

Something in my words made them freeze where they were. Their faces showed a sudden confusion; they turned and looked at one another.

"Well! Why are you stopping, friends— come on," I said again.

They remained rooted and stared at me with those skewed faces. I made a beckoning gesture inviting them, but none moved.

I struck a match and relit the fire. They snarled at the light, certainly, but still did not advance.

A thought— perhaps mad in that moment— flashed through me: why should only spirits frighten humans? A man can do the frightening too. So I rose, put on a predatory expression and leapt toward the nearest one like a prowling leopard.

The moment my hand touched it, the creature dissolved into a black smoke and dispersed into the air. I steadied and lunged for the second; it too evaporated. One after another, the others chose the same fate and vanished.

The strange whistling began again, but now it was a chorus of low growls, and shadows appeared on the ruined walls standing far off. I raised the middle finger at them in a provocation and sat back down.

They growled louder, and the air around them wrapped into eddies. When the fire faltered beneath a gust and cooled to barely glowing coals, I didn't bother relighting it. Instead, I sang loudly— a Bengali song— as if to needle them. The eddies struck me but could not unseat me; their blows only shook my clothes. Then a sharp, icy gust struck my head from above, as if someone had emptied a large drum of cold air over me.

The cold touch chilled me to the bone and numbed my mind for a moment.

When I regained my senses, the place had changed— it felt as if I had been transposed, sitting in the same posture but in another reality. This could mean only one thing: while my mind had gone numb, something had pulled me into a different realm. Who had pulled me?

I looked around. I found myself in what seemed like a human-made cavern. Cut passages branched out, possibly vents punched through to the roof. Torches, set in the ground at intervals, burned with some resinous fuel, giving both light and a little warmth.

Directly opposite where I had appeared stood what looked like a tree whose upper trunk pierced the roof; its roots and buttress formed a crude dais at its base.

This was the very place where, the previous night, I had peered into Maling's made reality— trying to view a future vision like the eye of a camera— and where Maling had sensed my presence.

Today most of those people were gone… yet looking closely I saw someone bound inside the roots and tangles that encircled that dais: a body cleft into a thousand pieces. Bones dangled like part of the roots themselves. Among the roots hung a heart that still thudded, and two eyes were fixed within the tangle, staring at me.

Among the fibrous roots a thin-branched, brush-like section blinked faintly with a pulsing light, as if an electric current ran through it— perhaps the mind of that body.

So, this was Maling's fragmented form— the body he wished to complete and return to youth; the body he hoped to anchor forever.

Yet because he had, so far, helped me in certain ways and because his action had given me the confidence I now had, I owed him some respect. I folded my hands and offered him a namaste.

"Namaskar!" There was no sound anywhere, yet I felt a strange, unfamiliar voice reverberate inside my mind.

"Why did you call out to me?" I asked aloud.

"To make you understand this much— that do not fall into the illusion that I seek to acquire Agashi's powers through you, so I may reclaim a young body and bend things to my will. I desire none of that. I do not want Agashi's powers. This very condition of mine is also her doing— that I remain alive in this state, with death denied to my fate." The voice echoed again.

"Then what is the truth, munivar?"

"I want you to defeat her without hesitation, and I know you can do it. If you win, you will be able to do what your father wished, what all his companions wished, and what Saavri wishes. That is what I want as well. I too live a cursed life, born of Agashi. When you send her into the darkness of the netherworld, the influence of her powers will end. Not only will your father and his companions be freed, but I too shall attain liberation and leave this mortal realm. My purpose is not to grow powerful in this world by using her strength, but to be released from this world with the destruction of her powers. So, brave young man— do not grow weak through confusion, do not commit an error by sinking into doubt. Focus instead upon your goal. That pishachini who stands beside you holds an incorrect notion about me, but she is certainly your well-wisher, hoping for liberation through you, just as I am. She can prepare you well against Agashi. Do not hesitate— fully partake of her body and, through her, practice how to give yourself completely in union yet still retain such control that you can grant Agashi ultimate pleasure. She will come to you only in the form of Saavri." The answer rang directly inside my mind again.

"So you will not seize control of my mind at the moment of victory?" I expressed mild surprise.

"Absolutely not. The moment you absorb her power, you yourself will become so powerful that it would be impossible for me to do such a thing. Think for yourself— if I were that capable, would I not have entered Agashi's world against her will? Even for that, I must wait until she weakens. And once you alone possess her powers, how could I possibly gain dominion over your mind?"

I nodded— his reasoning was sound.

"Close your eyes and return to your place. Be fearless and practise with Saavri. You will face no obstacle— I promise." came the mental command.

I obeyed: I shut my eyes and emptied my thoughts, and then a bat-like shriek echoed— and my eyes flew open.

I was back at my camp. The forest was still as if no time had passed; the spirits had withdrawn. I relit the fire and sat, thinking over what had just happened.

Could what he said be true? His words had force: if I did manage to defeat Agashi, her powers would become part of me— and if that happened, how could Maling possibly seize control over my mind?

If he could do that after her power had been absorbed into me, then why, the last time Agashi had been weak in front of my father, hadn't he simply taken control of her mind then? If that had been possible, then when Agashi had weakened the last time before my father, he would have taken control of her mind directly. And if control over a weakened Agashi was not possible for him, how could it ever succeed over me after I had grown stronger? Something was clearly amiss. Either I could not see through his stratagem, or he was speaking truth.

My mind wrestled with the question for a long while and mulled over every possibility. When sleep finally crept up on me, I returned to my camp and lay down.

The dread that I might be dragged into another dangerous reality the moment I closed my eyes had receded; instead, a strange eagerness filled me. At least this gave me a pretext— practice with Saavri. My head was heavy with exhaustion and, within moments, I fell into sleep.

I don't know how long I actually slept, but soon I found myself in the very kind of reality my father had sketched in his diary— that beautiful, picturesque lake.

Flowers lined the banks; flocks of swans and ducks drifted about; and out on the water there was a small islet of four plane trees that Father had called Adan Bagh. At the bank where I stood, Saavri sat poised in a boat, looking toward me. Her gaze was a quiet invitation. She wore not her modern Western clothes but an old-world princess's garb: saffron and silk embroidered with delicate thread that both covered and revealed.

A Jeweled necklace lay at her throat and flowers were woven into her hair. Her arms gleamed like marble; bangles glittered at her wrists. She was more beautiful in that hour than in any other I had seen her.

I leapt into the boat and she took the oars with a smile.

"You took your time getting here," I said, feigning chide.

"You're too eager," she smiled playfully.

"A man's wedding night— if he's not eager, then what worth is he? Listen, after you left something happened to me: I saw Maling in his true form."

"Sh-sh— Maling or any other talk has no place here. This is not the time for stressful, mind-tugging matters. Remember why we are here— focus only on that. Everything else belongs to the outside world." She shook her head, shutting the subject down.

"As you command, ma'am." I complied with mock ceremony.

"Perhaps this is the very place where Agashi sang to your father in the guise of your mother… You'll be surprised, I sing well too— Bengali, Assamese, Bhutanese, Kashmiri… want to hear?"

"Kashmiri too— how is that possible?" I blinked in surprise.

"Shh… no questions. Will you listen?"

"Sing."

She rowed and began to sing in soft, measured notes that seemed to steep the air in honey. Language hardly mattered; whether I understood the words or not, her voice had me spellbound. I let myself dissolve into that listening; all else fell away.

The trance broke when the boat drew up at the little Adan Bagh. I came back to myself with a shiver.

"Wonderful… I did not know you sang this well," I said, praising her.

"I was trained to entertain my master with music," she said — "Shh— don't ask. Keep what I tell you in your heart. Come; look how beautiful it is." She reached for my hand.

I took it, and we climbed ashore. We walked a little into the grove, she close against my shoulder; I slid my arm around her waist as we went inward. Trees draped with fruit and flowers arched over us. Petals lay thick upon the ground, as though spread in welcome. The air, heavy with perfume, grew dizzy with sweetness. The light felt as bright as day, yet its source was nowhere to be seen. A gentle breeze stroked like silk.

"If one could spend an entire night in such a place within a made reality, what then matters where the physical body lies outside? This is like heaven, and an apsara lies in my embrace." I pulled her closer and pressed kisses to her cheeks.

She laughed mischievously.

We wandered deeper into the bed of flowers and found a chamber-like clearing where a floor of petals formed a bed.

She collapsed onto it laughing, breath quickened and gorgeous. I lay beside her and turned to look at her.

"You are beautiful," I said.

"If we have all night in a pleasant made world, you won't sit philosophising— remember why you came. Practice restraint." She cautioned, and a jolt went through me.

"My fault," I admitted, sheepish. "Alright. For now, remember: until the new moon I am on a mission that requires putting aside private feelings."

She draped her arms around my neck and pressed close; our lips brushed and I tasted her. Now the real test began. I had to give myself wholly to union and yet not lose myself; I had to practice surrender and command at once. It was not an entirely new art.

I had tried such experiments before, but then the sentiment had been different. Now the balance had to be struck between feeling and discipline.

She kissed me from head to toe and I undressed her. I knew from research and experience that foreplay— the entire play before intercourse— is the essential part of this craft. For many women it is the central thing; coitus itself is only the culminating act. There are infinite ways to excite a woman, and countless tender points. I had to learn how Agashi or Saavri might be aroused; I poured myself into the effort.

Because of that careful attention, the coupling lasted long. We both reached the peak together, and after the first attempt there was much room for improvement. We rested briefly and prepared for a second round. The second time lasted longer still; again we reached climax together and then fell spent. For a first lesson it was not bad; two rounds had left me pleasantly exhausted, and we slept.

●●

CHAPTER 13

It was Friday— the day of the new moon. The day that would decide my fate. What would be written— victory over Agashi and deliverance for all, and a safe return? Or death at the hands of Agashi or Maling? Tonight, the answer would come, and by morning there might be either a dawn I would not see or a liberation I had hoped for.

Tuesday night we had spent practicing the act in that made-up world with Saavri, and the next two days and a night flowed by in the same pattern until every limb of our bodies grew accustomed to it.

Though we reached climax a dozen times in that stretch, most of our practice remained in the foreplay and the restraint before ejaculation— the kind of repeated starts and stops you see in some animals, beginning again and again but deliberately never going all the way.

In other words, for roughly forty-eight hours straight, in both the real and the unreal worlds, we had been engaged in sex; by the last night I had grown almost weary of the act itself, as if there were nothing left in me to ejaculate, and a strong aversion to the very idea had set in.

From the second day onward, I began to gain the upper hand in the game with Saavri, and by the end she had come to trust that I was ready to face Agashi. She was satisfied with my preparation.

The following day I told her about my meeting with Maling and tried to understand his real intent. Saavri said that because Maling had first tied himself to my father's mind, he had been able to break into that mind repeatedly, and in the same way my father and his companions had tried to learn Maling's mind.

According to her, Maling had spoken as he had to lull me — to keep me from suspecting him and to stop me from abandoning my purpose. He wanted me to go after Agashi with full confidence; if I succeeded, he could immediately seize control of me and bend everything to his will.

"How could he control me once I had Agashi's power," I asked, "when now his influence doesn't hold over Agashi herself? If he couldn't seize control of a weakened Agashi back then, how could he possibly dominate me after I absorb her power?"

Her answer was blunt: Agashi is not a mere human but an ancient spirit, and controlling such a spirit is beyond a human's capacity.

She can be weakened, subordinated, even deceived, but not possessed because she lacks a physical substrate the way a human has. I— being human— would still retain a physical body even after taking on her power; that corporeal anchor would allow Maling to exert influence. The logic made grim sense, and the same rotten conclusion returned: even if I won, I might yet lose— because we had no clear strategy to rid ourselves of Maling.

During those two days we spoke little beyond necessities: food, relieving ourselves, the all-consuming fatigue. Outside of that, our time was taken up by the sex games which had become our priority.

After a last session near midnight, we flew toward Agashi's temple. Saavri could take the form of a large bat and carry me by her claws, but even she had limits: she could not transport all our gear. So, she carried me first to a point within a few hours' walk of the temple, left me there, and returned for our packs; by the time she had fetched everything, it was already the third watch of the night.

We reached the place, spent what remained of the night sleeping, and lay in bed until late morning.

I did not feel right about barging into the temple in the middle of the night. If a son is to watch his mother pass into her fate, it seemed fitting he should face that moment in daylight; I did not want to steal her sleep or deny her those last waking hours. I therefore resolved to arrive at the temple by day.

Saavri agreed. She had found a safe cave near the temple for that last night— a place where we could spend the remaining hours properly and then reach the temple quickly enough in daylight to give me, if possible, some time with the mother whose face I had once seen and then forgotten.

The cave lay geographically closer to Bhutan; the temple itself stood at a higher altitude within the compound.

When the sun rose, we rose too, did the morning things, swung our packs and rifles onto our shoulders, and set off. As the last stretch of the road approached, a number of questions hovered in my head.

"Saavri," I said, "have you thought that tonight's companionship might be the last time we meet in this guise? If I defeat Agashi, your existence will end. If she consumes me, my existence will end. If Maling gains control, he will recover a body and kill me. If I achieve a half-success like my father, I may no longer remain human— just as you would not. Then we would both become machines of a sort."

"I understand," she said quietly.

"Before we go, answer a few questions for me— small things that still matter to me now, as a man. Afterwards they may have no meaning at all."

"Ask."

"You may be whatever you are, but while living beside you I have developed feelings for you that I can't name other than love. Have you felt anything like that?"

"Don't you think an answer will change what you decide to do before Agashi?" she countered. "If I say yes, will that make you halt and spare me?"

"No. I owe my duty to the man who placed his hope in me— my father. I have decided that our bond ends here. If my choice causes me pain, so be it. I will not be selfish out of affection. My ultimate aim is to send Agashi into the darkness and free everyone. I will not be diverted." I spoke with a firmness meant to settle her fear.

She studied me for a few long beats, exhaled, and turned her gaze to the path ahead.

"In my state," she said, "human feelings like those mean little. We live as hunters; we perform tasks like machines. Still, there are moments when even we forget ourselves and begin to think like humans. Then those human sensations touch us, and we feel them the way a human would. I have roamed this body for perhaps three hundred years, and I never once met someone who made me feel any hope. Every encounter was a hunt.

You are the first to awaken in me something like your father's faith. If you stirred that hope, it is not surprising I formed an attachment. You are not only decent but brave in the way a man should be. I began, slowly, to feel human sentiments— I began to care. I did not want you to weaken, so I helped. I know if you lose, Agashi will punish me cruelly for trying. Despite that risk I chose to help you; some attachment to you grew. You can call it love if you wish, but the name is awkward for me; I cannot say it so plainly."

"Is that why you savaged that chain-man so brutally at the rest house on the Narayangudi road?" I asked.

"Yes— I felt that much hatred toward him," she said.

"Tell me— you said you can see a little of the future sometimes. How could you craft the visions you showed me? My father's diary claimed Agashi's sphere of influence prevented such powers. Yet during the train incident and at Bodhanbari I saw future-visions— and in that first vision I encountered Maling. How was that possible?"

"Wrong— You were not seeing your own visions then," she answered. "Maling showed them to you."

Another question surfaced. "When we went to Deepdas babu's place in Calcutta, I had to give my locket to get the diary— how did you know the locket would be demanded?"

"Because that was known to your Boyal maama, and through him it reached your father, it was only natural that I would know as well— what is so remarkable about that?" She shrugged.

"Hmm. Fine. You said one is vulnerable to being pulled into the unreal only when one is unconscious or in a trance.

But Maling pulled us from a waking state at the rest house and at the ruined place too. How did he manage that?"

"His mental force is vast. He doesn't pull a man out while he remains fully conscious— he uses his power to make the mind briefly oblivious. In the rest house you were unconscious later; in the ruined place there was that cold gust of air that shocked your awareness— in that lapse he drew you in."

"Suppose tonight I don't sleep at all— neither you nor anyone else manages to render me unconscious, and I keep watch: what then?"

"You won't succeed. Maling will make you unconscious by force, or Agashi will put you to sleep herself. In any case, you cannot avoid it— and besides, why would you try? Your aim is to go into Agashi's realm."

"I only wondered if it would be possible. Tell me one last thing: how, after centuries wandering as you do, do you speak modern modes, know English words, and carry such a range of folk songs— Assamese, Bengali, Bhutanese, Kashmiri? And how do you know Urdu?"

"So you won't believe me without knowing my past."

"Then tell me, so no thorn remains lodged in my chest. I am already proceeding on the assumption that either I am going to die, or that tonight is the last night you and I will spend together. If I die, it hardly matters. But if I survive and you leave, this question will remain with me like an unhealed sore."

She looked at me and, for the first time that morning, a thin smile crossed her face. Then she began to speak, and I listened.

"Hmm… all right, I'll tell you. I was born a Kashmiri— so long ago that I hardly remember much. Perhaps my parents died or were killed when I was very small. I was then taken and sold to a jagirdar. In those days the Pathans held sway there; a woman was little more than a plaything. From the earliest age I was trained to entertain that jagirdar— a libertine, cruel, yet fond of music.

My voice pleased him, so they taught me singing and instruments so I could charm him. I stayed with him until I came of age… suffering every kind of exploitation, but still alive. Strange, when I think of it now: having lived such a wretched life, I was grateful just to be alive.

One day some Pathans murdered him; they kept me as their concubine. They went on an expedition to Punjab and I went with them. There their company met with misfortune and the Pathans died, while I escaped. But where would a lone girl flee?

Those were the days of Aurangzeb's reign and the English were spreading their foothold. By some chance I fell into the hands of an Englishman traveling from Lahore to Delhi on official business. He employed me as a servant; I became part of his household. There too, besides singing, I was used for that Englishman's pleasures— just as I had been for the jagirdar.

We stayed in Delhi for maybe three years. Twice I conceived, only to have the pregnancies terminated by the so-called doctors with their potions. I was a thing to them, yet I was alive; for that I even offered thanks to God. Later they left Delhi and moved to Bengal, took up quarters in Chittagong.

These men were agents of the East India Company, whose work was to curry favor with regional rulers and commanders to ease the Company's trade. They moved from one capital to the next, setting camp wherever they went.

After two years in Chittagong they moved toward Cooch Behar to approach the royal household. One day, while on a hunt in the Manas forest, a terrible storm scattered them. I was with them and wandered in the dangers of the jungle until we met a band of Deori people.

They killed my companions, but left me alive and took me to their encampment. There they treated me like an animal— no food, beatings, lust. For them mere intercourse was insufficient; they derived pleasure from inflicting pain. In ten days they had reduced me to a state where I longed for death. Then came a dark moon; they took me to a temple-like place

— you can guess it was the same site where your father later rescued your mother and Maama.

They planned to sacrifice me to Agashi. I prayed with all my heart that Agashi might not spare me, but would at least destroy those monsters.

Something in me must have snapped into emptiness in that hour, for Agashi pulled me into her otherworld. She was willing to save me— on one condition: I would dedicate my life to her. I agreed without fully grasping the meaning, and she pressed herself into me so utterly that it felt as though she breathed into me and became part of me.

I lost consciousness, and when I returned, endowed with many of her powers, I tore into those men. I killed all but their leader, whom I rendered unconscious so that Agashi could draw him into her realm and consume him. When Agashi took him, she consumed him as a sacrament. At that time only Sachi and Nimbuja were there with me.

For the first time I tasted raw human flesh— a satisfaction unlike anything I had known. The message was clear: this would be my food henceforth, and my life's sole purpose to bring victims to Agashi so that she might constantly regain and increase her powers. By day I would wander in human shape; by night I would take the form of some predatory bird or beast and hunt.

Year after year— from Narayangudi to Domka, from Dechling to Gelephu— I roamed and learned peoples' languages, their gestures and customs. That is why I speak so many tongues, and because I lived long with those Englishmen, I know their dress and manner as well." She fell silent after that.

"Who among you is the oldest?" I asked.

"Nimbuja— perhaps in Agashi's service for four hundred years. Sachi joined some fifty years later, then me, then the others."

"And Agashi—how old is she?"

"No idea… she never told anyone anything herself. What Nimbuja knows must have come from the people of her own time— back then Agashi was known only as a specter that used to overpower people. As her powers kept growing, she created her own realm of illusion and confined herself to it. She began hunting there, and at first it was a problem that she had to wait for prey— sometimes for years. Then Maling built that temple, where in the early days he himself brought people and offered them in sacrifice to please Agashi, and before death could claim them, she would pull the prey into her realm and drain them.

For this service, Agashi granted Maling enough power to save himself from death. Later Nimbuja fell into Agashi's hands and began bringing her prey every new moon. Maling was no longer as necessary, so he withdrew into austerities. His aim was to become as powerful as Agashi herself, but he was human, and humans have limits. While he was absorbed in his penance, beneath him— perhaps from a seed expelled as waste from the food he had consumed— a tree took root and grew, gradually absorbing his body into itself. Maling did not break his austerities, and in this way he succeeded in acquiring immense mental powers, even as his physical body disintegrated.

Had he been subject to death like an ordinary man, he would have died long ago. But since death was not destined for him, his body, though broken, remained beyond death. Not only did it endure— even in that state he used his powers, much like Agashi, to create a realm of his own, where he lives a passable existence with a projected body. He can control the minds of humans around him, so across different eras he enslaves ascetics and hermits who wander into the forest, draws them into that world, and lives an unrestrained life with them. Now it is impossible to say whether he truly seeks release from this cursed existence, or whether he intends to use you as a pawn to attain immortality in a young body of his own."

"So you are still not certain what his true purpose is… Fine. I had asked how old Agashi is."

"I told you— no one knows. Everything known about her came through Nimbuja. In Nimbuja's time she was regarded as a powerful specter. The stories attached to her were known, but how old those stories were— even the people of that era did not know. In those days, history was not recorded in a way that would allow common people to determine an exact time. Still, from roaming this region for centuries and speaking with people, we have gathered fragments of history, and by that reckoning, about a thousand years ago there was a kingdom and a city here that could have been hers."

"So, by rough estimation, she is about a thousand years old." I nodded, understanding.

"You can think of it that way."

Then we both fell silent… she drifted into her own thoughts, and I into mine… and the rest of the journey passed in quiet.

When we neared Agashi's temple, perched atop a high cliff, my heartbeat quickened without warning. From a distance itself, I could see those people standing on the outer platform of the temple— Saavri's companions, among whom my father was also present. In his diary, at one place, he had written that they could sense when Nimbuja had reached the temple with her prey, and that was why he was stopping his writing… which meant that even today they must have already sensed that one of their companions was bringing me to the temple, and they had all come out to see. Until now, who knew under what disguises they had appeared before the arriving prey, but at least with me there was no need for any disguise… yet did everyone know this?

When we reached the steps, the others' faces may have appeared expressionless, but my father's face seemed to tremble. As we moved upward, I observed the rest… Namgyal and Baro had ordinary faces but strong, solid bodies. As for the women with them, I could not identify them individually by name as Hirvi, Nimbuja, or Sachi, but each of them possessed striking physiques along with attractive features. All three were beautiful in their own way, yet in terms of facial structure, one appeared Bhutanese while the other two bore Assamese features. Beside them, Saavri— being of Kashmiri origin— stood apart from all of them, and was the most beautiful of all. Whatever their real ages might have been, they all looked young— my father too should, by all logic, be at least twenty-one years older than me, yet in appearance he looked no more than an elder brother, four or six years my senior.

As I came closer, I folded my hands and offered a 'Namaste' myself, but no one responded. While the others continued to look at me with interest, it was difficult for my father to contain his emotions.

"Perhaps you are unsure how to deal with me… because until now, whoever came here was prey— someone who knew nothing at all. Neither who you were, nor why they had been brought here, nor what was going to happen to them… but I am not unaware. I already know everything. By your reckoning, you could say that I have knowingly walked into the mouth of death." I said, looking at all of them, with a faintly taunting tone.

"When you already understand everything, what is there left for us to say?" one of the three women spoke.

"Saavri— I can recognize my father, but at least introduce the others," I said, and at that Saavri introduced them to me.

Then I addressed my father directly and asked after him. He broke down, embraced me, and began apologizing for his foolishness. According to him, when he sent me to Calcutta with Boyal maama after writing the diary, he had no sense of what the future held. But later, once Agashi had learned everything, my coming here no longer made any sense, because if I could have prepared myself in advance against her, then she surely would have done the same. In any case, the arrow had already left the bow, and there was no turning it back.

When I asked where my mother was, he gestured toward the back. Did she know that this time I was the one being brought as prey? He said he had told her only yesterday, and since then she had been badly shaken, doing nothing but weeping. I moved in that direction to see her.

Behind the temple there was a small chamber, and at its doorway sat an older, distraught woman, her hair disheveled.

At the sound of my footsteps she looked up toward me. The moment she saw me, her body stirred, and she rose and rushed toward me. When she came close, trying to stop herself from crying, her face shifting and breaking, she began touching me from one side to the other, as if to reassure herself. What a mother might feel after cruelly sending away a piece of her own heart at her husband's insistence, and then seeing him again after years— I could understand that. And to see him now with the knowledge that he was today's prey must have been an experience sharp enough to tear at the nerves of her mind.

There was nothing more I could do to console her except step forward and hold her to my chest, and that is exactly what I did. The dam of her restraint broke, and clinging to me, she began to weep uncontrollably.

●●

CHAPTER 14

The new moon had already set in; dusk was falling. I chose a place inside the temple and sat like Lord Shiva— cross-legged, eyes closed, folded as if in meditation.

By everyone's account— and somewhere in my own sense too— perhaps my last day had already passed. The moment had come when the struggle between my life and my death would begin. I spent that whole day mostly in my mother's lap. She fed me with food she'd made herself and talked about my life, over and over.

I tried, repeatedly, to convince her that Agashi could not kill me and that I would return victorious, but perhaps even that would not comfort her— for if I won then my father would gain release, and she would lose him. We had reached a crossroads where only one of us could remain; that truth was painful for her whatever the outcome, and there was nothing to be done.

I was lucky that she did not know of Maling and his designs, or she would have been even more tormented.

While she cooked and moved about I slipped away to speak with my father, gathering what information I could— among it the question of how I might stop Maling if I did manage to win.

None of them had an answer. I knew their story of survival, but I wanted to know how Namgyal and Baro had escaped— it turned out that, like my father, they too had only partial knowledge, and so most of the night they were awake and alert; Agashi could not drag them entirely into her otherworld.

When they finally entered that state through their own trance, Agashi had not had enough time— dawn came, and the incomplete contest ended for them as it had for my father. The difference in their case was that Maling's people had disrupted events and saved them; otherwise their deaths would have been certain.

Now the sun had set and Agashi would have become active. It was up to me whether I let her take the chance or whether I followed Namgyal and Baro's example of waiting — though Saavri said that when Namgyal and Baro had succeeded, Agashi had not been able to render people unconscious and pull them into her realm; now she was capable of doing so, of dragging me against my will into her world the way Maling had twice done.

In other words, in a sense nothing was in my hands— it depended on when she chose to pull me. What little time I had was for thinking how to stop Maling inside that otherworld.

I embraced Saavri for the last time, kissed her, and sat in that chamber— everyone else remained outside, restless. I had given my father a task that would defy Agashi and for which he might pay later, but it seemed necessary as one desperate attempt to hinder Maling.

My mother's rule was to lock herself in her room at dusk and not appear before those people— and though she was in terrible shape, she, crying, said farewell and shut herself in.

According to my father, this was the first time anyone had said that if I lost to Agashi and she managed to consume me, the people outside would not accept my dead body as sacrament. Instead, they would burn me. They would do so even if that brought them Agashi's punishment.

Seeing my mother's state grieved me sharply— and letting Saavri go from my embrace hurt the same. I felt that this was our last embrace— my final touch with Saavri. She might never meet me again, whether I won or lost. I could only hope my fate would not be my father's— yet I knew his courage, his knowledge, and his limits were not mine; I had to go all or nothing.

Putting all other thoughts aside I focused on Maling. Why should I assume that he, like the rest, wanted release? He wouldn't need anything special if Agashi were buried in darkness— that would free everyone, including him.

I only needed to act differently if his aim was to gain control over me; my preparations had to reflect that possibility. Whatever plan I had urged my father to set in motion might have any outcome— I could not be sure of success— so I concentrated on what I could do if it came to it.

I plunged into thought but kept checking myself that I would not slip into a trance and be dragged into Agashi's world— I made small movements, opened my eyes occasionally to remain rooted in the real.

The confrontation was inevitable, but I did not want the fight to stretch all night; the shorter the time I spent there the better. I also wanted to see whether Agashi could yank me into her world against my will as Maling had done.

Waiting like that, midnight must have already passed, when Agashi was finally forced to become active. Maling had anesthetized my mind with that cold wind; Agashi struck the brain with a sudden shock.

The shock was so violent that sweat broke out on my skin; despite all my efforts to stay conscious I fell into darkness.

When I returned to awareness it took a moment to register what had happened. The final moment of my mission had come— I had been drawn into Agashi's realm— and I woke up with a jolt.

Consciousness returned with a roar: a kettle-drum sounded and a proclamation rolled out. Astonished, I looked around and found myself not in some edenic valley or the flowered garden vision, but in a kind of ancient arena— a circular stadium with galleries on three sides.

Thousands seemed to throng the seats, shouting together the same name. I listened: they were cheering— "Agashi." On the far side a great gate stood open; soldiers were posted at the entrance, and two ranks of mounted horsemen flanked the doorway. Two powerful men stood on either side of me holding the chains that bound me.

Directly ahead, at the center of a dais, sat an unmatched beauty— she could only be Agashi— and on either side of her were two elephants. Drums and kettle-drums beat; the public in the galleries roared.

What was going on? My body reacted as if struck— my head spun and sweat ran cold. I touched the chains at my waist: they were not dream-phantoms but solid, real. I could not fathom how such reality could be conjured.

I looked, panic-struck, toward the throne where Agashi sat erect with a murderous smile.

Everybody had told me that victory or defeat with Agashi would be decided by physical union— and yet here I was stripped down to a dhoti at the waist and bare above, the garments of another age.

Agashi had drawn me back to the era when she was a princess. I tried to make sense of the hills and landscape visible in the arena's panorama, but they might have shifted with time: earthquakes, landslides— the world had changed and could not be read as easily now.

Suddenly Agashi raised her hand and all the drummers fell silent— the kettle-drummers had already finished their part. As the drums died away the crowd quieted too, until such a hush spread that even from so far, I could hear her clearly when she spoke.

"So, you think you can challenge me?" she said in a strange tone— I could not tell whether she was asking or declaring.

"Yes— but you hold the contest through intercourse, don't you? Then what is all this?" I asked, confused.

"My throne is reached by passing through this arena," she said. "First you will be tested, young man— if you survive, then you shall earn the prize of my embrace." Her voice gathered force as she spoke.

My head went numb— she would not take me straight to the throne but would try to bring me to death first, or to wear me down so much that when the real contest began, I would have lost half my strength.

Father had been right: if I prepared against her, she would prepare against me. She had placed me not in a garden but in a battlefield, and she herself stood before me in her true form rather than hiding behind any mask to startle me. If both of us knew each other's games, there was no need for guises.

"And how will this test be?" I asked after a cold breath.

"First you must fight these two champions together—then all those mounted soldiers, and if you survive that, you'll have to deal with it," she said, pointing to a closed barrack—when I glanced that way I saw a leopard behind bars. "and if you are still alive after that, you will certainly get the chance to defeat me on my own bed," she finished.

"And if I die, what of your harvest this Amavasya? You'll be left thirsty." I replied, a touch mocking. She only smiled mysteriously; finding no answer I pressed on, "Is this a fair fight?"

"Think," she said, the secretive smile still on her lips.

She was right— I could not rush in without thought. I dropped to my knees on the earth and closed my eyes, truly thinking how I could stand against mountain-sized demons, armed soldiers and a leopard.

Could she really prefer to kill me rather than consume me? Saavri's stories came back to me— how for centuries she had sometimes gone years without prey, until Maling and then Nimbuja arranged her quarry and, in time, her own army formed. It was possible she had long fed on humans and that missing a single Amavasya would not kill or weaken her.

So perhaps from the start she had judged me a threat and meant not to fatten herself by my embrace but to end me outright. The game might be designed merely to kill me.

That was her side— now what of mine? I had never truly seen any benefit in the boon of Goddess Sainvani, for which my father had undertaken such a long and perilous journey to Africa… but now, at this stage, its meaning was suddenly becoming clear to me. Maling had prepared me entirely within this framework. Here or anywhere else, in any illusory world, whatever beings existed— regardless of their size or form —were not real people of the physical world.

They were creatures of a realm of illusion, a virtual reality, whose strength depended not on themselves but on me. If I feared them— if I doubted my own ability against them—

then even while being smaller and weaker than me, they could overpower me. But if I faced them without fear, with complete faith in my own capabilities, then no matter what their size, shape, strength, or speed might be, they could not get the better of me.

They were not real people, so their numbers meant nothing. Even a hundred of them amounted to no more than one against me, and even a single one still made for an equal contest. In other words, they could be anything, anyone— but they were never stronger or faster than me. This was what my father had failed to understand till the very end, but the experiences recorded in his diary, along with Saavri and Maling, had already prepared me mentally for all of this.

I had made up my mind— the point was clear to me.

When I opened my eyes, I stood up, and a smile came to my lips. I glanced at Agashi— she watched me now with a hint of perplexity.

I bowed my head once, placing a hand on my chest as if to accept her challenge. The two champions then unclasped the chains at my waist— they did not remove them of their own accord, which meant Agashi would use them against me.

No matter— let us see how long they hold before me. To wonder whether I could stand would be to admit doubt, and doubt would hand them victory. But there is a fine line between confidence and overconfidence. I must not rage blindly; instead, I must keep my mind cold, anticipate each blow, and strike with calculated force.

We faced one another like true opponents. They twirled the chains in their hands; I had nothing. From the look of it the battle was lopsided— but I knew their size, shape and weapons were irrelevant here. They stood to my sides so that if I focused on one the other could strike— but that was a familiar ruse that would not fool me.

One of them cracked his chain toward me like a whip. I watched the arc and sidestepped, then launched myself toward the other. He, too, was whipping his chain and before he could finish, I collided into him— his mountain of a body did not intimidate me for an instant; my momentum upended him and he crashed to the ground.

I did not pause to watch him fall; landing on him I drove my fist toward his skull with every ounce of force. Saavri had taught me that in the real world a fist against iron breaks the hand, but in a world shaped by thought the mind is the hammer— strike with certainty and the steel shatters.

My blow met his forehead like a blacksmith's hammer; blood spurted, and he writhed. I stepped off.

By then the other champion had risen, furious, and spun his chain with all his rage, but this time I did not dodge— I watched the chain's path and, as it came near, caught it in my hands.

The man had intended to hurl me into the air with that loop— the chance came to him, but not for long. He had not expected me to seize his own weapon; as he lunged he tripped into his momentum and I wound his chain about him so tightly his hands became entangled. I ducked onto his shoulders, pushed him backward until he lost balance and smashed him down.

With his legs trapped he could not recover; I pinned his chest and threaded the chain around his throat, pulling with all my strength— there was no escape.

He died quickly.

I freed myself and took his chain, winding it across my torso like a harness so that no straight blade could slay me. Before the two corpses could be cleared the mounted soldiers spread out around me; the crowd watched with bated breath. For a moment I met Agashi's eyes— her face was expressionless.

Now I was among those mounted soldiers, which meant they could easily take aim at me. There were about a dozen of them; ten held swords while two carried spears, and from where I stood those two looked more dangerous than the rest.

I understood then that I couldn't survive by staying between them— I would have to become one of them, so why wait for them to come to me; why not move forward and join them myself.

With that thought I lunged at a cavalryman. The two or three men on that side immediately brandished their swords, but I had expected as much, and I dodged the blades in their arcs. I reached the rider and used the chain to parry his swing, then shoved his horse with all my strength.

Here my power was far greater than in the outside world; the horse went down with a whinny and dragged its rider. When you fight many at once, trying to face them all is foolish — you must focus on one at a time and neutralize him, even if you take a few wounds yourself in the process.

With that aim I had gone after the rider.

His horse collapsed and he was down, but I grabbed his leg and pulled him toward me; he could not recover as I seized his sword-arm, drove him backward and forced his own blade through his back into his chest— that ended him.

I had taken his sword before he fell, and with the same speed I plunged it into the horse's neck; the beast reared and the rider was flung down. Before he could rise, I cut his throat. It wasn't that I'd become careless of the others while taking those two— I was watching them all, especially the two spear-men who could strike me from a distance.

The man whose horse I'd pushed was dead; his mount tried to stand and the reins slipped into my hands, so I vaulted up to its back.

A spearman lunged and his spear grazed my moving body, struck the horse and set it wild. The other nearby horse startled and its rider lost balance, giving me my chance. I leapt onto that rider's horse, caught his head with one hand, and with the sword in the other I slit his throat.

With that done I shoved him off and took the reins. Rather than sheathe the sword I swung the chains hard so no blade could reach me and urged the horse forward.

My eyes were fixed on the other spearman— the one who had driven the spear— while the man who'd thrown the spear had drawn his sword.

I rode the horse toward the spear-man, who readied another throw. Before he could release it, I folded the sword's hilt into the rein-hand, uncoiled part of the chain I wore across my chest and sent it at him.

The chain diverted the spear's trajectory toward my chest, and when he came close I looped that same chain around his neck; the horse stumbled, he was thrown, and I dragged him past the others. I pulled him under my horse and crushed him.

He screamed, frenzied. His comrades ran to him, so I bit the rein in my mouth with one hand, took the sword in the other and began to whirl the chain— six feet of iron now— so none could reach me. Those the chain struck I hauled in close and cut down with the sword. They hacked and slashed wildly but could not touch me at distance.

Had we all been on the ground they might have had the advantage; mounted, I was the heavier force— and I had taken four men out of the fight. Whether those four later lived or died I could not say.

Only four were left then, and sensing the risk, they attacked the horse itself to unseat me. The maneuver worked.

I was thrown off and scrambled for the spear that lay nearby. Two cavalrymen charged, trying to trample me. Before they reached me I targeted a horse's face with the spear and struck so it reared and froze; at the same time I sent the chain looping to entangle another horse's legs so it fell. I too went down and skidded, but it was soft ground and I was lucky to escape worse injury. As I freed myself, I drove my sword into the belly of the fallen rider who had been thrown from his mount.

By then the remaining mounted men and the man who had fallen from the other horse were on their feet.

The mounted duo flanked me while the dismounted man stood before me. They sprinted in; I let them come close enough so they could not change direction, I hurled the chain toward the soldier in front and leapt at him myself. He was expecting me, but the chain reached him first. Startled, he swung his sword to knock it aside— and by then I was already upon him. A hand once set in motion at such speed cannot be drawn back in time. Before the thought could even form in his mind, my sword had already driven into his neck.

After he fell there were only two left. They advanced in such a way that I could not dodge around; I let them come nearer and when they were almost within reach, I released the other end of my chain so it lengthened to some six feet, then swung both ends toward them.

The chains wrapped around their wrists and swords before the blades could reach my head; the weapons passed through the air and missed me, the chain entangled them, and both riders were toppled from their horses. They had not expected it. Scrambling to rise, they found me already upright with sword in hand, and within moments both were hors de combat.

The crowd erupted.

I stood straight, bowed slightly with a proud smile, and glared up at Agashi— her eyes were narrowed, jaw clenched. I doubted she had expected so much from a twentieth-century youth. It must have surprised her.

As the last opponents fell, other soldiers rushed in to clear away the dead and wounded. The horses, both injured and intact, were removed. One thing, however, seemed wrong to my eyes: though they had left the chains with me, they had taken my sword. So now, by the time I faced the leopard, I had only those two chains— a formidable weapon, yes, but how to confront a creature whose teeth and claws could shred me?

How could I face it? I sat down to think. The beast was no mere man whose gambits I could read; it would not hesitate or falter— it would give its all, like me. The only option I saw was make-or-break.

When they released it from the cage, I took my stance: one foot as balance, the other digging into the soil for support; one arm ready in defense, the other poised to strike; my eyes alert enough to sense the slightest change in the air.

As expected, it flew at me like an arrow once freed. My heart thudded once, then I bit down hard. I felt it close and, the instant it reached my circle, I sank every ounce of power into a punch straight between its eyes. The beast's momentum multiplied my blow; my fist struck like a hammer. No one recoiled, no one yielded, but the force landed— the creature's body stilled, astonishment and then blood filling its eyes.

Its hindquarters carried it up by its own force and then it crashed down; a strangled growl escaped and it fell still— its skull split.

The audience went wild.

Standing there, chest heaving, I bowed once to the crowd and then looked toward Agashi— she rose and turned away with a strange look.

Now I stood before her throne.

After my victory in the arena, they had escorted me away with the same respect a conquering warrior receives before being offered to the queen.

From the field I was taken to a magnificent palace adjoining it, where nearly naked attendants bathed me in perfumed, lukewarm water, cleansed every trace of blood and dust from my skin, and draped me in a silk dhoti. Then, after rubbing fragrant oil over my body, they led me to the inner chambers— the zenana— where a vast marble bath awaited.

Before me lay a rectangular pool, its warm surface steaming faintly.

The slope descended gradually into deeper water, and at the shallower end two attendants sat, their bodies glistening under the torchlight. In the deeper part stood Agashi— and even beneath the water her naked form shimmered like some sculpted divinity. When she noticed my arrival, she moved towards the shallows, and as she emerged knee-deep, the water tracing silver trails down her curves, I saw her fully for the first time.

It was impossible not to stare.

From head to toe she seemed carved by the hands of an artist obsessed with perfection— hair dark as a rain cloud, face bright as a new moon, a neck as slender as a swan's, shoulders smooth, arms like marble columns, and those taut, full breasts rising with every breath.

Her waist narrowed like a flute, melting into the round fullness of her hips and thighs— a body designed to unmake resolve. I had sworn to remain untouched by her beauty, but my pulse betrayed me; every beat came quicker, louder, more uneven.

She walked with the slow, intoxicating grace of a lioness, settled on a low marble seat where her lower body remained underwater while her upper half gleamed in the dim light. The attendants began to stroke her skin with soft cloths.

"May I ask what this spectacle is meant for?" I said, trying to sound stern.

"Of course you may ask— go on," she said, mocking me with a smile that burned through my restraint.

"If my victory truly meant something, I should already have received my reward."

"It does mean something," she replied, "and you shall have your reward. I am only being prepared for it. But tell me, why must everything unfold by your wish?"

"So, you truly intend to take me to your bed?"

"Yes. Why should that surprise you?"

"You know everything— my purpose, my intent— and yet you arranged my death in that arena. If you meant to claim me, why all that?"

She tilted her head, amusement curving her lips. "And would you rather I had you killed without a fight?"

"I only ask— if in the end you were to take me to your bed, what need for that trial? And if death was your goal, why this reward now? You seek not my valor or my courage— you seek only my blood. Whether you drain me yourself or have your soldiers do it, what difference would it make? So why the charade?"

Her smile deepened; it was the kind that hides knowledge rather than emotion.

"Is it because you wish to keep everything contrary to what I expect— to confuse me, to weaken my mind?"

"If I were to call Saavri your teacher, I wouldn't be wrong," she said quietly. "You've forgotten one of her greatest lessons."

She turned away, rose from the water, and at once the attendants splashed a final shower over her gleaming body. I felt a shock— what was I missing? My thoughts tangled as she began walking away, hips swaying, attendants trailing her. I followed, half dazed.

They entered a chamber lavishly adorned. Several other attendants awaited there. I stopped by the doorway and watched as they began to prepare her. They dried her body and hair, perfumed her locks with scented smoke, rubbed fragrance into her skin, and dressed her in a fabric so thin and sheer that it revealed more than it concealed— silk spun from moonlight itself.

Jewels were clasped around her neck, her wrists, her waist; her face was painted with the patience of a sculptor perfecting the final stroke.

And I— I stood thinking, What lesson had I forgotten?

Then it came like a flash— impatience. Saavri had warned me again and again: whether in combat or in passion, no victory belongs to the restless.

Impatience is the enemy of every discipline— and this contest was nothing less than my ultimate discipline. I had been growing restless, desperate for answers, eager for the bed that waited beyond the door. That was my mistake. In the temple I had fought to remain awake, to deny Agashi time; now she herself was giving me that time, and I was about to squander it by rushing toward her.

Why had she reminded me herself? Why offer her enemy a chance to steady his ground? Unless… the test had already begun.

Before I could think further, she and her attendants began moving again. She turned once, casting me a glance that gleamed like a blade under moonlight— a silent invitation. Come. The time has come.

I followed.

Up the wide stairway we went, into a high chamber dressed in silk drapes and flowers. Every object there— carpets, lamps, canopies— whispered of wealth and seduction. In the center lay a bed of blossoms and silk, curtained by petals hanging from the chandelier above, enclosing it like a fragrant cage.

The attendants guided Agashi onto the bed, bowed low, and withdrew, closing the door behind them.

She looked at me— eyes deep, luminous, inviting. But my mind was clear now. I would not be hurried. I stepped slowly to her, took her hand— smooth as carved stone— and kissed it lightly. Then, pressing it gently, I urged her to rise. She understood and stood before me.

My palms rested on her warm, radiant shoulders; I met her gaze, steady and dark as a lake at midnight.

"May we talk a while?" I asked softly, lacing my tone with warmth.

"Why not? Between us there are no veils now. Your fate lies in your hands," she said, stepping back toward a corner where heavy curtains hung.

She drew them aside, revealing a balcony overlooking the valley. I followed her out. We were high above a chasm where, far below, a river roared unseen through the dark. Mountains stretched like shadows to the horizon. Above us, a star-scattered sky gleamed— moonless, because Amavasya had no use for light. Only moments ago, I had fought beneath a burning sun; now it was deep night.

But in Agashi's world, such shifts were effortless.

"What did you mean," I asked, leaning against the railing beside her, "that my fate depends on my will?"

"You may lose to me in union and die— that is one path. You may flee and let my guards tear you apart— another. You may try to kill me and perish in turn— a third. Or, if you choose, you may spend this night untouched and live to leave this place alive. But then you will carry my mark— my essence. You will live as my kind— as your father does, as Saavri does."

"And if I choose otherwise— if I choose not to die at all, if I choose to defeat you?"

"Then defeat me," she said simply, pointing behind her toward the bed— "The couch waits."

I said nothing, only looked at her. Her calmness unsettled me more than any threat could. Who would believe that a woman so serene, so tender in her beauty, could hold death itself in her hands?

"Why do you wish to defeat me, truly?" she asked after a pause.

"So that I may cast you into the dark," I answered quietly. "So that those bound to you— my father, your followers— may finally be free."

She didn't turn; her hands rested on the railing, eyes fixed on the endless black. After a long silence she spoke— her voice low, almost weary.

"You must wonder why I chose you for this Amavasya," she said. "If I hadn't sent Saavri to you, you would never have known of me, of your father, or of the past. You would have lived your life in Calcutta, died an ordinary death, and I would have gone on hunting souls as before. On the surface that seems the truth— but destiny had already chosen you. You would have found your way here, one way or another. I only chose to guide that path, to know you before you arrived.

It is true— I can see the future, and most events come to me before they happen. Yet strangely, I have never seen beyond this night. That does not mean it is my last; it means this night is the barrier of my existence. Tonight, I must face you— and in doing so, either I will sink back into the shadows, or I will transcend this limit through you. Whether by your death or your becoming part of me— that, I cannot see. The event is clear: we will unite. But its end… remains uncertain."

Hearing that gave me an odd peace— proof that hope was still alive. And with that realization, my resolve hardened. The night was not over yet.

"You know how many centuries I have wandered like this… twelve! In these twelve centuries I have faced thousands of men, and except for your father, Baro and Namgyal, none has ever been able to stand before me— and even those three survived not because they were unmatched heroes but because chance favored Baro and Namgyal, and your father was spared by Maling. In all these hundreds of years you are the first man I have met who stands before me utterly fearless, overflowing with such confidence that there is no trace of worry or dread— you. I have not seen such courage in twelve centuries." This time, when she looked at me, there was admiration in her eyes, and I liked it.

"That's because I was warned of everything beforehand and they trained me thoroughly for it." I did not hesitate to own the truth.

"Even so— a reasonable, brave man can falter before the unexpected. I gave you such an unforeseen test, yet you met it admirably. That is why, for the first time from the moment of my birth to the fading of existence in that world, from an ordinary spirit to a goddess, a human heart has touched me." She did not look at me as she said it, but her voice held a strange tenderness.

"Fine— it pleases me that you are impressed. Since you are impressed, think of some middle path instead of choosing to take my life. Let my purpose be fulfilled and yours remain unharmed." I seized the chance and laid my cards on the table.

"How? Even if I wished it, I cannot free your father by myself. The way out is one-sided— one may come here, but one cannot leave. They can be freed only if I return to the darkness where I was first cast— only if my powers are undone. Why would I want that?"

"Then what does being impressed by me mean for me?" I asked bluntly.

"This is my world, the world over which I am queen. I shape it as I will. To sustain it, I require energy once every month; for that I need one man, and I have many to claim. You must have wondered what I do the rest of the time. When your daylight falls, that is the time I sleep— our sleeping is not the same as a human's. When your night comes, I awaken and craft a perfect day, a perfect night, a perfect instant and setting— and I drink it in. It is like living in the heaven men dream of. I am its queen… would you like to be the king of it?" she asked abruptly, and I was stunned.

"I— I don't understand," I stammered.

"You asked just now what meaning there would be to my being affected after all this— so this proposal is the answer to that. If you wish, you can become king and enjoy this heaven forever. Whatever is happening outside will continue as it is. Your body in the outer world will live out its natural span and perish, but here you will remain immortal forever — just as I am. Tell me— do you accept?"

For a moment, I found myself unable to speak. I had come with the intent of destroying her world, and here she was, trying to make me a part of it instead.

"What are you thinking— I have never made such an offer to anyone before. You want to bring me to my peak, absorb my powers, and make me obedient to your will, don't you? I am still offering you exactly that, with just one change: this realm of illusion will not be destroyed. Instead, you too will enjoy it like a paradise. The life of Saavri and your father in the outer world feels like a curse to you, doesn't it— that destiny you do not wish to endure. Then you will be given a level of immortality beyond that, where you yourself will be god, shaping everything around you as you please. Humans perform countless rites in their longing for heaven… I am offering you heaven itself. So what is the problem?"

The temptation was immense, and for me it was another unexpected situation— one I had not prepared for at all. When nothing like this had ever crossed my mind before, how could I give an immediate answer? I had only just steadied myself by telling myself that I was here in a state of inner discipline, where impatience is the greatest obstacle— that whatever I do, whatever decision I take, must be done calmly and with careful thought.

"We'll see… by the way, what do you think about Maling? Does he want to absorb your powers through me, regain his body, and rule your world, or does he seek liberation like the others?" I asked, clearly trying to change the subject.

"I don't know— I cannot look into his mind… but I do not think he longs for liberation."

"It is strange— the body with which my father had union… the thought of it makes me sick." I could not help the disgust that surfaced.

"You should not feel that," she replied gently. "Those are the laws of the human world; physical ties and proprieties matter there, but not here. Emotions have different measures. For your father I was only a mission, and for me he was only prey. For you, you are more than prey. Your collision with me was different."

"Then tell me why you and Maling have paid so much attention to me. Yes, you see in me a possible uncertain challenge for this Amavasya, but why was I singled out? Why did fate, in one way or another, ensure I would come to you?" I pressed the one knot I could not untangle.

"Do you believe in rebirth?" she asked, eyes probing mine.

"No." I answered bluntly— "I may be a Brahmin by birth, but my thinking is of another sort. Memory dies with the brain; when the body perishes, what is left for rebirth?"

"Consciousness," she said— "Can consciousness be destroyed?"

"Consciousness is tied to brain— when the brain ends, it ends," I replied.

"No," she said slowly, "consciousness is energy, and energy does not perish. Look at me. I was once bound to a brain that has long since turned to dust, yet I was not destroyed. I wandered in darkness for centuries, learned to practice, and in time became more than a body. When one gains such power, the body becomes incidental, and consciousness continues." She named the examples— a pishach in my father's case, and Maling as a man who survived by other means.

"Fine," I said— "But tell me plainly."

"That consciousness does not end," she repeated. "Even after centuries in darkness, consciousness may find a new dwelling— that is reincarnation. You were right that memories tied to a brain are lost. So, a reborn consciousness usually carries no recollections. Rebirth, therefore, often seems pointless, but sometimes it matters. It mattered in your life."

"Do not say I am a rebirth," I heard myself protest. The notion sounded absurd.

"Look into my eyes." She placed her hands on my shoulders and drew her face close. There was no escape but to meet what she sought; I looked, and suddenly the world around hummed. I felt as if a multitude pressed in.

I blinked; the scene before me had changed. She had said she could fashion her realm. The valley, the balcony— all vanished. We stood again on the royal stage of the arena where I had first seen Agashi enthroned.

The silk-draped balcony was gone; it was the dais itself. The attendants bowed, soldiers stood with spears, and the crowd roared. Ten half-clad young yogis were bound in chains in the ring; their faces were fierce as they stared up at us. There were elephants and mounted warriors in the ground below.

Some strange, terrible logic suggested this was the same yogic order that had once challenged Agashi— and, after their defeat, she had made them trample their would-be saviors, turning resistance into submission.

"Look closely at the man in front," she said softly. "He is Biraman— their guru. See him well."

When I focused, my breath caught. The man's face was my own. Though wild beard and hair framed him, the features were unmistakably mine. I had worn a yogi's disguise once; after the artifice of beard and robe, the face that had emerged was this very one. Recognition was immediate.

"This is exactly like me," I said in astonishment.

"Yes… that was you, twelve hundred years ago," she said. "Listen; hear what you said then." She nodded toward the arena.

"You wicked woman— you broke your vow. If you could not give up this kingdom, this pomp and pleasure for which you broke your promise, then go… we curse you that this crown, this splendour you take pride in, shall be destroyed. Nothing shall remain of what makes you proud… You have spurned us despite our victory, and for the crime of sentencing us to death— this shall be your curse. You love death, do you not, to visit it upon others? So we curse you to live free from death, but that life shall be your punishment. Neither shall you live among the living nor rest among the dead… you shall dwell in the underworld's darkness with a deathless body, and you shall never come back out.

If ever you attempt it, I will cast you back into that darkness again. Remember— those darknesses will be your fate. For a while you may cross them, but your permanent abode shall be those shadows." The yogi called Biraman thundered the curse.

As soon as the meaning struck me, I stared at Agashi in shock— she sat before me with an unreadable face as the soldiers threw the chained yogis to the ground and elephants moved forward to trample them. Even as they died, they repeated that curse; then, one by one, their bodies turned to smoke.

The words hung in the air… and, little by little, that whole scene dissolved into deep black fumes which, as they thinned, revealed again the nightscape that had been there before: those dread mountain-forms wrapped in dark and the sky studded with bright stars.

"So, it was I who cursed you, and because you crawled out from those darknesses and managed to found your own separate realm, I was reborn to thrust you back into that blackness? But I don't remember any of this." I looked at her, bewildered.

"What does it matter whether you remember or not? The truth is this. Now you understand why you are so special. I don't know who this Devi Sainvani is or what boon she granted your father— Baro and Namgyal reached that state somehow without any boon. Whatever it was, you thought it had transferred to you from your father; that was an illusion you accepted. The strength you showed— its source was what you have just witnessed, not some goddess's gift."

"Oh." The thought had flickered through my mind earlier. "But those visions I saw in Calcutta— the glimpses of the future— on what basis did they occur?"

"Perhaps it was the effect of merging with a great yogi's consciousness, or perhaps Sainvani's boon did indeed work in that case. But your fearlessness and the ability to brace yourself in any situation are the reasons you were born for this purpose." She was blunt and decisive.

"I don't know what to say— these matters are beyond my understanding. Anyway… after those men were crushed by the elephants, what happened to you?" I asked.

"The night those men were meant to die, the weather turned violent. An enormous earthquake tore everything to pieces; then the skies burst and floods swallowed whole towns. I was up above— when I tried to flee the palace the earth split, and I fell into a deep darkness.

It felt as though I plunged down a bottomless well and struck something, bone upon bone shattering. I could not move; death did not come. I lay there, and year after year passed. There were no scavengers to finish me off; death would not take me, nor could I die.

Time passed and I learned to practise restraint: if a yogi could, by mental power, bend nature, then perhaps I too could. So I began to cultivate my consciousness. Many decades— centuries— went by. Slowly I learned to leave my body, though still bound to that abyssal dark. After many more years I crossed those depths, and though I returned to the world as a spirit, I was not free.

I kept experimenting, met many yogis and spirits, learned, failed and learned some more. Over time I wove a realm of my own and made humans the source of my strength. In the early days prey was scarce and I remained weak, but once feeding became frequent my powers swelled. Now I can do almost anything— I remain here. I no longer feel the need to walk the outer world."

"And where is the body that escaped death?"

"It lies far below, in such depth and darkness that none can reach it."

"If you became so powerful that you could do anything, how then could someone come and take your powers by bringing you to climax?"

"Even the most unimaginable thing follows some rule. Your body derives energy from food, but it can neither preserve that food nor retain the energy itself— both must ultimately be expelled. My power, too, is siphoned from humans. If I am brought to my peak before I can devour, then those powers can be drawn back by the victor. Like your practice, this union is also a ritual— victory yields the vanquished's power. I have won for so long that I persist; if I lose, control will tilt to the winner."

"So, the curse functions like a law. Maling may exploit that. But there's a way to free others— by casting you back into darkness so your influence ends. Is there no way to free you?"

"I do not wish for freedom. Once I lay in those depths yearning for death; now I have tasted the world beyond suffering. How can one forgo the bliss of being a deity? Great power demands a price— I pay it gladly. Yes, you can defeat me and send me back to the abyss, but that will not end my being. I will have another chance later to regain what I lost— whether that takes two hundred or four hundred years, it will happen." Her voice showed no remorse.

I fell silent. Sympathy was pointless if she found contentment even in her punishment. My mind returned to the vow I had made to my former life: I must send her back into those darknesses.

"Tell me then," she said, "only a little night remains. Will you squander it and become my consort, entering this new existence— or will you attempt to fulfil that ancient vow and send me back?"

"That you broke your vow in mortal life and thus fell— can you now give me a promise you can keep?" I asked; this was the essential thing.

"What sort of promise?" Her tone hardened.

"When, in our intimacy, I first left the arena, you could take me— kill me if you wished. I would not complain. But if you are defeated, then in the event of my victory, you must obey one condition I command before we begin. You must pledge to it." I spoke with iron calm; my demand was angled at the danger of Maling seizing power over me afterwards.

She thought as if weighing my words against some great scale. Finally, she smiled and nodded consent.

"Agreed— if it lies within my power," she said.

"Just one demand: you will return to the darkness, and after that no order I give you will be binding upon you. Once the game begins, not a single word of mine will hold authority over you. You will do only what I have just stated— nothing beyond that." I wanted to prevent any scenario where Maling could seize my mind after I had absorbed her power.

She looked at me as if trying to read the depth of my purpose, then, smiling, signalled assent.

We came inside, took each other's hands, and drew back the curtains so the outside world disappeared. The chamber was as before: curtains, flowers, the soft bed. For the first time in two days, I felt a pang of distaste recalling Saavri's body, and an odd reluctance stirred.

Her touch, nonetheless, was new— different from Saavri's. As she kissed my arms and neck the sensation startled me like the touch of a stranger, but I forced my mind to transform that stranger into Saavri: convince myself she was the same woman I had been with these two days. The body might feel strange; my mind must keep insisting that this was not Agashi but Saavri, and so steady the spirit.

Her skin had a freshness; her hair, the curve of her shoulders, the slope of her waist were all unfamiliar. Yet I received those touches and translated them into memory— Saavri's face, Saavri's rhythm— until the strangeness dulled and the practice I had spent days on took hold: to give my body, but not my will; to surrender in flesh while keeping the mind's reins taut.

We lay down. The night drew on.

This was no ordinary act of lovemaking but a struggle of victory and defeat, a contest both of us tried to prolong as long as possible.

I tore at her clothes with a show of impatience; reflexively she ripped free my dhoti. I seized her, kissed her savagely; sometimes I dominated, sometimes she did. It was an aggressive, violent erotic game in which I tried, through prolonged foreplay, to carry her most of the way— and she, for her part, strove to make sure I did not reach the end. How successful I was I cannot say; what I could be sure of was that she had not succeeded, because my actual arousal remained under control and my body responded only as much as I willed it to.

It felt like one body with two operating units— body and mind running on different tracks.

Alongside that, she started another move: altering reality itself. That threw me off balance at first, which actually worked to my advantage.

We began by grinding and pressing and kissing one another on the bed, but within moments the chamber became a whirling sand desert… then, the next moment, a rain-soaked jungle… then a sandy shore by a placid lake… then, suddenly, a hell of fire and smoke where people screamed as they burned. From there we were transported to a garden of fountains, full of flowers and fluttering butterflies— then onto a battlefield where swords rang and soldiers hacked at one another.

We were washed by a torrent at a waterfall, and when we plunged we found ourselves in a graveyard where corpses rose out of their tombs and moved toward us.

The dead encircled us— and then, as if by snapping fingers, we were back in the same chamber of the palace where the game had begun.

Through all of that, neither of us let our rhythm break. Our limbs were used and our bodies ground together in the same measured way I had practised with Saavri— assault and counter-assault begun and then left unfinished, a thousand small stops and starts, so that the mind always had some chance to steady itself on the slippery slope.

On the surface I remained outwardly unaffected by the shifting scenes and stayed with her; underneath, my mind kept connecting to each new scenario so it would have the repeated opportunities to regain balance.

What she held in her mind I could not know— perhaps she meant to live this final union through every shade of experience. Otherwise, being as experienced as she was, she must have realized that these repeated shifts of reality would keep jolting me out of my trance, giving me chances to regain my footing.

There was an enormous, almost carnal joy in that violent coupling— no denying that— but even after giving so much of myself physically, my mind never surrendered; orgasm did not edge near. Partly that was because over the previous two-and-a-half days I had exhausted my body: there simply remained no immediate reservoir of the energy that would flood me to release.

In those circumstances, even a few drops after hours of digging felt like a plentiful yield.

Undoubtedly she, too, was working the same way with her mind. A normal woman, under the ferocious foreplay I gave her, would likely have reached climax three or four times. Even Saavri might have given out a while ago. I had to concede her extraordinary control over her senses— she too was clever with her mind, and yet in appearance surrendered as fully as I did, wholly engaged in the act.

Then I felt a tension build inside her— and hope took flight in me. My heartbeat leapt; I drove harder. At that instant her control seemed to falter. Seeing her weakening inflamed me further; I redoubled my efforts to enter her. When her hands clenched, I felt them dig into my back, her nails biting into flesh— but I refused to let go.

At the precise moment she stiffened, I withdrew from inside her— but not in the way she expected. I did not release my hold; instead I gripped her so fiercely it felt as though I meant to snap her bones. In that condition she could not stop herself, yet my withdrawal at that final instant enraged her; she convulsed and flailed.

"Th-this... this is an insult," she murmured, barely forming the words.

She had not even finished speaking when she freed herself from my grasp, shoved me away, and began to convulse in an uncanny way. I felt the chamber tearing— walls and roof disintegrating; everything came apart in shards and collapsed. For a moment panic rose, but I steadied myself, wrapped the dhoti tight round my waist so I would not be left naked.

The world she had built relied on the strength of her mind — once that strength faltered and her mental state became unstable, how could that fabricated reality stay intact?

The roof and walls collapsed and we stood in the open. The whole scene looked as if a world had been living in the sky and, with a single shudder, was falling into a black earth. Stars flickered; night reigned; the place beneath us was a dark city crumbling into ash.

I could see the palace and the mountains break apart, sliding down into the void below. If some cosmic dissolution were to happen, perhaps it would look like this. I braced for the impact. If gravity worked here, the fall would end in a terrible jolt.

After what felt like five minutes the fall halted. Before we struck the ground, all the material had turned to vapor; only the two of us remained, and then the sudden collision: a violent thud as our bodies hit the earth.

I had braced my feet to absorb the shock; it was brutal but not bone-shattering. She hit the ground on her back and for a moment lay so still it seemed as if there were no life in her — yet I knew that was not possible. I wrapped the dhoti tighter.

As I watched her lie quiet, the devastated city around me matched the sketch my father had made in the diary— an ashen metropolis with pockets of lava, rivers of molten rock and pockets where people were trapped, clawing to escape. We had fallen upon a ruined palace; the ground steamed under our feet.

Then my head grew heavy. My limbs trembled and thought would not stay steady. In that bewildered state I leaned toward Agashi and attempted again to sink into her. At that instant she was not the lovely woman I had known— she had been transformed during the fall into a monstrous, nightmarish shape.

She was no longer human: towering easily ten feet, broad as a boulder, her face a hideous hybrid of wolf and human, nose and jaws elongated, fangs bared like knives. Her hair writhed as if alive; parts of her skin looked less like flesh than a crawling mass of smoke and worms. Tentacles crowned her body, tipped with needle-like points.

Her eyes had swollen large and glowed red, as if embers burned inside them.

Even so, like a man possessed, I tried to re-enter her. Though the falling had dulled my arousal, when I felt that tension return, I forced myself into her— only to be pushed away as her consciousness snapped awake.

"Not now— you had one chance to take my powers, which you have wasted. Now you must die." She rose with a guttural roar.

In that instant a compressed air seemed trapped inside my body, pressing to get out. I pitched and twisted on the ground as if something were splitting me apart. Then, as though forced from within, another figure tore free of me— he fell away, writhing and disconnected. It was none other than Maling.

"If I had not separated myself from you then, Maling would have taken your powers— not me." I panted and looked at Agashi.

"That was your problem— not mine." She answered in the same low, growling voice.

"You thwarted me." Maling's voice, like embers being chewed, reached me and I turned my head toward him.

His face looked as if it were filled with boundless rage— his eyes spat sparks. He advanced, lips drawn in hatred, and delivered a heavy kick that sent me tumbling away.

I fell, but I stood up at once. I knew very well what even a tenth of a second meant for me here. Both of them, seething with rage, were advancing toward me. Watching them, I closed my eyes for a moment and convinced myself that whether it was the effect of Goddess Sainvani's boon or the ascetic power of a past life, in that place all my opponents amounted to a single unit of strength, and I was not inferior to them in any respect— and this was a truth I had already tested. Even if there were sixteen of them against me alone, I could fight them. In fact, their anger was only making the battle easier for me. I had to avoid anger at all costs, keep my mind cool, anticipate every possible strike, evade it, and counterattack— while keeping my eyes and ears fully alert.

It was true that the night was wearing away, but there was no knowing how much time remained before dawn— so escape was not an option at all. I had to fight, no matter what. For now, there were two before me, whose roles, by every prior estimate, were bound to be hostile, but now both of them were my enemies— and all their companions would prove enemies to my life as well— whether they were those Aghoris who had once protected my father from Agashi and her followers, mere pawns of Maling… or Saavri… or even my father himself.

Maling drew close first and aimed a punch at my face. Watching it closely, I tilted my head just enough to let it pass, and as his fist flew by, I grabbed his arm, spun him, and, with both hands, thrust him toward Agashi who had now come near.

The two of them tangled; before they could steady themselves, I sprang and landed a solid kick on Maling's back. They both staggered and went down. I fell too, but rose quicker than they did and ran into the crumbling ruins of the palace. Agashi, seeing Maling on her side, flung him away in annoyance.

I ran, but not to flee— from the ruins I would face them one by one rather than all at once. In the arena among a dozen armed soldiers an open-field battle would have been far tougher; here, among rubble and broken halls, I could use the place to pick my fights. Agashi, in her own way, had created that advantage for me.

As I entered the ruins, aghoris dropped from the sky around me— exactly where I was headed. That was expected; I had prepared myself for them.

The first aghori I met I kicked before he could plant his feet; he crashed against a fallen wall. I snatched up a large slab of masonry and flung it at the next man's legs. He screamed and crumpled at the first step. Five more landed around me. Behind, Agashi and Maling loomed; Agashi's soldiers— those animated idols— had regained life and were awakening to move toward me. Saavri and my father were among them.

I searched for a club or rod to use as a weapon, but the place offered nothing. It was fortunate the site was such that they could not all assault me at once. I'd learned to dispatch each incoming enemy in turn. That tactic worked: I drove my boot into the first aghori before he could steady himself; the second one had a piece of masonry dropped on him and was out of the fight.

More kept landing; one by one I dealt with them as they arrived. The advantage, in this melee, lay with me because almost all of them— Maling's followers included— were linked to him and to Agashi mentally; their frenzy strengthened their puppet-like aggression, while I had no such fury to destabilize me.

I stayed methodical, struck hard, and put each opponent out of action for a time.

The conjured wolves— Agashi's fierce, oversized creatures— were harder, and even when badly hurt they could recover. They inflicted wounds on me too, but none that would put me out of the fight. As blows landed and blood and dust mixed, the palace walls groaned and collapsed faster.

At one point my father came at me; Saavri stood before him. Their faces were blank— there was no recognition in them. It pained me to strike those I loved, but survival left no choice. Besides, my mission required that tonight every thread be severed. Wounded or dying, they would not matter in the end.

I did not escape unharmed. I took my share of wounds, and the fight was fierce. Yet fortune leaned my way: Maling's four lieutenants had been crippled enough by then that they were effectively out of the battle.

Once, when he leapt at me from behind and we both fell through a collapsing wall, I had grabbed a brick and struck him while we hurtled down— before he could steady himself, the blow crashed into his shoulder. I did not know then who lay behind me when the wall gave way, but the strike shattered his balance; his right shoulder was crippled.

That injury weakened him, and before reinforcements reached us I struck again and crippled him further.

Even after taking grievous punishment, Maling managed to shove me and send us both sliding beyond the palace limit — into a basin of molten rock.

I had braced for scalding heat; the stone did not melt, but the heat burned like coals. I managed to steady myself for less than a breath when he seized me and tried to push my body into the molten basin.

The basin's surface was layered; occasionally trapped figures writhed beneath, unable to break through. They reached for us with eager hands, striving to drag us under. Maling was on top of me; his leverage meant my strength had to double. Below and above forces tried to tear me apart.

With every ounce of gathered strength I struggled to wrench him free.

Two of his companions rushed in and a third arrived at that moment; together they overwhelmed me and bore me toward the molten edge as if to throw me in. I was losing: the combined force above and the hands below would have dragged me under. Then smoke began to pour from Maling's body. He felt it too— panic flashed across his face. His grip weakened.

Seizing the opening, I used every muscle to wrench them off and break their hold.

Maling's expression changed to raw terror. He tried to pull himself free from the basin, but I would not let him go. I sank my hands into his throat and locked my grip. He writhed, smoke billowing ferociously from him. For all the struggle, I held fast.

Two of his companions who had been inside the molten depths, along with the third who had just arrived, surged to free him.

They attacked me with kicks and blows. But by then I had no intention of letting go; their rescue attempts were in vain. The three who had been in the lava were weakened; they were giving off smoke too— and then the smoke from Maling's body burst into flame.

The fire licked him, and heat seared me in return, but the blaze did not consume him in the usual way. As he began to falter, I shoved him down into the basin, and the grasping hands pulled him under.

At that instant the three companions who had been in the basin recoiled from the edge; their bodies began to smoke violently.

The smoke kindled into flame, and like men struck by sudden combustion they were swallowed by the molten mouths beneath them. Their screams became hissing embers as they vanished into the lava.

I stood among the ruins, breathing hard, the taste of ash in my mouth. Around me the palace continued to crumble. The survivors— those who had been puppets of Agashi— retreated in chaos or lay twisted at my feet. For a moment I had nothing but the silence of that burning, broken city and the knowledge that I had, for now, prevailed.

Then I turned and walked on.

A party down— now I could turn my full attention to the others. By the time Maling was finished, Saavri had reached the place, and there were three of them.

When I crawled out from that pool of lava, I'd thrown them into, I sprang at Saavri and slammed her against a collapsing wall. Hirvi and Namgyal lunged at me from behind, and the four of us crashed through the ruins together.

Before they could pull themselves free, I had seized a chunk of debris and struck Namgyal across the face. They may have been monstrous, wolf-bodied beings in size, but I refused to pamper the women— my focus was on crippling Namgyal, Baro and my father.

After disabling Namgyal I threw Saavri with all my strength; she sailed, arms splayed, and landed in the same molten pit that had become the graveyard for Maling and his crew.

No sooner had I tossed her than I grabbed Hirvi by the neck and tried to snap it. Her ironlike claws scratched at me, but they could only injure as much as ordinary hands would. I broke her neck, then hurled Namgyal away with a chaos of blows; I gouged his eye with my thumbs until he howled in pain.

He was staggered enough to be out of the fight, and then I charged at my father.

We plunged into a stream of lava, and the hands from inside it reached up to drag us under. There was no time to consider filial feelings— survival came first. I struck like a whirlwind, slamming my father again and again. The submerged dead made the fight worse, thrashing and trying to seize us.

I shook them off and crawled out, only to find Saavri and the others already crawling through the ruins. I leapt at her again and drove her into the molten trough; she was half-frozen in its grasp, and I left her there, then dashed off into the collapsing structures.

They roared in anger and gave chase.

With Maling gone from the arena, a weight lifted from me; I could savor their hunt. The ruins offered plenty of cover despite their collapse. I hid, grabbed bricks, struck when the moment came.

They searched for me like hounds while I picked them off one by one, aiming to break skulls or blind eyes so they'd be out of the fight for a while. Fear was a stranger to me that night; doubt had long since been burnt away. I'd seen them grow weak before my eyes, and that bolstered my confidence.

Sachi was the first to fall to my brick— she didn't have time to cry out before I smashed her skull. Baro attacked and briefly overpowered me, but he wasn't as skilful as Maling; I beat him down, then when I turned, Nimbuja was next and I crushed her eyes out. I did not bother to finish many of them — maiming was enough to remove them from the field.

Agashi herself did come at me, but I did not want to end her then; instead I defended and maneuvered. Baro fell next — I reduced his head to pulp.

Only three were left; two of them were dear to me, but duty demanded I separate them from the battle. In the meantime, Saavri and my father had escaped the lava and were stalking through the ruins. I pulled Saavri close and, with a single brutal jump, we plunged fifteen feet down where a jagged spike jutted up from the rubble.

I had chosen that drop on purpose. Saavri hit the spike square on her spine— the sound and her strangled scream told me all I needed. Her backbone was broken; she writhed and shrieked.

I moved away. Her wound pained me— but she had asked for freedom, and sometimes freedom exacts a price.

Those two survivors dove down after us, but I slipped into the lower caverns of the ruins and they had to chase me. In the shelter's shadow I confronted Agashi first, though I meant no lasting harm to her at first; I fought to save myself. When my father approached, I used the falling walls as weapons and smashed his knees with a brick; he crumpled, crawling in agony.

Now only Agashi remained, and I no longer had reason to run. I stepped into the courtyard where we had landed. She emerged and attacked; I let her come. When she tried to twist away, I pinned her legs with my own, forced her down, pressed her wrists to the earth and kissed her face— over and over— until she struggled, then grew still.

I pressed my legs across her feet, held her wrists, and began to kiss her throat, shoulder, cheek. She thrashed and howled, but the signs of her weakening showed: she could no longer steel herself as she had before. I felt the moment shift.

"Come on, Agashi," I murmured between kisses. "This doesn't have to be a one-time thing for you— we can try it again. I won't pull away. I'm not afraid now."

She snarled and writhed, trying to wrench free.

I was exhausted, wounded and panting, but I had decided the night would be decisive. Despite the disgust her transformed body inspired— tentacles, writhing skin, the smell of something not quite human— I had to become unfeeling. I held her face and kissed the torn, split lips until she shuddered. That strange paradox worked: when I tried to think of her as anything other than the beautiful woman I'd known, my body's response steadied. It was a terrible, clinical intimacy: I treated her like the practice Saavri had given me — to drive the mind to discipline the body.

Gradually her resistance thinned. She twisted, then went limp. For the first time she offered no more fight; she surrendered to the contact.

Her body responded to warmth and touch, wave after wave, sometimes human, sometimes monstrous, until the sequence began to resolve back into her older, more familiar form.

I kept the rhythm, pushing and pulling, until at last she gave herself over entirely. The old strength slipped away, and the beast receded. In that collapsing ruin of gods and stone, something fragile and cunning softened: Agashi, in pieces and whole, yielded.

Even in whatever monstrous shape she had taken, she must have sensed that despite her horrific form, the friction of our bodies still carried pleasure. Inevitably, that pleasure would lead her to her peak.

For me, though, the sight of her disfigured body was an obstacle— it pulled my mind back from release. It was necessary, therefore, that she return to her human form— that same mortal beauty whose softness and allure could draw me to my own climax.

She was lying on her back on the ground, and I was over her. From the angle of our bodies, I could see a faint light shimmering in the distance— as if there were an invisible wall holding it back, and that wall was straining to collapse so the trapped light could burst free.

She couldn't see it, but I could. It made me realize that I had little time left. That was perhaps the difference between us— she was utterly absorbed in the act, while I was battling the awareness that every second was slipping away. Yet I kept myself moving, wanting her to believe that I was lost in the same feverish trance.

Earlier, when she had all her powers intact, she could prolong her climax indefinitely, but now, half-drained of her strength, she had lost that control.

I could feel the rising tension in her veins— the rhythm of surrender building within her. That realization filled me with sudden, wild energy. Without giving her a moment to recover, I drove deeper, faster, with reckless abandon.

And finally, with a cry that trembled between pain and bliss, she clutched me tight— the sound of her surrender, my victory proclaimed. I felt the convulsion of her body, the liquid warmth that came with release— yet there was no surge of power, no spark transferring to me as I had imagined.

Nothing extraordinary happened. I had won, and yet it didn't feel like victory.

She held me for a few more breaths before her arms loosened, and she fell back— utterly still, utterly spent. I sat beside her, staring at her face. There were tears in her eyes. I didn't know what emotion had brought them— remorse, exhaustion, or relief— but they were human, and that alone meant something.

"You must go back," I said, holding her limp hand in mine.

"Yes… but before I leave, I want to give you something," she whispered. Her voice trembled. "If you accept it, it will please me."

"What is it?" My heart skipped.

"Saavri," she said softly. "I know what she means to you. When you entered this war against me, it wasn't your father's loss that pained you most— it was the thought of losing her. I am giving her to you. She will live in your mind— you can summon her whenever you wish, share with her every joy, every moment. She will stay with you for as long as you live… and when your life ends, she will go with you."

"Wouldn't that be selfish of me?" My voice shook. "To keep her bound, when her soul deserves release?"

"No," she said, her tone pleading. "In the physical world she is free. Her body will no longer exist. She will dwell only in the realm you create— your own mind, your illusion. I can already see it… the sun is about to rise. Accept it."

Her voice trembled with hope.

"I… I accept," I said at last, surrendering to the temptation.

And the very moment I spoke, that invisible wall shattered. The trapped light behind it burst forth with a blinding brilliance that swept across everything. The world dissolved into vapor— the ruins, the darkness, even Agashi herself. The radiance grew so fierce that it consumed my sight until there was nothing left but light.

••

Chapter 15

The battle was over. Agashi had been banished back into the abyss. Those bound under her power, condemned to live cursed half-lives, were finally free.

When the light cleared, I found myself in the same chamber of the temple where I had first taken my seat. I stepped outside and saw seven figures— five of them reduced to skeletal remains. My father was not among them, nor was Saavri's body.

Their bones were too ancient to tell apart; some were a century old, some four. The moment Agashi's power had broken, their bodies had aged to the time of their real deaths, leaving only bones.

Only my father had belonged to the present age. If he had been there, his body would have remained intact— though aged, perhaps, to its rightful years.

But since he wasn't, all I could do was gather those ashes, preserve them, and promise myself I'd carry them to the Ganga.

Mother was awake in her small room when I returned— weak, but alive. Seeing me brought her joy, though the news of Father's final passing struck her hard. Still, when I explained, she understood: that he had, in truth, died nineteen years ago, that what lingered since then was a cursed existence — and that his liberation was his own wish. It was peace, not loss.

I could have left that very day, but exhaustion and injuries forbade it. I decided to rest one more night.

That night, as my mind drifted into sleep, I found myself once again in that garden of Eden— where Saavri wandered, singing a sorrowful tune. The same garden that had once filled me with rapture now felt steeped in melancholy.

"Saavri," I called out. She stopped, but did not turn.

When I reached her and stood before her, she finally lifted her eyes— they were filled with tears.

"What happened?" I asked gently, resting my hands on her shoulders. "Aren't you happy?"

"Why did you do this?" There was reproach in her voice.

"What… what did I do? Didn't you attain liberation?" I was completely taken aback.

"No… my body may now lie somewhere inactive and safe, but I have stepped into the very role she once occupied," she said in a voice drained of hope.

"What— but why? She herself said that you too would be freed like the others, and that you would exist only within my mind." My head began to spin.

"Everything in creation is bound by some rule. For Agashi too there was a rule— that if she could gain power by forcing a man to climax during union and then consuming him, then a man could also bring her to climax first and absorb her power, at which point she would be bound to obey him. She could not escape that rule— but there was nothing stopping her from lying. By lying, and with your consent, she could still do something that would ultimately serve her own interest… and that is exactly what she did. You fulfilled her desire of your own accord." There was bitterness in her voice— resentment, accusation.

"I don't understand— tell me everything clearly." I grew restless.

"She may not have known how last night would end, but she certainly knew the possibilities. So there was always the chance that you might win and send her back into the darkness. She prepared for that in advance. She knew I could become your weakness, so before the game even began, she ordered me to secure my body somewhere deep within the womb of this land, and then return to her realm of illusion. You rendered my body inactive, and since Agashi's influence has ended, it can no longer recover. Then she made you accept that you wanted Saavri for yourself— and I was left deprived of liberation, like the others. What she said was technically true: with my body inactive and vanished from the world's sight, I am nowhere, and my existence is now confined only to your mind and to the realm of illusion you create or I create. Without understanding the full truth, you gave your consent and, even as she was leaving, allowed her to have her way."

"But how does my remaining alive benefit her at all?" I still could not grasp the whole picture.

"She had already taken a vow from me— that I would do exactly what she used to do, that while remaining in this realm of illusion I would consume one prey every new moon, increase my power, and make myself strong enough to one day pull her out of the darkness and bring her back into her world. She lived in the forest, so she needed Maling or people like us to provide her prey. I don't need that… because I will live inside your mind, and you will live in Calcutta, surrounded by people everywhere. There will be no shortage of prey."

"You will do this?" I stared at her, eyes wide.

"It is the same rule. The power you absorbed from her is, in essence, the power of the mind— and she placed me there. If I do not do this, I will grow weak and one day be destroyed. And if I die now, you will die too. Consuming humans, in one form or another, is our sustenance. To keep you alive, I must keep myself alive, and to keep myself alive, I must continue hunting. And when I become strong enough to pull her out of the darkness, I will have to do that as well. The reason for that— you may consider it a vow I was made to give."

"Why did you give such a vow at all?" I snapped, irritation breaking through.

"She was terribly afraid of you— I don't know why, but that fear was pushing her to abandon her own game for that one night. Nothing would have gone wrong if she had let a single night pass without hunting. Whatever her intentions may have been earlier, as you kept growing stronger she lost faith in her own victory. Instead of giving you even a chance in union, she wanted to finish you off outright. She had decided that she would not summon you into her realm of illusion at all, but have you eliminated in the outer world itself, through all her companions. Believe me— you could have faced everyone in the illusory realm, you could have defeated them all. But in the outer world, you could not have stood against people like us, and you would have died. She gave me two choices: either I chose your certain death, or I agreed to these terms, by which she would draw you into her realm and give you the chance of union. I chose that option believing that if you won, you would free everyone outright, without falling for any of her words. But you listened to her — and ruined everything."

"But you exist only as long as my mind exists. Even if it never meets with an accident, it will last, at most, fifty or sixty years. After that, it will end— and with it, you will have to die too, won't you?"

"You saw what became of Maling, didn't you? You have received the same power from Agashi. Even if your body were to be torn apart and scattered, you cannot die. You too will remain alive for centuries, just like him."

"Don't forget that despite all her powers, I killed her. If I can kill her, I can kill myself in the same way."

"No… that is precisely why Agashi placed me inside your mind. I am with you not only in a senseless state within a realm of illusion created by you or me, but even in your waking state— so that I can stop you from taking any such step."

I let her go and sat down, clutching my head in both hands. What kind of victory was this? A moment of my own attachment had turned into a torment for me. What had begun as a mission to free my father had ended with me trapped like this. She too sat down beside me, subdued, and rested her head on my shoulder.

"What power did I actually gain from her— apart from this cursed immortality?" I asked after a while.

"Like her, you can create a realm of illusion by your own will. The moment the consciousness of any person within your sphere of influence goes blank, you can pull them into that realm. You can love them, have intercourse with them, rape them, injure them, or take their life— and its effect will manifest on their body in the outer world as well. How you use this power is up to you… exactly like Agashi."

We fashioned in our minds a crimson, sinking sun on the distant horizon and sat through the night watching it, lost and sullen.

That night weighed heavily on me— I didn't tell Mother anything. Next morning we prepared and left. The forest dangers remained, but we had to travel. Mother had grown up in these woods, so she was more at ease than I was.

On the third evening we reached the ruins where Saavri and I had spent our honeymoon period… the whole area around the ruins had been burned to ashes. There we also found Father's body— though charred, he had not burned completely. His broken knees bore the marks of the blows I had given him; that filled me with deep remorse, yet there had been no other option.

As expected, freed from Agashi's sway, he had returned to his true age and looked middle-aged. I gathered some dry wood and made a pyre and handed his body to the flames. The place was haunted by spirits— a potential trouble for Mother— but surprisingly no one came near. That night Saavri told me that my own presence now radiated a deterrent: spirits would not come close to me easily. That was something positive.

After many days of travel, we reached Narayangudi and from there the journey to Calcutta was not difficult."

With the story finished, Saumitra babu fell silent and turned his face towards Debu.

Even with curtains at the window, it was clear the night had fallen and lights were being switched on outside.

"So— what happened next?" Debu asked, sitting up.

"Mother stayed with us while she lived, and when old age took her, she passed away— they were the parents who had reared me, and they left having lived their term. I could not change what I had become, so I tried to be happy with Saavri, but that was insufficient for a human life.

There are many things to be done for society, for maintaining status, for continuing one's lineage as tradition demands… I too had to do them. I married. The early years were tolerable, but I had forgotten that I carried Saavri in my mind— and she had grown so attached to me that she could not tolerate another woman in my life.

She began to influence the mind of the new wife the way Maling had influenced my father's. By then I had two children, but my wife's behaviour deteriorated— sometimes she harmed herself, sometimes the children were endangered. Gradually she went dangerously mad and one day she disappeared. I searched, the police searched… she was never found.

Sometimes she appeared as a spirit in the house and frightened the children horribly. Though Saavri denied everything when I asked, I knew Saavri's presence had caused this ruin. For the children's sake I married again; that second wife I drove to suicide. Then I realised my children were at risk, so I asked my English father's cousin to take them— he agreed and the children were sent away.

As long as my parents lived, I did not remarry; after they passed, I wed a widow in later years hoping she might show mercy, but she too died within three years. I lost the courage to try again, and nobody now would give me a bride. I lived dependent on Bhagtrām, and he loyally looked after me."

"And Saavri… did she really do what she said she would?" Debu asked.

"Yes. There's no lack of humans in Calcutta. People come here from everywhere. For her, one dead man a month is not a big deal, especially when those victims are the homeless, labourers, pavement dwellers. Who asks after them? The municipality disposes of stray corpses. So, she took from them."

"Now one crucial question remains unanswered— what mission had you sent your father on that would offend Agashi and bring her wrath, and how did Maling die?"

"You'll remember I told you: when Saavri told me about Maling, she said that if anyone approached Maling with the intention of harming him, he would first take control of that person's mind. That meant that though Agashi's boon might make him immune to natural death, someone could still kill him by other means.

If that was possible, then I could do it too... The first need was to locate him. When Maling had pulled me into his realm in the ruins, I had seen a particular kind of pillar down there — the same one I had seen above as well. During our talks he had said, 'Go back fearlessly and stay here— no spirit will trouble you.' From those two things it was clear he himself was located in that place. The next day I found the tree whose roots held his body.

I told Father the location and asked him simply to go there at night and remain near it. If Agashi weakened at any hour of the night then Maling would certainly reach her— he needed to get there immediately, or else he would lose the chance to take her. They might arrive slightly later, since their job was to aid Agashi, while Maling had to arrive on time, because through me he planned to seize her power.

When he moved toward the mayalok, they would first set fire to the tree and the surroundings and then enter her realm. Father did exactly that. Maling was intent on punishing me and his companions didn't notice the changes around their physical bodies. By the time they realised, it was too late and Maling paid with his life."

A silence fell between them for a few moments as both considered the matter.

"So, this means you yourself now suffer a curse: your body is free from natural death, but do you want such a life? Is this your desire?"

"Absolutely not— if I had wished this, I would have accepted Agashi's proposal. I always wanted an ordinary human life: to grow old and die. I still want that. I have lived my life; now I seek release."

"And how will that come?"

"Saavri lives in my mind almost constantly, and in that state she will neither allow me to commit suicide nor let anyone threaten me. Still, each month a time comes when she is separate from me for a while— the new-moon night, when she needs to hunt. Coincidentally, tonight is such a night. I had asked her permission once to share my feelings with someone and she left me alone.

Even so, her gaze was on me… Our talk is nearly over; through most of it she saw and heard everything, and now her work is about to finish. Now I can both speak and act on my true feeling.

Here is a secret— we have never actually met in the waking world. You are asleep in your home and I drew you into my crafted mayalok. It will seem to you that you spent the day with me, but in the real world you spent the night. I can see many events of the future— so I foresaw the big accident that would happen tonight in Calcutta: an oil tanker crash on the road near your house.

I came early to be at the right place at the right time. Then I used my power to find, among the sleeping people, one human suited to my purpose— you— and at the bus stop I built this mayalok and drew you in… so you could learn what I alone knew, and through you the world might come to know it.

Now my hour of release has come… the tanker is close by. I will be consumed in its fire, and Saavri with me. Farewell, Debashish… be happy."

No sooner had he finished speaking than a thunderous sound erupted in his mind and he sprang awake as if an earthquake had struck, the room trembling. He sat up drenched in sweat. The explosion had also woken Aparna beside him; she looked at him groggily.

"What happened?" she asked.

"I don't know— maybe some explosion," he answered uncertainly.

He slipped into his slippers, went to the window that looked onto the road and peered down. There, at the bus stop a little distance away, a tanker lay overturned and blazing, smoke pouring up. Fuel had leaked and fire spread a considerable way. Across the road a car had smashed into the scene— perhaps the cause of the crash. At the bus stop itself a person was burning in the flames; by the time he saw it the figure had gone still. Debu raised his gaze to the far east— a pale light was beginning to appear on the horizon.

(The End)

Acknowledgments

No story is ever written alone. Saavri may have unfolded within a single mind, yet it carries the weight of many unseen voices— of myths whispered across mountains, of faith and fear that coexist in every Indian night, and of those who dare to listen to the silence between words.

My deepest gratitude to every reader who believes that stories are not meant to be escaped from— but entered, lived, and sometimes, feared.

And to the shadows that waited patiently while I wrote— you were right. I did return.

••

If these pages touched you, please consider sharing your thoughts on Amazon, Kindle, or wherever you found this book.
Your reflections are the embers that keep this fire burning.

••

www.ingramcontent.com/pod-product-compliance
Lightning Source LLC
Chambersburg PA
CBHW031339230926
51848CB00002B/307

* 9 7 8 8 1 9 9 5 6 2 0 0 4 *